New York Times Bestselling Author
HELENA HUNTING

As an NHL player, relationships haven't been my thing. Shrouded in secrecy and speculation, they never last very long. But then that's what happens when you require an NDA before the first date.

Until Charlene. She's like a firefly. She's elusive, and if you catch her she'll burn bright, but keeping her trapped dulls her fire and dims her beauty.

I caught her. And as much as I might want to keep her, I'll never put the lid on her jar. Not at the risk of losing her. So I've let her set the rules in our relationship.

But as long hidden secrets expose us both, I discover exactly how fragile Charlene is, and how much I need her.

We're all broken. We're all messed up. Some more than others. Me more than most.

ACKNOWLEDGMENTS

This was quite a journey, from Violet and Alex all the way to Charlene and Darren, I've had an amazing team of people supporting me through this series. Sebastian, you said this was the book and you were right. Sometimes I just need to write with my seatbelt off and The Pucked Series has given me that freedom.

Huge love to all the people who have made this possible. Mom, Dad and Mel, your love and support mean so much to me. Debra, for being my rock, Leigh for being my faith when I couldn't manage it on my own, Kimberly for letting me write all the crazy on with this book.

Endless love to Nina and Jenn and the team at SBPR, (Sarah F and Bex, you rock my socks) for all your hard work with me on this series.

Sarah P, you're a gem and I'm lucky to have you and the Hustlers with me on this.

Shannon, I know this cover was tough, but I think you rocked it ;) thank you for making these covers truly shine, Teeny, thank you for always making the inside so pretty and Jessica, thank you for always cleaning up my grammar and commas and all the other things I'm so terrible at.

Bloggers, without you, the love for Alex and Violet wouldn't have had a chance to blossom, so thank you from the bottom of my heart for following this cast of characters all the way here with me. Readers, you're amazing. Thank you for embracing the insanity of the Pucked Family. I love your love for them, which makes it hard to say goodbye.

To all my author friends who have been with me along the way, through the ups and downs and all the in-betweens, thank you for holding my hand. Kellie, thanks for the brainstorming session that started this all, Deb, Leigh, Tijan, Kelly, Susi, Ruth, Erika, Katherine, Marine, Julie, Kathrine, Karen, Marty, you're my tribe. Thanks for pointing out I'm Violet and loving me anyway.

For my Pucked Series readers: this one is like reading with your seatbelt off.

PROLOGUE

NDA COFFEE DATE

CHARLENE

I breathe into my palm to check for freshness. I brushed my teeth less than ten minutes ago, but I pop two Altoids anyway. Fresh breath is crucial. I crunch down and spread the fiery-cold bits over my tongue. The burst of mint makes my eyes water, so I have to dab at the corners with my sleeve and breathe through my nose to avoid making it worse.

Darren Westinghouse is picking me up for a coffee date. *The* Darren Westinghouse, Chicago's NHL right wing and the most mysterious man in the league. There are loads of rumors about him. His dating history is unclear and based mostly on speculation and conjecture. I'm excited to get to know the man behind the intense, stoic mask.

My palms are sweaty, and my panties are inappropriately

damp as I wander around my kitchen. My reaction to anxiety is weird. And rather inconvenient. I've already changed my panties once in the past half hour.

"It's just coffee," I scold my crotch.

It doesn't seem to matter, though. She's preparing for all possible scenarios.

I introduced myself to Darren when I went with my best friend, Violet, to an away game. He was gentlemanly and sweet, offering to walk me back to my room. I went in for a goodnight kiss that turned into an epic make-out session. We kissed like teenagers until my lips were raw. It took a week before they finally stopped peeling.

Today I'm wearing shiny gloss that tastes like cotton candy—my hope is that Darren likes the flavor and will want to kiss it off more than once. I smooth my sweaty palms down my jean-covered thighs. I'm going for casual—except under my jeans I'm wearing a nice pair of lacy panties, just in case his hand happens to find its way into them. My bra matches, of course.

I check the time. It's nine forty-nine in the morning. He's picking me up at ten, but those eleven minutes feel like they're taking an eternity to pass. I mentally scroll through the approved topics of conversation: obviously hockey, weather, my job, and my college experience are all approved.

I've learned that it's best to give people the barest of facts and then shift the topic away from the really personal stuff. People usually love to talk about themselves, so it's not all that hard to do. At nine fifty-three I do another breath check and startle as my doorbell chimes.

"He's here!" I whisper-shriek to no one. Or maybe I'm addressing my anxious vagina. I take two deep breaths and count to three before I open the door.

I'm still not adequately prepared for the vision taking up my front porch.

Darren's in jeans and a long-sleeved shirt—so different than the suit he was wearing the last time I saw him. His short hair is styled neatly, and his hard, icy blue eyes move over me in a casual sweep that I feel everywhere. Darren is intense. He's lightness and darkness fused together. And he's unearthly beautiful. It's a lot to process.

A half-grin tips his mouth and quickly becomes a disarming full smile that transforms his face from severe to stunning for as long as it lasts.

"Hi." It's almost a moan it's so breathy.

"Hello, Charlene."

I have tingles below the waist from those two words.

"Hi." I'm repeating myself. Not smooth.

"I'm a little early," he says. "I hope that's okay."

I snap out of my Darren-induced daze. "Yes! Yeah, of course. Just let me get my purse." I turn, prepared to grab it from the kitchen, when I realize it's already hanging from my right arm. "Oh, never mind. Looks like I'm all set." I hope he doesn't think I'm a complete idiot.

I shrug into my coat with Darren's help—so courteous—grab my keys from the hook, and step out onto the porch. It's a crisp morning, but the sun is shining, so it takes the edge off the chill in the air.

Darren is ultra-polite, opening the passenger door and helping me in before he rounds the hood and takes the driver's seat. We make small talk as we drive toward the water.

I'm a little surprised when Darren pulls into a Starbucks and heads for the drive-thru. This isn't quite what I had in mind when he proposed a coffee date. I figured we'd go to some quaint, cozy little café and stare into each other's eyes.

"I thought we could go to the park."

"Oh, sure. That would be great," I say. Parks can be romantic. Especially since it's kind of chilly today. Maybe he'll have to put his arm around me to keep me warm. I can totally get on board with that.

Once we have our coffees, Darren drives to the water. He parks the SUV, but leaves the engine running. I assume we're going to get out and stroll the boardwalk, but instead we stay where we are and chat while we people-watch. Also not what I was expecting, but he smells great, so I guess I'll take it.

He's a quiet guy, so I end up doing the majority of the talking. Instead of rambling about myself, I regale him with Violet stories, which make him chuckle—a sound I like a lot.

After an hour or so, during which my stomach starts to grumble since I was too nervous to eat this morning, he shifts to face me. He skims my cheek as he sweeps my hair over my shoulder.

I lean into that touch, willing him to lean in, too. And he does. His thumb rests against that soft spot under my chin.

"I would like to kiss you," he says.

"I have coffee breath."

"As do I."

I consider offering him a mint, but decide I don't care. I tip my chin up. "Okay then."

His smile is soft and warm, in stark contrast to his hard features and icy eyes, and his lips feel like silk against mine. I have no idea how long we kiss, but it's enough that my neck starts to get a kink. He finally pulls back, those icy eyes heavy with the same lust that's ruining my underwear.

"Would you like to have lunch with me?"

In my head I turn lunch into extended foreplay, but either way, spending more time with him is on my yes list. "Definitely."

"Great." That smile of his makes another appearance, shorting out all the connections to my brain and redirecting the energy to my lady bits.

He reaches into the backseat and retrieves a messenger bag. He then produces a file folder with my name printed neatly on the front of it. Well, that's kind of . . . odd. Although that seems to be the way this date is going: nice, but odd.

"What's that?" I ask, the lust and excitement I was feeling a few seconds ago transforming into anxiety.

4

"A non-disclosure agreement," he says breezily, as if he's telling me the name of a flower.

I've signed plenty of non-disclosure agreements during my time at Stroker and Cobb Financial Management. It's necessary when working with famous hockey players and managing their finances. But unless I've read this whole thing incorrectly, Darren isn't going to ask me to manage his finances. At least I hope he's not.

"I'm sorry, why would a non-disclosure agreement be necessary?"

His brow furrows, making the sharp lines of his face even more severe and slightly ominous. "Because I'd like to have lunch with you."

I surreptitiously place my hand on the armrest, near the door handle. Just in case. "You need a non-disclosure agreement for lunch?"

He runs his hands down his thighs. "I'd like to take you to my house."

"For lunch?"

"Yes."

"Is *lunch* code for something?"

I get more of his furrowed brow. "Code?"

Maybe the rumors about him are true. Maybe he really is some kind of Dom and he's looking for me to be his next submissive. I'm not sure how to feel about that. I've read all the Fifty Shades books, and sure, some of that stuff sounds like a fun time, but I don't like to sign contracts for anything outside of work and banking. Even then, it makes me uncomfortable.

"Yeah, like, is *lunch* a code word for some kinky sex games or something?"

His furrow turns into an arch, and a slightly sinister smile tugs at the corner of his sinfully sexy mouth. The same mouth that was recently suctioned to mine.

"No. Although I'm certainly not opposed to kinky sex games if that's what you'd prefer in lieu of lunch."

I pick up the folder, which he's left on the dash between us and flip it open. The agreement is several pages long.

I glance at Darren and raise my own eyebrows.

"Take your time. I can wait." He smiles again, but it seems more like a grimace.

I scan the contents. It's incredibly thorough, with a whole bunch of clauses. There's even one pertaining to a credit card and a budget for clothing and lingerie. *What in the actual fuck?*

I close the file folder and pass it to him. "I'd like you to take me home."

He grins widely and produces a pen. His smile is so pretty I almost forget why I want to go home. Then I remember the pre-date paperwork.

I hold up a hand. "No, you're not understanding. I'd like you to take me to my house, not yours. I'm not signing an NDA agreement for a lunch date—especially this type of NDA."

That smile of his drops, and he blinks rapidly, fingers tapping against the manila file folder. "But I thought we were enjoying each other's company."

"We were. But there's no fucking way I'm signing this, so if you want to have lunch with me, you'll have to do it without an NDA."

He's clearly experiencing some conflict over this because he stares at me long enough that my skin grows hot before he finally says, "It's meant to protect us both."

"It's not a condom, Darren. It's an NDA. The next thing I know I'll have some kind of tracking chip and I'll be tied to your bed."

He tips his head to the side and seems to be fighting a smile. "Would you like to be tied to my bed?"

"Not if I have to sign an NDA."

"And if you don't have to sign an NDA?"

The answer to that question is still *no*, I think, but I shrug, because even him asking makes things happen in my panties.

"I'm a very private person, Charlene."

"So am I. Doesn't mean I make all the people in my life sign an NDA because of it. If you want to have lunch with me, you can do it without asking me to sign away my rights."

He regards me for several long, intense moments in which I have to fight to hold eye contact. Jesus, I'm nervous.

"Okay, no NDA," he finally concedes. "But I have rules for dating, Charlene."

"So do I, and we can discuss them over lunch."

MISCOMMUNICATION

DARREN

TWO YEARS LATER

Wᵉ arrive at my house, two huge vehicles filling up the driveway. Normally, we'd go to Alex's house after practice (my best friend and teammate), but his wife, Violet, is working from home today, and he doesn't want us to pose a distraction. My place is the second closest to the rink, and I don't live with anyone, so I'm the default.

My house is a modern build with solar panels and floor-to-ceiling soundproof windows you can see out of but not into, because I like my privacy. I also like having sex with my girlfriend against the ones that overlook the front lawn.

Our teammates, Lance, Randy, Miller, and Rookie, pile out of

Lance's Hummer while I grab my stuff from the trunk of Alex's muscle car. I key in the code, and they follow me into the foyer, where I dump my hockey bag.

"I'll grab some beers, and we can head out back."

It's early April, but the weather has been unusually warm, so at least we can get some fresh air while we discuss the impending expansion draft. Vegas is starting a new team, which means they'll be cherry picking a player from every established team in the league. So far, only Alex and Randy are safe from the draft with their no-trade clauses.

I stop short and breathe a curse when I reach the living room. My erection is nearly instantaneous. It's also very confused because I shouldn't be seeing what I'm seeing.

"Holy shit," Alex says from my right.

"What the fuck?" Randy bumps into me from behind.

"I *knew* you were into some kinky shit!" Lance's thick Scottish accent makes me acutely aware that what's supposed to be for my eyes only is *not*. I consider, very briefly, the ramifications of scooping out my teammates' eyes with a melon baller. I decide it's in my best interest not to act on that impulse. I don't think prison suits me, and it's hard to play hockey without eyeballs.

A low whistle comes from my right. I glance over to find Rookie blinking rapidly, his bewilderment apparent. "Dude, are you having some kind of fucked-up party? 'Cause if you are, I might want to get back on the bunny train for a night."

Randy smacks him across the back of the head. "That's not a bunny, asshole."

He's referring to puck bunnies, the groupies of the hockey world.

"Ow! Fuck!" Rookie rubs the spot.

In the middle of the room, halfway between kneeling and standing, is Charlene. My girlfriend. Naked. Well, apart from her pearl necklace and a pair of fuck-me heels. Her gorgeous hazel eyes are deer-in-the-headlights wide as they meet mine, and then they dart down to her naked form. Seeming uncertain how to proceed, she stumbles a few steps and drops back to her knees on the pillow. She bars one arm across her chest, the other moving to shield the apex of her thighs.

Rookie seems unable to process the scene with anything but stupidity. "Is that a ball gag? Who the fuck wears that mask? How do you even breathe with that on?"

"Shut it, Rook," Miller says.

I hadn't even noticed everything else. But I pull my gaze from Charlene and look at the items littering my living room. This is pretty damn far from ideal.

"Everybody out," I snap as I cross the room, nab the throw from the reading chair—*Charlene's* reading chair—and step over the dragon dick dildo Charlene purchased when she was in her *Game of Thrones* phase. I drape the blanket around her, which sends some of the light, lacy pieces of lingerie fluttering across the floor. But the blanket does the job, hiding every inch of bare skin covered in goose bumps.

That my teammates have now seen.

I grit my teeth against the possessive anger and exhale a slow breath, trying to find some calm.

Here's the thing, finding Charlene mostly naked in any given room in my house is not necessarily out of the ordinary.

Even the selection of lingerie arranged in a very neat circle around her—everything from virginal satin to a studded leather corset—isn't particularly unusual. Charlene enjoys dressing up, and her choices often tell me a lot about what she'd like to have happen in the bedroom—or whichever room we're having sex in —and prove helpful in allowing me to gauge her expectations. Leather often indicates she's feeling feisty. It's cute when she thinks she wants to be in charge.

What *is* highly atypical is the second circle, which consists of a wide variety of assistive pleasure devices, many of which have been on Charlene's *I think I might want to try that eventually* list. It's a long list. Almost as long as her *I thought it would be fun but I changed my mind* list.

Charlene and I have been extraordinarily careful about keeping what she feels is our *sometimes colorful* sex life private. What happens behind closed doors should remain behind closed doors, as far as I'm concerned. It's the reason I've always insisted on an NDA—until Charlene, anyway. Not particularly romantic or enticing when starting a new relationship, but my privacy has always taken precedence.

In lieu of signing a non-disclosure agreement, Charlene promised not to discuss our details with her girlfriends. Those women love to share, especially her best friend, Violet, and I have a feeling they might not fully understand the complexities of our relationship, since sometimes even I struggle with that.

"I'm sorry," Charlene's voice shakes along with her hands as she clutches the ends of the throw.

"Stay here, please." I bend and press a kiss to the top of her head, hoping the simple gesture helps dispel some of her anxiety.

Her bottom lip trembles. "Okay."

I want to assure her my dark mood isn't directed at her, but I need to deal with my teammates before they run their mouths to someone besides each other, like their girlfriends or wives. This is why relationships are tricky. I may trust Charlene to maintain our privacy, but I can't be sure anyone else will—especially when we live in a world where people like to color inside the lines, and Charlene believes she likes to scribble in all the margins, when really she likes to get close to the margins and then run away from them.

I step over the sex toys, noting exactly how many are from her *I thought it would be fun but I changed my mind* box. Apparently she had big plans. I wasn't expecting her until much later, as she'd messaged earlier to let me know she had to work late. She must have rearranged her schedule to accommodate me.

I drag a hand down my face and follow my teammates outside as they head for their respective vehicles.

"Wait." It's more bark than word.

They turn as a collective, expressions ranging from curious to downright disturbed. I need to do triage and smooth this over. I slip my hands into my pockets, conscious to remain calm on the outside, unaffected. I think it's pointless to tell them it isn't what it looks like, because it honestly is exactly what it looks like, just not quite the way they think.

Instead I go with, "It would be ideal if we could all keep this between us."

"And you all think *I'm* fucked in the head? What the fuck is wrong with *you*?" Lance waves a hand in the air as I open my mouth to speak. "Never mind. I don't want to know." He spins around and stalks to his Hummer. "I'm out."

"It's really not . . . ." I don't know how to finish that sentence without compromising Charlene more than she already has been, so I don't.

"We'll talk to Lance. You don't have to worry about him saying anything." Miller thumbs over his shoulder and then motions between himself and Randy.

Randy lifts a finger, looking like he has something to add, but he stops and strokes his beard, gives me a nod, and follows Miller to the Hummer. Of all the guys, Randy is probably the least likely to get on my ass about this. Last month he and Lily did five grand in damage to a hotel bathroom when they ripped the sink off the wall during one of their own sexy funtimes and flooded the room.

"I always thought you were so . . . normal." Rookie rushes after them. He doesn't even have the door closed before Lance starts backing up.

Alex is the only one left. We watch Lance's Hummer peel out of the driveway.

"What was that about?" I ask.

Alex glances at me, his expression flat, lips mashed into a line. "I don't know."

I don't like the way he's looking at me, like he doesn't know me. And in some ways, he doesn't. He only knows the sides of me I let him see. And now he's seen one that's not easy to explain.

"Let Charlene talk to Violet, please."

He huffs out a small laugh and shakes his head. "What Charlene tells Vi isn't your problem right now, Darren."

"It's not what it lo—" I stop, because it's pointless to say that. "It's complicated."

"Well, it just got a fuckload more complicated." He runs a hand through his hair. "I'm gonna see if I can catch up with the guys and make sure they keep this to themselves, maybe find out what's got Lance so riled."

"I should come with you."

I take a step toward his car, but Alex slaps a palm against my chest. He gives me a look, somewhere between disbelief and disgust. "Are you fucking serious right now? You can't leave Charlene in there on her own after that. Where are your priorities? Manage your relationship, Darren, or whatever the hell it is."

He's right. Of course. But what he doesn't understand is that Charlene is my priority, and making sure the guys keep their mouths shut is more about her than it is about me.

2

OH. NO

CHARLENE

Well, this certainly didn't go as planned. I had great intentions when I came here today. Violet is the one who made the suggestion. Well, she didn't suggest I surround myself with weird sex toys and hang out naked in Darren's living room. She thought it would be a good idea for me to be here when he arrived home so I could offer to relieve some of his stress. With sex.

I glance around at the sex wheel of fortune. Individually, the toys might not be that shocking—except maybe the dragon dildo, the crotchless black latex bodysuit, and possibly the mask that looks like it belongs to the lizard man or something—okay, maybe it's a bit more shocking than I originally thought. On a scale of one to ten, I would classify this as an eleventy-billion of epic clusterfuck.

Playoffs begin in a few short days, which is both exciting and stressful. Chicago has had a great season and is in a good position points-wise. But the excitement over making it into the playoffs this year is dampened by the looming expansion draft.

Today they had a team meeting about it, and Darren doesn't have a no-trade clause like Alex, so he must be worried. I know I am. It doesn't matter that he's older than a lot of his teammates; his stats are great—better than they were last year, which puts him at risk. Especially since the owner of the expansion team has been interested in Darren before.

So I came up with an awesome plan to surprise him. Or it would've been awesome if he hadn't brought half his team home with him. I'd wanted to provide all the best distractions for Darren tonight in the form of every single sex toy and apparatus he's ever seemed remotely interested in. In hindsight, my choices might have been a little over the top.

I clutch the blanket Darren draped around my shoulders and stare at the empty space where his teammates—our friends—stood moments ago. The front door closes with a slam. I jolt and clench below the waist, as if it's echoed in my clit.

Which it kind of is. Whenever I get anxious, I feel it in my vagina, like my clit is the Grand Central Station for my nervousness. It's rather inconvenient, and it can be embarrassing. It's also not a normal reaction to stress. I know this, but there's nothing I can do to stop it.

I finger the pearls at my throat, their smooth surface strangely calming as I debate whether I should clean up the kinky evidence, or wait for Darren as he requested. Another wave of anxiety slaps me right between the thighs. My eyes roll up, and I exhale a shuddery breath.

I don't have a chance to make a decision about putting away the sex toys, because the front door opens and closes—much more gently this time. Darren appears at the threshold of the living room a few moments later.

"I didn't think you'd be by until later," he says, low and even, despite the dark look he's wearing.

I swallow thickly as he approaches, my body lighting up like an arcade game. A bead of sweat trickles down my spine and I shiver, clutching the blanket tighter.

"I wanted to surprise you. I thought it would be okay since the guys never come here. I'm so sorry."

"You've already apologized." He steps over the dragon dick again—it's ridiculously huge, and not at all useful—and skirts a pale lace teddy until he's standing in front of me. His rough finger rests gently under my chin, and he tips my head up. His expression is intense, as is typical of Darren. "And you're certainly a surprise."

Instinctively, I want to issue yet another apology. My lips part of their own volition, and Darren tilts his head ever so slightly. It feels like a warning. I have to remind myself to breathe. Shadows dance across his face, sharpening the angles and making them more severe. He's terrifyingly beautiful. Quietly stunning.

He caresses my cheek, the touch so gentle it's entirely possible I imagine it. "We need to talk about how this changes things." He holds out his hand. "And I would prefer if you weren't on your knees for this discussion."

My panic takes over, and the worst possibilities bubble up in my head. The weight of his words feel like anchors wrapped around my heart. The only thing Darren has ever asked of me is to keep our private life private, and now it isn't anymore.

I slip my shaking, clammy fingers into his warm palm. I'm stiff from kneeling for so long, and I wobble unsteadily as Darren helps me to my feet.

The uneasiness that's settled low in my belly flares and claws its way up, twisting through my stomach, into my chest, until it clamps around my throat. My pearls feel too tight and not tight enough.

What have I done? What if he breaks up with me over this?

My lashes wet with each frantic attempt to blink back the tears. All it took was one mistake to unravel two years. I feel as though I've tried to build a house of cards on the precipice of a mountain.

"It was an accident." The words crack like shattering glass.

"I'm aware it was unintentional." Darren frowns. "Why are you crying?"

"I broke a promise."

He inclines his head—it's more acknowledgement than it is agreement. "And what do you think that means?"

I lick my lips, my mouth dry, palms sweaty. "That you're going to . . ."

"I'm going to?" he prompts.

The words stick in my throat, like I've tried to swallow a pill without water. "I shouldn't have listened to Violet. I should've messaged you first. I didn't think. I-I-I—"

"Charlene, stop." He places his wet thumb against my lips, and I taste my own sadness.

Darren takes my face in his palms. I memorize the feel of his fingers sliding along the edge of my jaw, consider what the absence of his touch will be like. Remember how the fear that Darren could be traded at the end of the season has plagued me all day.

I brace myself as he tips my head up. "Look at me."

I have no choice but to comply. I try to stop my chin from quivering, but I'm too unnerved to manage my emotions.

He sweeps his thumbs under my eyes as new tears free themselves. "Do you think I'm angry with you?"

"I don't know."

"Then what are you so upset about?"

Now it's my turn to frown. "I-I—" I have to take several deep breaths to calm down and organize my thoughts. "You didn't want anyone to know." I motion to the lingerie and surrounding sex toys. "And now they do. So I thought maybe . . . it might mean that you'd—"

He waits for me to go on.

"End this." The words barely carry.

"End this?" His expression shifts to confusion.

"Us. End . . . us." My stomach churns at the thought. Losing Darren would mean giving up a lot more than a boyfriend. He's connected to almost every single important person in my entire world.

His eyes flare. "Do you honestly believe I would walk away from you over something so trite?" His jaw tics. "Have I ever been that rash in my decision making?"

"No, but—" I bite my lip and drop my gaze. It's hard to look at him when he's this intense. His severe beauty is more than I can handle sometimes.

"Is it unfortunate? Yes. Will it create unpleasant questions? Most likely, yes." He traces the contour of my eyebrow, sweeping along my temple. "Help me understand what's happening in this beautiful head that would make you come to such an extreme conclusion."

"I just thought, I don't know. I broke a promise. The *only* promise. I guess in my head it's the same as if I'd gone back on an NDA."

I've taken great pride in my ability to keep our private life private. Well, I mean, obviously I talk to Violet about the things I can, but I never tell her what *really* happens behind closed doors.

"Did you happen to write an exposé chronicling our sex life in an attempt to blackmail me in addition to this?" He makes a sweeping motion to encompass the circle of toys and lingerie.

"No, I just gave all of your closest friends a very vivid peek into what we do when no one else is watching." Now that I'm not quite so worried about Darren breaking up with me, embarrassment is setting in.

His cheek tics, not with a smile exactly, but a hint of mischievous humor makes his eyes glint. "I'm sure they're having a very interesting conversation about it at this precise moment. And I'm even more certain questions will follow for both of us, which is why we need to discuss how this changes things."

"Oh." Wow. I went way overboard with the internal drama on this one.

"Come. You're shaking; you need to sit." He keeps hold of one hand and wraps his other around my waist, guiding me to the couch.

I drop to the cushion and immediately spring back up, face mashing into Darren's chest. His fingers curl around my arms. "Are you okay?"

"Fine. I'm fine." *Shit*. I forgot how thoroughly I prepared for *any* possible scenario this evening, which is saying something about my state of anxiety and might explain why it's been bouncing around in my clit so hard.

"Between the tears and how jumpy you are, I'm going to disagree that you're fine." He smooths a palm down my back. I try to shift away before he reaches my ass, but my calves are pressed against the couch and I'm wearing sky high stilettos—which accounts for the sore ankles—so my coordination is somewhat lacking. I accidently step on the end of the blanket, tugging it free from my grasp, which means I'm once again naked—apart from shoes, and pearls. At least this time there are no other witnesses.

"Maybe I should get dressed before we talk about how to deal with this," my suggestion is super pitchy.

Darren's eyes narrow as I attempt to untangle my heel from the blanket. It's one of those soft, hand knitted ones from a super-cute store downtown. I pointed it out to Darren once when we were out for dinner, and the next time I came over it was draped over the reading chair he bought me last year. The chair doesn't often get used for reading, and the blanket doesn't match Darren's décor, but it's sweet that he bought it for me.

Unfortunately, I'm now caught up in his thoughtfulness.

Literally.

"Turn around for me, Charlene." Darren's voice is low, commanding.

My entire body flashes with goose bumps. *Oh shit.* His expression is no longer serious. Instead a dark smile appears briefly. I can't decide right now if that's a good or a bad thing.

I turn slowly, fighting the urge to crane my neck so I can see his face. I shudder as he drags a single knuckle from the top of my spine to my tailbone and then lower. Fanning out his fingers, he skims the pink, fuzzy bunny tail—which is attached to a butt plug that's currently parked in my ass.

"I see you had expectations for tonight," he murmurs.

"No expectations," I breathe.

"I don't think that's true." His lips are at my ear, his fingers spread across the underside of my jaw, palm resting against the base of my throat as his other hand trails along my hip, palm flattening under my navel as his chest comes flush with my back.

His shirt is cotton, soft and warm, his belt buckle is a cold shock resting against my low back. I exhale on a whimper when Darren's fingertips graze the crest of my pubic bone, the heel of his palm pressing firmly against my low belly, his thick erection putting pressure on the plug through the barrier of his jeans.

"I wanted to be prepared for whatever you needed tonight," I whisper.

"Ah, you were being thoughtful, then?"

"I know today was stressful for you." It sure was stressful for me, even more so in the past twenty minutes.

"All this trouble you went to." His teeth graze the sensitive skin at the side of my neck. "It was definitely a stressful day, and you would've been the perfect surprise had circumstances been different."

"I'm sorry." I need to stop saying that.

"Actions always speak so much louder than words, don't they?" His voice is a shadow looming. "Why don't you show me how sorry you are?"

ANXIETY ORGASMS

DARREN

It's a good thing Charlene can't see my face right now. It's difficult to not smile, which is the reason I have her in this position. Of all the relationships I've been in—which isn't all that many considering most women aren't excited about signing an NDA before the first date—Charlene is hands down my favorite sexual partner. She's my favorite everything, really.

Her throat bobs with a nervous swallow under my palm. I bite the shell of her ear. "Whatever shall I do with you?"

She stumbles forward a step when I release her. She doesn't turn around, doesn't ask any questions, simply waits for instructions. It looks like she's giving me the reins tonight. I bite my knuckle as I consider the plethora of sex toys and then Charlene.

She really is gorgeous, with her long auburn hair piled on top of her head to expose the gentle line of her neck, slender shoulders rolled back, and that pink bunny tail peeking out from between her ass cheeks is just . . . adorably sexy. If there was a sex toy that could encapsulate Charlene's personality, it's that goddamn butt plug.

Here's the thing about Charlene: I know what she wants better than she does. And it sure isn't that fucking mammoth dragon cock sitting in the middle of the living room floor. Charlene has an incredibly wild imagination, and she loves to read every dirty, smutty book she can get her hands on.

She also thinks she wants to try everything, but sometimes she jumps in head first and then realizes what she thought, and what truly is, are not the same. So she'll come at me with the most extreme of extremes, and I've learned from experience and trial and error to feed into it, then dial it all the way back until we're a few shades out from vanilla. That way she's not at risk of having a full-on panic attack over the possibility that I might try something she's not ready for.

It's clear my needs were her priority when she set this up today, which tells me more about her frame of mind than she realizes. Charlene is worried, just as I am, about the expansion draft. I know better than to expect her to say it outright, but her concern is laid out in the offerings surrounding us. What Charlene doesn't understand is that my needs end and begin with only her.

Starting at her shoulder, I drag my finger along her skin, following the contour of the pearl necklace, and slowly circle her.

Her hazel gaze rises to meet mine, lashes fluttering. It's filled with need and uncertainty and desire. My worry is echoed in the parting of her lips, in her shallow breaths and her tiny hum of longing. I want to take her to the edge and hold her there. I want to make her understand that there is no end to us, that I will never willingly walk away from her—not unless that's what she wants.

Charlene is like a firefly, and sometimes that's what I call her. She's elusive, and if you catch her she'll burn bright, but keeping her trapped dulls her fire and dims her beauty.

So I don't trap her. Not for long, anyway. I might enjoy watching her burn for me, but in the end I always set her free. Over and over, I let her fly away, even though it goes against every instinct I have.

So far she always comes back. I keep waiting for that to change, and hoping it won't. The expansion draft could be a potential threat to this thing we have, and it makes me edgy.

I dip down and press my lips to hers, flicking my tongue out to taste her, but not slipping inside as I'm sure she wants. Her lips are like candy, but I taste the salt of her uncertainty, tracked in tears over her cheeks. Charlene stumbles forward, chest meeting mine as she grips my shirt.

I drop one hand to her hip to prevent contact from the waist down, and to help keep her upright. She moans against my lips, the sound sweet and needy. As much as I'd like to deepen this kiss and make it last for hours—and I truly would—she needs to be taken care of. And so do I.

I pull back, stroking her cheek as she whimpers her displeasure. "You should choose something from your circle of sex toys so we can play."

I allow a half-smile to form as I drag a finger from the center of her clavicle, down between her breasts, going lower to circle her navel before I finally dip between her thighs. She sucks in a tremulous breath as I skim past the hood piercing—the one she opted to get during a long stretch of away games. Her legs shake as I brush the inside of her thigh.

"What are you waiting for?" I cup between her legs. "Make a choice, little firefly. Or maybe I should call you little bunny, all considering."

"But I—" Her eyes roll up as I drag my fingertips past her entrance. She's so wet. I can feel myself unraveling—the stress of this day, the possibility of potential loss too much to handle. I need to drown myself in the certainty of her.

"Unless you'd prefer I make it for you."

She exhales a quick breath as I remove my hand from between her legs. I grip her hips to keep her steady and glance to the right. Her eyes follow mine, landing on the ball gag, and dart back to my face.

She tips her chin up, so determined, even though her voice wavers. "I want whatever you want."

I tap the end of her nose and smile darkly. "I guess we'll find out whether that's true or not, won't we?"

TWO HOURS LATER, Charlene is stretched out along my side, her head resting on my chest. Her manicured nails trace the dips in my abs. When she reaches my navel she circles, the sensation sending a rush of goose flesh over my skin. She flattens her palm and smooths it all the way back up, as if it will erase the imaginary lines she draws on me.

"Keep doing that and you're going to wake the beast," I warn.

She lifts her head, resting her chin on my pec, her wide hazel eyes meeting mine as she drags her finger back down the center of my chest.

Somewhere downstairs a cell phone buzzes across a hard surface.

I grab her hand before she reaches my navel and thread my fingers through hers. "We need to discuss how to handle our friends." I bring her fingers to my lips, kissing the tips of each so she doesn't take it as rejection.

"I'm spending tomorrow afternoon with Violet and the girls."

"Which means you'll be fielding questions, I'm sure." I understand that asking the guys not to say anything excludes their significant others. Charlene is always the exception to every rule, it seems. I'm aware it's no different for my friends, hence the reason I asked Alex to allow Charlene a chance to talk to Violet—I'm not sure that was a reasonable demand, considering.

Charlene chews on the inside of her lip. "What should I tell them?"

"What do you want to tell them?"

She lifts a shoulder. "I don't know. I mean, it's not like we're superfreaks or anything."

I fight a smile. We're far from superfreaks, although Charlene's collection of toys, outfits, and props would lead some to believe otherwise. "So maybe that's what you tell them."

"Violet might be upset."

"Why?" Violet doesn't strike me as judgmental. From what I understand, she likes to dress up Alex's cock as a super hero, which is fucking weird. But then Alex is also a little off center, so there's that.

"Because she's always been open with me, and I haven't been the same with her. I sort of let her come to her own conclusions. I let all the girls come to their own conclusions, but now they're going to have all these ideas. It's one thing for them to speculate when there was no evidence to support it, but this is different. It was kind of fun to keep them guessing, and I never figured they would take me seriously. Now they'll want to know what's really going on."

I trail my fingers down her spine, enjoying her shiver. "I can take the blame for all the secrecy."

"I like the secrecy. I liked that what we had was just ours." Charlene murmurs, eyes on my chin. "I just don't want Violet to be hurt."

"And you're worried about that?" I prompt.

26

"It'll be fine. She'll be fine," she says, possibly as much to herself as to me.

"You're sure?" I don't understand why Violet would be hurt, but then she's a woman, and sometimes I don't understand their reactions to things. Even Charlene, who I can read fairly well most of the time, has odd reactions on occasion.

She nods pensively. "I mean, I guess the most awkward part is that all my girlfriends' significant others have seen me naked. But it could be worse, right? At least it wasn't the whole team."

Charlene is referencing the time Alex and Violet were caught fucking in the locker room. Alex had been ejected from the game for beating the shit out of a Toronto player. The guy had been taunting him, so it was somewhat understandable. The entire team walked into the locker room as a woman was screaming her way through an orgasm. That woman turned out to be Violet, now his wife.

All I saw were her legs wrapped around his waist.

In this case, all of our closest friends have seen Charlene's pierced nipples, so it's a little different, but I'd prefer to lessen her anxiety over this, rather than make it worse, so I don't point that out. "Fortunately it was only a few of the guys."

"What're you going to tell them?"

I lift a shoulder. "I don't have plans to tell them anything."

"But won't they ask questions?"

It's my turn to shrug. "They can ask, doesn't mean I'm going to answer."

"But you can't tell them nothing."

I don't understand her sudden panic. "Is there something you want me to tell them?"

"No. I don't know. Just . . . all that stuff in the living room sort of paints its own picture, doesn't it?"

"And that concerns you?"

"They're going to think you use all that stuff on me."

"You're the one who surrounded yourself with it."

"It was all stuff I thought you might be interested in," she mumbles.

"Ah, now the truth comes out, but I'll keep that little detail to myself, if that's what you prefer." I untwine our hands and hook her leg over my hip. "We can discuss details later, over dinner. Right now I have plans to fill you up again."

GIRLS BE GOSSIPING

CHARLENE

Ever have one of those dreams where you know it's not real but you can't seem to pull yourself out of it? It happens to me all the time. I have this recurring nightmare where I'm locked in an RV and there's no way out. The RV gets smaller and smaller, like I'm Alice in Wonderland and I've eaten the wrong thing. I'm growing, growing, growing while everything else is shrinking, shrinking, shrinking.

I wake up and instantly go into panic mode because I can't move. It takes me several blinks and just as many seconds to realize I'm not in my bedroom, I'm in Darren's, and it's him I'm trapped under. Well, I'm not exactly under him, but he's wrapped completely around me, which is . . . abnormal.

Usually Darren sleeps like Dracula, on his back with his arms crossed over his chest, and I starfish on the other side of the bed. But not today. Today we're spooning.

I try to slip out from under his arm, but it tightens around me. "Oh no you don't." His voice is gravelly in my ear, and his lips brush my neck. "I'm taking full advantage of the fact that you being here means I don't have to rub one out in the shower."

"I'm so glad I can be helpful."

He smiles against my shoulder. "Tools are helpful, Charlene. You in my bed this morning is a treat."

My heart flutters at his words and the warmth of his lips on my skin. That fluttery feeling echoes through my body as his palm glides down my stomach.

"And I plan to enjoy you as I would the most decadent dessert," he whispers in my ear before he bites the lobe.

By the time we're done I've had two more orgasms, which Darren happily adds to his running tally. He quite literally keeps track of my orgasms, like they're part of our sex stats.

I curl up against his side, blissed out enough that my brain and my mouth are on a disconnect, so I ask a question I'm not so sure I want the answer to. "Did you find anything out about the expansion draft?"

"Just that Alex and Randy are safe. The rest is up in the air until they announce the other players they want to hold on to."

"Do you think you'll be one of them?"

He runs his fingers through my tangled hair. "It's hard to say. At thirty-four I'm closer to the end of my career than I am to the beginning, but that doesn't necessarily mean anything."

"Because the Vegas team owner has a hard-on over you?"

Darren sighs. "Yeah. Here's hoping he doesn't throw away one of his picks on me, but if he does, I guess I spend a year in Vegas playing like shit so they don't renew my contract."

I don't know whether he's intentionally left me out of the equation or not.

He checks the clock on the nightstand. "Fuck. I didn't realize it was so late. I need to go. I have practice in half an hour."

I regret bringing up the expansion draft when we don't have time to really talk about it. He rushes to get dressed and gives me a quick peck on the lips as he shoves his wallet and phone in his back pocket.

"Your face smells like my pussy!" I shout as he rushes out of the bedroom.

"It's my favorite cologne," he calls back.

I expect to hear the door slam shut, but instead he pounds his way back up the stairs. He appears in the doorway, expression unreadable as he tosses my phone on the bed and then climbs up after it. "You have a thousand messages from Violet. She'd like to know if you're being kept in my lair and if so, do you have a cage, or are you allowed to sleep in my bed." He straddles me, eyes dark as he leans down, fingers sliding into my hair at the nape of my neck. His lips ghost over mine. "Feel free to answer that however you like."

I wait to see what he's going to do. Apart from a few brushings of lips and teasing of tongues, there wasn't much kissing last night. Our mouths were too busy on other things.

He sucks my bottom lip between his and then his tongue flicks out, stroking along the roof of my mouth, causing me to jerk and flail. He pulls back, eyes searching my face as one side of his mouth twists in a malevolent smile. "Change the setting on your phone so there's no preview of the messages, Charlene. Unless you want me and the rest of the world to know the content of your conversations with Violet."

With that he releases me. I flop back down on the mattress as he gracefully rolls off the bed. He pauses at the door. "Next time I'll kiss you for hours before I let you come."

And with that, he disappears down the hall. I cover my mouth with my palm and smile behind it. I don't care if our relationship is weird; I wouldn't trade it for all the normals in the world.

I pick up my phone and key in my password. Darren wasn't lying. I have a million and one messages from Violet. Half of them are gifs of the Fifty Shades movies. Most of them feature Christian Grey half naked, so I get distracted by the pretty as I scroll back through them. They stopped from midnight until eight this morning, and then started up again. The most recent ones are requests for proof of life.

I'm about to take a selfie, but then I realize I look like I could be a kidnapping victim with how messed up my hair is, so instead I search the internet for pictures of sex dungeons and send that to her instead.

I love Violet, and she knows more about me than anyone else in this world—except maybe my mother, and in some ways, Darren. But after my mom and I left The Ranch when I was a teenager, it was drilled into me to gloss over personal details. The less I share, the easier it is to keep myself and the people around me protected from my past. It's part of the reason Darren and I work so well. We're both private people when it comes to our pasts, and that makes him safe in a way a lot of other people are not.

Almost as soon as I hit send, my phone rings. "You do realize Darren and I have been dating for two years. I think you'd know by now if he chained me up and kept me in a cage," I say by way of greeting.

"Alex said the living room looked like a BDSM porn set."

"It was just a few toys and some lingerie." I'm downplaying it, by a lot, but Violet is prone to exaggeration, and those two are pretty vanilla—apart from the costumes she makes for Alex's penis, anyway.

"Lies. Go wash Darren's pearl necklace off your chest and get your ass in your car. I need to know exactly how much you've been keeping from me so I know how angry I'm supposed to pretend to be when the rest of the girls get here. Oh, and pick me up a dairy-free latte on the way over." With that she hangs up.

I'm relieved that she doesn't seem nearly as upset as I expected. I take a quick shower, not because there's jizz on my chest—although there might be some in my hair—but because there was a lot of sweating between last night and this morning, and I'm a little ripe. I also smell like I bathed in sex perfume.

I put on my dress from yesterday since my bag with extra clothes is still in the car. I have an extra outfit or two in the trunk of my car at all times. And an emergency escape kit, just in case. I think it might be a PTSD thing from the whole fleeing The Ranch when I was a teenager, but I'm not willing to unload it on a therapist, so all I can do is hypothesize.

For years after we left, my mom and I always had a bag of essentials packed: three changes of clothes, hair dye, toiletries, Miss Flopsy (I will love that stuffed bunny forever), five thousand dollars in cash—obviously small bills, a burner phone and new identification, and a few other essentials. Was it overkill? Probably. But then my mom isn't playing with a full deck. She's missing pretty much every face card there is. But I still love her.

I'm on my way downstairs when I hear a code being punched into the front door. I freeze on the stairs. It can't be Darren coming back; he has practice. The front door opens, and the warning alarm beeps.

"Mr. Westinghouse! It's Gertrude. I am here for the house-keeping!"

I let out a relieved sigh. Gertrude has been Darren's house-keeper for years. I take the rest of the stairs at a light jog, my calves tight from last night's awkward, but fun, sex positions. Gertrude appears in the hallway as I reach the bottom of the stairs.

Now here's something interesting about my relationship with Darren: we don't have a lot of sleepovers. He's a light sleeper, and I'm a flailer, so I feel bad when I wake him up with my acrobatics routine in the middle of the night—at least this is the excuse I usually give him.

I mean, I do feel bad when I accidentally elbow him in the face, and once I charlie-horsed him with my knee, but sleeping beside someone else is . . . strange. You really need to trust someone to be unconscious next to them for a lot of hours in a row. Waking up the way I did this morning, with Darren wrapped around me, makes me feel vulnerable, and also protected, which doesn't make a lot of sense, but there it is.

"Hey, Trudes!"

Gertrude startles and nearly drops her cleaning gear. "Oh! Miss Hoar! I am sorry to surprise you!" She looks past me, up the stairs. "I can come back later if now is a bad time."

I wish she would just call me Charlene. She always forgets the H in my last name – Hoar –is silent. "You're good," I sigh. "Darren's at the arena, and I'm on my way out."

She smiles, looking a little relieved. I don't think she likes cleaning when Darren's home. He makes her nervous. He makes a lot of people nervous because he's so quiet and intense, sometimes even me. But it's the good kind of nervous.

"I will get started right away then." She heads for the living room. Two seconds later, she shrieks.

I rush to find out what happened and cringe. The remains of the kinky sex toy wheel of fortune are still scattered around the living room. The dragon dick stands majestically in the middle of it all, right beside the ball gag and the latex body suit. I don't know what I was thinking when I pulled all that stuff out yesterday, other than I wanted to erase my fear and make Darren happy.

I scramble for a reason all of this stuff to be here. "I'm so sorry! We had a party last night."

She glances at me with wide, horrified eyes.

"I mean with my girlfriends."

Now she looks downright disturbed.

"Shite McCockslap," I mutter. "It was a joke. One of my girlfriends is getting married, and we had one of those bachelorette sex toy parties, but the host brought all this stuff. Crazy, right? I'll just put it all away for you." I put my hand on her shoulder and turn her away from the sex prop trainwreck. "You can start in the kitchen."

She nods mutely, lids fluttering as she fans her face with her feather duster. I snap a photo of the living room before I put everything away. Darren has more than one special trunk in his walk-in closet, complete with padlocks, where we store all the toys for exactly this reason.

Gertrude is in the kitchen with her cell phone plastered to her ear, speaking in German, since that happens to be her mother tongue. I lean casually against the doorjamb, don an icy smile, and clear my throat. She startles, again, and drops her phone on the floor.

"Oh! Miss Hoar! I did not realize you were still here." She bends to pick up the phone, says something into the receiver, and ends the call.

"I'm on my way out now." I tip my head to the side, exactly the way Darren does when he's measuring his words. "I think now might be a good time to remind you of the NDA you've signed and how it pertains to all facets of Darren's life within these walls."

Her eyes flare until I fear she'll be unable to blink ever again. "Of course, Miss Hoar. I will not breathe a word of your sex party to anyone."

"Bachelorette party. Have a lovely day, Trudes."

I spin on my heel and sashay to the garage, where my car is parked. I waffle for a moment over what I should do about the Trudes situation.

I don't typically text Darren directly after a sleepover. I don't ever want to appear clingy, so I try to wait until he messages me, but it isn't easy. By the twenty-four-hour mark, my anxiety gets pretty bad, and no amount of marble rolling seems to calm it down.

I decide it's in my best interest to let Darren know what Trudes saw this morning. I send him the picture of the living room pre-cleanup, along with a message to check his voicemail. Then I leave him a voicemail and fill him in on Gertrude, suggesting he call and remind her of the NDA himself, because he's a fuckton scarier than I am.

I stop on the way over to Violet's, pick up coffees for us, and order myself a breakfast sandwich, which I scarf down in less than a minute. I'm always super hungry after a night with Darren. It's better than a boot camp workout, that's for sure.

I pull into Violet's driveway and take a deep breath, aware that I'm walking into a conversation that's going to be awkward, especially with Violet.

The door opens before I can even knock. "Took you long enough. Did you have to free yourself from Darren's elaborate restraint system to get here?"

I pass her the dairy-free latte. "Haha. There was a line at Starfucks."

She checks the label before she takes a sip, since there have been occasions when they've gotten the order wrong and Violet has paid the price for consuming dairy. She arches a brow at me over the lip of her cup, moaning her latte love.

"Thanks for this. Now get in here and give me some details."

I follow her down the hall to the kitchen, where a pile of takeout bags sit unopened on the counter. Violet doesn't cook, which is a good thing because she's horrible at it. She and Alex would starve to death if she were in charge of meals.

She plunks down on a chair and slaps the counter. "Well?"

"Well what?" I'm not going to make this easy for her.

Darren suggested I tell the girls whatever I damn well please, but I don't know how much I want to share. I've enjoyed how private our relationship has been up until now. Darren definitely has a commanding presence, so it's not hard to imagine that extending beyond his performance on the ice.

"Alex said there was a ball gag, and some weird latex stuff, and a fucked-up giant dildo, or butt plug—he wasn't sure. I hope you're happy with yourself because thanks to you, Alex spent an hour on some online sex toy shop and asked me fifty times if I wanted an anal training set." She taps the counter with her manicured nails.

"You're going to need a hell of a lot more than an anal training set to get that dick in your ass," I scoff.

I've accidentally seen Alex's hard-on—through the barrier of boxer shorts, but still. It was enough to know Violet isn't exaggerating his size. Darren is well-endowed, above the national average for sure, but Alex's dick is terrifying. I have no idea how Violet walks without crying most days.

"No shit." Violet wrinkles her nose. "Anyway, Alex's Area 51 mission aside, I'm kind of pissed at you. I can't believe you've kept this from me all this time."

I sigh. This is what I was worried about. "There really isn't anything to tell."

"Uh, pretty sure that's a lie with all the freaky deaky Alex saw. Clearly there's a lot more to it than Darren jizzing on your chest and getting into your Access Denied hole."

"I promised Darren I wouldn't say anything."

She frowns. "But I'm your best friend. Those promises don't apply to me."

I give her an apologetic smile. It's not fair to use Darren as a copout. "Darren is private about this kind of thing, and so am I."

"But we always talked about boyfriend stuff before Darren."

"Before Darren it was different. I didn't want to risk him getting asked questions by anyone, so . . ."

"I wouldn't have said anything if you'd told me not to."

I give her a look. "Not even Alex?"

She starts to speak but makes a face. "Okay, you have a point. I'd probably tell Alex because husbands fit under the same cone. Alex was pretty freaked out last night. I mean, those guys have been besties for as long as you and I have been besties, and he had no clue Darren was such a kinky fucker. We thought you might be a little off-side, but not all the way out in left field."

"It looked a lot more extreme than it is," I offer. "Most of it is the stuff my mom sends me from all her dominatrix conventions, and the majority of it I haven't even considered trying out. I guess I went a little overboard yesterday."

37

"Well, that's going to take all the fun out of the kink inquisition."

"Kink inquisition?"

"Yeah, the girls are freaking out over this. They started a group chat last night asking me all sorts of questions. I didn't pull you in because I figured you didn't want to be bombarded with text messages, and you were probably busy with Darren, doing whatever." She crosses over to the fridge and produces a couple of bottles. She holds out the champagne. "Pre-inquisition mimosa?"

"That's probably a good idea."

"I figured."

She hands me a glass and pours herself some sparkling grape juice since she and Alex are actively trying to get her knocked up, and she doesn't want to drink until or unless she gets her period. Then the doorbell chimes. I exhale a nervous breath. This is probably going to be uncomfortable, but if I can deal with wearing a butt plug for several hours, I'm pretty sure I can handle a few questions and dispel some misconceptions.

Sunny, Lily, and Poppy appear in the kitchen a minute later. It's awkward times a million. Especially since the first thing out of my mouth is, "Sorry all your significant others saw me naked yesterday."

"Everyone except Lance has heard me come," Violet says, because she's my best friend and is happy to offset my humiliation with her own.

"Um, Lance has heard you come, Violet, and so have the rest of us," Poppy, Lance's fiancée, says quietly.

Her face turns the color of her name. She's so stinking cute. It's amazing that someone so sweet could end up with one of the most volatile players in the league, who was also dubbed a notorious womanizer—although the media likes to twist things around. And from what I know, Lance is actually a little broken, kind of like me and Darren both seem to be. His childhood wasn't the best either.

Violet looks confused. "Since when?"

"When we went to the cottage over winter break and you and Alex had sex in the outdoor shower," Lily replies when Poppy doesn't respond right away.

"Ooooh, right. Lesson learned on that one, I guess."

"And only Darren and Miller haven't seen me naked, so don't feel too bad." Lily gives me a side hug.

"Wait, what?" Poppy suddenly looks like she's ready to go a round. As sweet as she is, she's a massage therapist, so she's strong, and dating Lance means she has to have a backbone of steel. She also has a fiery personality to match her hair.

"It was an accident. Randy came home from an away series, and I answered the door wearing a bow like a necklace. I didn't know Lance was with him until it was too late," Lily explains.

"And Alex saw her naked when she was six, so that doesn't really count," Violet adds.

"Oh. Right." That seems to calm Poppy down.

"My boob popped out when I was breastfeeding Logan at a team BBQ last summer." Sunny pats her little baby bump. "But only Miller saw, so I guess that's not the same."

"It's a good one, though." Violet claps her hands. "Okay. Who needs a drink before the sex-quisition?"

"The what?" Sunny asks.

"The sex-quisition. The sex inquisition. I'm sure everyone has questions for Charlene after last night. I figured nothing goes better with uncomfortable questions about our sex lives than booze! Sunny, I have dealcoholized champagne for us. It basically tastes like fizzy grape juice, but we can drink it out of fun glasses and pretend we're getting drunk, too."

Sunny shrugs. "I don't need to pretend to be drunk, but I like fizzy grape juice."

Violet serves everyone drinks, and we all head to the living room. This whole thing makes me nervous. I mean, they're all my friends and we're all pretty open with each other, but with all the focus on me, I realize that *they're* open, while I've spent the past two years saying little about my sex life. I wish we could go back to the way it was before all my secrets were spilled out with the dragon-shaped plastic schlong.

I root around in my purse for one of my candies and pop it into my mouth. I need all the calm I can get. I don't care that the candy is going to make my mimosa taste like crap.

"I have a question." Lily drops into the chair parallel to mine.

"Oh, I bet you do." Violet grins.

"Randy wants to know where you go lingerie shopping."

That seems to break the tension a little. "Depends on what I'm shopping for, but I can give you a list of places."

"Or maybe we can go together," Lily says.

Poppy raises her hand. "I would like to go lingerie shopping."

"I need new maternity lingerie. I don't think the ones from Logan's pregnancy are going to fit for much longer." Sunny blinks a few times and then sniffs.

Lily and Poppy are out of their chairs with tissues and hugs before the first tear falls.

It's another minute of consoling before Sunny is okay again. "Sorry," she sniffs. "I'm already showing, and I just found out there's a baby in there. I can't imagine how big I'm going to be this time around."

Lily and Poppy murmur their understanding, even though Lily is the size of my wrist. Poppy is curvier, but being able to see her toes isn't an issue, and likely won't be for a while yet. At least I don't think she's going to jump on the baby train, but then who knows?

Darren and I have never talked about kids. He held Logan when he was born for, like, a minute and a half or something. He doesn't seem to have anything against kids, but he's never mentioned wanting them. Personally, I'm on the fence, mostly because my childhood was seriously fucked up, and I worry no matter what I do, I'll mess my own kid up by default.

Darren grew up in a very strict house with a lot of rules

about what constituted acceptable behavior, which may account for how private he is and his sometimes commanding presence in and out of the bedroom.

Sunny's mini-breakdown seems to have shifted the subject away from my unconventional sex life. For a few minutes, anyway.

"Once the playoffs are over, we should plan a trip to the cottage," Violet says.

"That would be so great! I want them to do well, but it would be nice if they were finished before June so they get a bit more of an off-season and Miller can spend more time with Logan," Sunny agrees.

"We could roll it right into a birthday celebration for Charlene or something!" Violet flaps her hands excitedly and nearly topples her sparkling grape juice.

"Aren't there a million black flies up there at the end of May?" I ask.

Once we left The Ranch, my mom and I never made a big deal about birthdays.

"Fine," Violet says. "We have the party here and plan a weekend at the cottage for later in June."

I wave off that idea. "I don't need a party."

"That's what you said last year. You're turning twenty-six. It's your champagne birthday, so we need to do something fun." Violet bounces, making her boobs shake and my mimosa slosh perilously. "It should be themed! We can all wear leather chaps!"

"Could you be any more cliché?" I roll my eyes. "Just to be clear, Darren doesn't own chaps."

"Just a ball gag and a mask with no eye holes, according to Alex."

And we're back to my sex life. I knew I was getting off so easy.

I wonder if Darren is catching this kind of heat today. I seriously doubt it's worse than what I'm getting since I don't think his friends are likely to push his buttons, but I'll have to ask when I speak to him next. I'm not sure when that will be, either. The message I sent about Gertrude was pretty straightforward and doesn't necessarily require a response. Maybe I should've worded it differently.

Sunny raises her hand, like we're all still in middle school and she's waiting her turn to speak. "Wouldn't a mask with no eyeholes be dangerous? You wouldn't be able to see where you're going." Her eyes widen, and she looks around the room. "And what's a ball gag?"

I honestly love that Sunny has grown up in this highly over-informed society and still manages to be innocent. I was sort of like that, at least until we left The Ranch. Then I went from blissfully innocent to exceptionally knowledgeable in a very short span of time. The internet, while helpful for finding information, is also not the best place to learn about things like sex. It was a rough transition.

"Yeah, Char, wouldn't a mask with no eyeholes be dangerous?" Violet props her fist on her chin and smiles. "And please, do explain what a ball gag is."

"I'm not sure you really want the answer to that, Sunny." Poppy gives me a look I can't quite decipher.

Sunny twirls her hair around her finger. "Why not?"

"Where's the harm in a little bondage-sex education? It's not like Miller's ever going to go out and buy either item for her. First of all, Alex would murder him, and secondly, I don't think that's Miller's thing."

Sunny's face lights up, and she does jazz hands. "Oh! I think I know what Miller's thing is!"

Lily grins. "Eating your cookie?"

"He really likes to do that, a lot. When my belly gets too big I'll have to watch from the mirror." She gets a faraway look in her eyes. "But he has another thing! Kind of like how you and Randy are always getting it on in bathrooms, except I think it's a bit more sanitary."

"And it doesn't cause thousands of dollars of damage," Violet adds.

Lily throws her hands up in the air. "That sink was already falling off the wall. It's not my fault it broke!"

"That was one expensive orgasm," I say.

"And Randy says it was worth every penny." Lily's smile is devious as she bites her knuckle, then turns to Sunny. "Anyway, back to Miller's thing."

Sunny wiggles around excitedly in her chair. "So Miller paints my toenails for me."

"Miller's thing is painting your toenails?"

"Yes. Well, no. I think he likes my toes." Her fingers go to her lips, and she looks around the room, her cheeks flushing.

"Say what now?" Violet asks.

"Sometimes he kisses them." She covers her mouth with her palm and says something unintelligible.

Violet sits forward in her chair. "Hold on a second, does Buck have a foot fetish?"

"Um, I don't know." Sunny looks worried now. "Is that weird? Is it, like, mask with no eyeholes kind of weird?"

I dig my toes into Violet's calf, a warning for her to keep her mouth shut. "No, Sunny. It's not weird. Lots of people like feet."

"All our nerve endings are in our feet," Sunny says matter of factly.

"That's actually true," Poppy confirms. "I've taken a course on foot massage."

"Miller gives the best foot massages! Anyway, he didn't say anything about what happened yesterday apart from that he saw your boobs and some things he shouldn't have, so I want to hear more about that, especially the face mask and ball gag thing. Who else wants to know what they are?" She raises her hand again and looks around, expecting everyone to raise their hand, too.

"Am I the only one who doesn't know what this stuff is?" Sunny frowns.

"It's okay not to know," I tell her.

"But all of you know." Sunny sits up a little straighter and flips her hair over her shoulder. "I want to know then, too."

I look to Poppy and Lily, who both shrug. They spend more time with Sunny than me. They would know what could potentially upset her, which is not something I want to do to a pregnant woman—especially not one as sensitive, and obviously naïve, as she is. I'm almost sad that I'm taking this little piece of innocence from her. "I guess a ball gag is exactly what it sounds like. It's a rubber ball that goes in your mouth."

Sunny looks horrified. "Isn't that dangerous? You could choke!"

God, I love her. "It has straps attached to it, so you can secure it at the back of your head," Lily explains.

Sunny blinks a few times. "Why would you strap a rubber ball to your face? I don't get it."

"Maybe a picture would help." Violet performs a quick search on her phone, but I grab it from her before she can show Sunny the image. I would like it to be the least potentially scarring ball gag picture out there—which seems like an oxymoron. I find one that doesn't look too awful and show it to Poppy first. Her eyes flare, but she tips her head to Lily.

I pass the phone to Lily, who grins. "I think my question is, who wears it? You or Darren?"

Sunny throws her hands in the air. "Will someone show me what it is!"

Lily holds the phone out to Sunny. "Remember to keep an open mind."

Sunny peers at the small image on the screen. She frowns and brings it closer to her face. She twists her hair furiously around her finger until she's either at risk of knotting it or ripping out the entire chunk. "Wouldn't it be hard to talk?"

Lily coughs. "I think that's kind of the point."

Sunny looks from the phone to me and back to the phone. "But . . . why?"

"So no one can hear her scream." Violet's grin is evil.

"Don't be a jerk!" I jump in. "It's about trust, and heightening the experience. When you remove the ability to communicate through words, your partner has to be able to read your body and your reactions. Just like if you remove sight, it heightens touch, smell, and taste. You focus on feeling and being in the moment." I'm fidgeting with my pearls, nervous about the way they're all looking at me, maybe judging, seeing me differently. "Not that I have personal experience or anything."

"Wait, what do you mean, you don't have experience? Does that mean Darren is the one who wears the ball gag?" Violet's eyes light up.

I snort. "I'd have better luck getting a porcupine to wear a T-shirt."

"So what do you do with it if you don't use it?" Lily looks like she might be interested in taking that ball gag off my hands.

I don't want to explain where it all came from, but I've kind of boxed myself into a corner. I mean, some of the stuff I bought myself, but the majority came in the form of gifts—not from Darren. Violet and Darren know about my mother's unconventional career, but I generally don't broadcast that she's a Dominatrix. Usually I say she's in the entertainment industry, which is categorically true.

I have never worn that ball gag. It was one of my mother's gifts that ended up in my *this sounds interesting* pile on the heels of a super-smutty read. It always sounds so hot in books, but then when I tried it on, I didn't like the way the rubber tasted, and it was awkward. Also, I don't like not being able to talk. And I couldn't stop drooling, which is completely unsexy, so it went in my box of *no thanks* toys. It's a big box.

"We use some things."

"Like the mask with no eyeholes?" Sunny asks.

"Well, no, not that either."

"Wait a hot damn minute!" Violet slaps the arm of the couch. "Does this mean Darren doesn't actually have Area 51 access?"

"Oh, he definitely has Area 51 access, but I get why you don't want Alex in there."

"It's not that scary. You just need to work up to it," Lily says.

"Hold the fucking phone, you let Balls and his giant dick in your backdoor? How does that even happen?" Violet looks shocked.

"Lots of patience and lube," I reply.

Lily smiles. "Exactly. How do you think that hotel bathroom got destroyed?"

"I guess we know the value Balls puts on anal," Violet says. "All right, my butt is clenching just from talking about this. Let's move on, shall we? You know what I'm curious about?" She looks to me. "That necklace you always wear."

I finger my pearls. "This?"

"For a while there I thought maybe it was a collar and Darren was your Dom or something."

I roll my eyes. "That's because we went on a BDSM reading spree in our book club."

"What's the significance, then?" Violet asks.

"I bought them a long time ago, when I was a teenager, and I wore them until they broke. I loved them so much that I put them in a little bag and carried them around with me all the time anyway." Which I'm sure sounds silly, but they were the first thing I bought after we left The Ranch. I found them at a thrift shop and fell in love with them.

"Anyway," I continue. "One day Darren found them and had them restrung for me, and I've been wearing them ever since."

"Oh, huh. I made that into something a lot bigger than it was." Violet seems a little disappointed.

I'm relieved when no one brings the conversation back to the wheel of sex toys. Maybe it was the mystery and secrecy of what Darren and I do or don't do in the bedroom that made it more intriguing than it really is.

Phones start pinging mid-afternoon, signaling the end of

practice. Poppy checks her messages, a frown tugging at her mouth. "This whole expansion draft is crazy."

"It really is," Sunny agrees.

"Between that and playoffs, Randy's super stressed."

"At least he's safe, though," Poppy says. "I'm still trying to figure it all out, and getting Lance to explain it is maddening."

"What do you mean?" Violet asks.

"I don't get how it works."

"Oh, well, every team in the league can keep nine players safe from the draft. Players with no-trade clauses can't be picked up by Vegas, so Alex and Randy are automatically safe. That leaves the team with seven additional players they can keep safe." Violet pops a grape into her mouth and pushes it to the side, making a lump in her cheek. "There's no way they'll let Lance go."

"You can't be sure of that, though, since he doesn't have a no-trade clause." Poppy's anxiety is obviously shared collectively.

"From a pure numbers perspective, it makes sense, though, right, Char?" Violet looks to me, and I nod.

As an accountant and financial portfolio manager of NHL players, we know not just what kind of money they make and how to invest it, but also trends, stats, and player viability. We need to be able to look at career trajectory and performance in order to help make smart short- and long-term financial goals.

I've also been obsessed with hockey since I watched my first game, so I know a lot about this.

"Can you explain that? Because Lance is kind of freaking out a lot about this whole thing. I think he's worried he's going to be moved to Vegas and he'll have to start all over again."

I tap on the arm of my chair. "I can't promise I'm right, but based on Lance's stats over the past two years, he's likely to be safe. He's too valuable to the team for them to let him go. Same goes with Miller. They're the best defense on the team. They're not going to risk either of them."

"You think so?" Sunny twirls her hair around her finger.

"Logically, yes. When you take in points, age, team dynamics, and all that other stuff, it makes sense to keep them safe."

"What about Darren? He has to be safe then, too, right?"

I finger my pearls and shrug. "I don't know. It could go either way." I've reviewed Darren's stats incessantly since they announced the expansion draft, and the conclusion I've come to isn't great; despite his age, his stats have improved over the past two seasons, rather than declined.

"But he's been Alex's wingman for years. They can't trade him," Lily says.

"Who'll take us lingerie shopping if you move to Vegas?" Violet jokes, but her expression reflects my own worry.

I have no idea what will happen to me and Darren if he's traded, and our brief conversation this morning left me with more questions than answers.

Beyond that, Violet has been my only constant since freshman year of college. The idea of leaving behind the stability of my job, my best friend, and my independence is terrifying. Besides, I don't even know if Darren would want me to come with him. We don't have the same kind of relationship as the rest of our friends.

I'm independent, and so is he. I have my little house, and he has his big house. Hell, we haven't even met each other's parents. Until now it wasn't something I worried about.

With the expansion draft looming and the possibility that Darren could end up traded, I feel uncertain about everything. I don't want to lose him, but I don't want to lose anyone else either, or my job and my independence. It's been easy up until now, and suddenly it isn't anymore.

Even Poppy, the newest addition to our group, knows that no matter what, she's going where Lance goes. It's secured in the diamond she wears on her ring finger. Lily and Randy might not follow the wedding-and-babies path, but they live together, too, and they have a dog together, which is almost like having a kid. All I have is the pearl necklace Darren had restrung for me, and no real certainty that he'd want me to come with him. Or whether I'd be able to leave all of the other people I love behind for him.

I FEEL off kilter when I get home, listless and uncertain. While all the other girls had messages from their boyfriends or husbands this afternoon, I had silence from Darren. Normally it wouldn't be an issue, but with what happened last night and the discussion about the expansion draft, I'm feeling less than secure, which is not like me.

The reason Darren and I work so well is partly because he's never pushed to get serious. He seems content to keep doing what we're doing. Which is fine with me—or at least it was.

I drop my purse on the kitchen counter and scrub a hand over my face. I need something sweet. Well, what I really need is Darren and an orgasm. But since I saw him last night, that's not an option unless I want to look clingy—which is something I pride myself on not being—so I'll have to settle for hot chocolate.

I fill my milk frother, because I'm not ruining nice hot chocolate by using boiled water, and pick one of the gourmet tins my mom likes to send me. Every month I get a care package from her. Mostly it's herbal stuff likes teas and candles and creams for endless youth, but she also likes to send me whatever new sex toy she's found at whatever Dominatrix conference she's attended recently. She means well, but it's awkward.

I check the tin with the candies my mom sends me and frown. My supply is dwindling, which is yet another thing to worry about. I haven't been this anxious since . . . well, since we left The Ranch. I tap on the counter, waiting for the milk to froth. I could maybe try giving myself an orgasm to take the edge off, but I'm not sure that's going to be helpful.

I've just poured the frothy milk into my mug when my phone

buzzes on the counter. I snatch it up, but my smile fades as *Mom* flashes across the screen. I feel bad for being disappointed, but I'd hoped Darren might check in. I put a pin in my disappointment because it's nice to hear from my mom. She keeps busy, so sometimes it's difficult to find time to catch up.

"Hi, Mom."

"Char-char, how's my baby girl?"

"I'm good." I prop the phone on my shoulder, dump a handful of marshmallows into my hot chocolate, and head for the living room. "How are you?"

"Fantastic. Just wonderful! I can't talk long because I'm in between clients, but I wanted to let you know I'll be in town next week."

I sit up straighter, fingers of unease raking down my spine and slithering lower. It's such an uncomfortable feeling, especially when I'm talking to my mom. "In Chicago? When?"

"Probably not until later in the week. I'll know more soon, but I want to spend some time with you! I haven't seen my baby in almost a year, and I miss you. Oh! And I have some new fun things for you, too! Early birthday presents and such. You'll be around? I know sometimes you travel for work."

I hold in my sigh of relief. Darren leaves for the first two away games of the playoffs in a couple of days, so I don't have to worry about my mom being in town at the same time he is. So far I've been lucky that her infrequent visits have coincided nicely with his away games.

Also, I don't actually travel for work, but sometimes I go to away games with Violet when they're on the weekends or we can get a day off, especially on the long stretches when the guys are gone for more than a week. It's nice to break up the separation a little. I don't talk to my mom about relationships since she's very much against them. She hasn't had a real boyfriend since we left The Ranch, and that was over a decade ago.

"That would be great. What's in Chicago, other than me?" My mom wouldn't just come for the sake of visiting me. It's not that she doesn't love me—she does—but her life is . . . strange. She doesn't stay in the same place for long, moving around the country and refusing to set down any roots. She's not designed for parenting, something I learned once we left The Ranch. She's really good at a few things: getaways, making candies, and being a career Dominatrix.

"I have a work conference. It should be a lot of fun. Oh! My five o'clock is here! I'll call you when I'm in town."

"Okay. Oh, and Mom?"

"Yes, Char-char?"

"Can you bring me more candies? I'm almost out."

"Of course, honey. I'll bring lots."

I end the call and flop back on the couch. It's close to dinnertime, but I don't feel like making anything. I wonder what Darren's doing now. For the first time ever, I consider what it would be like to have someone to come home to, how I might like to curl up in that reading chair in Darren's living room and wait for him to walk through the door.

Sometimes I think it might be nice to be less independent and not quite so afraid of being trapped in someone's jar.

THE SAUNA INQUISITION

DARREN

P ractice is tense, as expected. I follow Alex to the sauna and drop down on the bench. Half the team is in here, and most of them are talking about the upcoming playoff game against Nashville. Not knowing who's safe and who isn't only adds to the stress.

After a while, the sauna clears out until it's me, Alex, Miller, Randy, Lance, and Rookie.

"So . . ." Rookie slaps his bare thighs. "You and your girl get freaky, huh?"

Of course he's the one to start off the conversation.

I shrug. "I guess it depends on your definition of freaky."

"Whatever floats your boat, right?" Miller glances nervously at Lance when he scoffs.

I don't know his whole story, only bits and pieces from time spent with him. But based on his previous on-ice behavior, his penchant for fights, his occasional destructive meltdowns, and his former reputation with women, I can take a stab in the dark.

I wonder if the ability to intuit brokenness in other people is a sixth sense only other damaged people are privy to. Like me and Charlene. Sometimes the most broken souls find each other, as if their missing pieces exist in another person. It doesn't matter what form the abuse takes. The holes it leaves in the psyche fracture the soul, too. It probably accounts in part for my instant attraction to Charlene. She's guarded and open at the same time. I might want more from her, but I won't take it at the risk of pushing her too far and losing her entirely.

"As long as you're both into it, it's cool, yeah? Consenting adults and all that." Randy runs his fingers through his beard thoughtfully. "Do you buy Charlene's lingerie, or does she do the shopping?"

I try not to envision all the lace and satin and leather we left in the living room last night. "I buy the lace, she buys the leather."

Randy's eyebrows pop. "Who's in control?"

"Who's in control in your bedroom, or bathroom, as it were?"

Randy rubs his bottom lip. "Both of us?"

"Why would you think it's any different for me and Charlene?"

"Good point."

"I gotta get home," Lance grumbles and pushes up off the bench. The massive cross tattoo on his back shifts as he punches the door open and disappears through it.

"He gonna be all right?" I ask.

Miller runs a hand over his buzzed head, then taps his temple. "I think he has some messed-up ideas about what's going on with you and Char." He turns to Randy. "I'll ride home with him."

"Mind if I come with you?" Rookie asks.

"If you want, sure." Miller shrugs.

"You think I need to talk to Lance?" I ask as Miller and Rookie get up to leave.

This is the exact reason I like my privacy, because people tend to jump to conclusions. Often the wrong ones.

"He'll come to you when he's ready," Randy says. "I'm hoping whatever conversation the girls have today will get relayed by Poppy and he'll relax a bit."

"If that's what you think is best."

Miller and Rookie take off, leaving the three of us.

"So, I have a question." Alex's knee is going a mile a minute.

"Fire away."

"What exactly are you and Charlene?"

"I don't understand the question."

Alex rolls his shoulders. "Like, is this a real relationship or is it contractual?"

"Contractual?"

"Like those books they all read—you know, they made some of them into movies, and those girls binge watch the fuck out of them every time a new one comes out, and then Violet wants to —" He pauses, maybe realizing it's not just the two of us, and he should probably censor. "Anyway, in the beginning the girl signs all these papers about what she will and won't do. Is it like that?"

"No, Alex. It's not like that."

"So then what's it like?" I can see the challenge in his eyes, and maybe a little mistrust, because I haven't been upfront with him about this, and we've been friends for a long time. But explaining how it really is exposes Charlene, and I'm not willing to do that, because it could compromise what we have.

"It's a real relationship. There's no contract, and whatever you think is going on, it isn't." I reconsider that, since Alex and Vi are pretty strait-laced, apart from the locker room sex and the dick dress-up games. "Well, it probably is going on, but not quite the way you think."

"I'm not judging. I'm trying to understand what this is. I mean, you and Char have been together almost as long as me and Vi, and it all seems pretty casual. What's your plan if you get traded—to Vegas or another team?"

This is the exact question that's been eating at me since the expansion draft was announced. I shrug, because I don't have answers to that. "I guess I'll have to wait and see what happens."

Do I want it to end? No. Not at all. Would I want her to come with me if I was traded, yes and no. Selfishly, I want to keep her, but is it reasonable? I don't know. I can give her what she needs physically, but I'm unsure if I'm capable of providing her with more than that, or if she'll even let me try.

Is it fair for me to take her away from everything she knows, everyone she cares about and keep her all to myself? I know Charlene, maybe better than she knows herself. If I took her with me, I'd be her everything, and she's made it very clear that's not what she wants. And I respect that.

Her childhood was bad enough that her mother took her and ran in search of a better life, and Charlene shuts down every time I try to talk to her about it, which admittedly hasn't been often. Most of the time it's enough that I know she's broken. But sometimes I want to know how closely our broken parts match.

Alex's brow furrows. "Haven't you ever talked about it?"

"About what?" I ask.

"The future, asshole. Your future with Charlene."

"She doesn't like being tied down."

"Uhhh . . . We've moved on from your sex life, Westing-house." Randy snorts.

I shoot him a look. "I'm not talking about my sex life. Charlene is . . . complex."

"She's a woman; of course she's complex," Randy says.

"Do you think I should talk to her about the future?" I look between Alex and Randy, who are both more than half a decade my junior, yet still manage to have a better handle on relationships.

"Probably? I have a hard time believing she's hanging around just for the orgasms at this point, man," Randy offers.

We hit the showers. The locker room is empty, everyone else long gone. I think about what's waiting at home for me—which is a whole lot of nothing—and how I'm going to be away soon and unable to see Charlene.

Typically after Charlene spends the night at my place, she's scarce for a day or so, depending on how the night went and whether or not I got all up in her personal space like I did last night with the accidental spooning. I don't like the space, but I also understand she sometimes needs it. Staying at my place makes her nervous. I'm not exactly sure why, but I sense it's because she feels trapped, much like a firefly in a jar.

Whenever she comes to see away games, I expect at least one day of silence for each night we've slept in the same bed. It's fucking torture, but I'm not the easiest person to be with, so I usually accept what she's willing to give.

It's a fine balance with Charlene, but with everything that's going on, I don't feel like toeing the line. Even if it makes her uncomfortable, I want to push, and honestly, it doesn't even matter if I do, because I won't be here for the fallout anyway. By the time I get back from the away games, she should be fine again.

I open my locker and find my boxer briefs. I look around and note that both Alex and Randy have their phones in their hands, and they're awkwardly trying to text and get dressed at the same time.

I scroll through my alerts—there aren't many since my people are all here, apart from Charlene. I freeze when I see that I have both texts and a voicemail from her. This has never happened before. Ever.

It's been less than twelve hours since I left her in my bed. That she's messaging *me* this soon afterwards is unheard of. I fight the initial shot of panic that something bad has happened and check the message.

The one from this morning is an image of the living room post wheel of sex toys and requests that I listen to my voicemail. Another came an hour ago asking how practice went. I can't decide if that's a good or a bad thing because it's so atypical.

"Dude, you okay?" Alex asks. "You look like you're gonna puke."

"Charlene messaged me."

"Did something happen?"

"I don't know." I listen to the voicemail, relieved it's just about Gertrude. I can handle that, but Charlene messaging hours after we've had a night together is . . . different. I can't explain that without it being strange to Alex and Randy. Which makes me question how fucked up my own perception of relationships is, and whether I've been doing Charlene a disservice all this time.

I care for her. About her. I don't want to be without her. But I have no idea if she feels the same way, and it's setting me off balance. Like I'm riding the Tilt-a-Whirl after drinking a bottle of scotch.

I send her a response:

> Practice was fine. Please let me know if you are okay.

"Just go see her if you're that worried," Alex says when she hasn't messaged back fifteen seconds later.

"Go see her?"

He makes a face, the same one he makes when one of our teammates makes a bad play. "Yeah. Like, if she said she needed you right now, you'd drop your shit and go, right?"

"Well, yeah."

"So go."

"But she hasn't messaged me because she needs me."

Alex exhales a slow breath. "Look, man, she's not going to say it outright. Is she messaging and calling when she doesn't usually message or call?"

"Well, yeah."

"Then she's asking you to be there when she needs you."

"But she hasn't asked me to be there for her at all," I argue.

Alex rubs the space between his eyebrows. "Look, I get that maybe this isn't familiar to you, but you can't tell me you don't know when Charlene is asking you to be like . . . on for her." At my confused expression he shakes his head. "Do I even fucking know you?"

I scrub my hands over my face. "Look, I'm emotionally stunted. I don't understand how this whole thing works. I want Charlene, and I don't want to lose her. The possibility is actually my worst fucking nightmare. I didn't grow up in a home with two parents who cared about me and whose entire existence was based on my success as a human being. You had that. I didn't. I don't know how to do this and be successful, and Charlene is just as fucked up as me, so any normalish perspective you can give, without judgement, would be really helpful right about now."

"I don't—"

I grab him by the shoulders. "Just tell me what the fuck to do!"

"Go to her house. Go see her. Make her happy, however you do that."

"Make her happy?"

"Yeah, man, like, however that works for you, make her feel good."

"You mean sexually, right?"

Alex frowns again. I don't like that expression on his face. It makes me question things. "If that's what works, then yes. But considering how long you've been together, I'd say it's probably beyond just where your dick goes."

"My dick goes in a lot of places." I figure honesty is important here.

Alex scoffs. Maybe that was the wrong thing to say. "Can we think beyond your dick, Darren?"

"Of course. What would you like me to think in terms of?"

"Charlene. Think about her."

"What about her, specifically?"

Alex stares at me and says nothing for a long time. "Other than your weird-ass sex life, what does she like? How do you show her you care about her and that she's on your mind? What do you do for her?"

"I buy her things."

"Such as?"

I consider that for a moment. "Usually clothes or lingerie. Sometimes I take her out for dinner, and there was that time I sent her to the spa with Violet. That was good. She liked that."

"Aside from clothes and lingerie, is there anything else?"

"I bought her a chair."

"Please don't tell me it's some kind of fucked-up sex chair."

"There are fucked-up sex chairs?" Randy asks, reminding me this conversation isn't private. Jesus, I'm offering up an awful lot of personal details to these guys in the name of making sure my relationship with Charlene doesn't get messed up.

"No. Well, yes, there are fucked-up sex chairs, but I didn't buy one of those for Charlene. I bought her a chair to read in. And a blanket for when she gets cold."

"Which I bet is pretty often if she's only allowed to wander around your place naked, eh?" Randy says.

"She doesn't need my permission to put on or take off clothes." I turn back to Alex, because Randy's commentary is unhelpful. "Should I buy her something else along those lines— maybe a footstool, or a pillow, or a side table for her tea? That could be good, right? It'll show her I'm thinking about her for reasons that don't pertain to sex."

Randy shakes his head. "Or you could just buy her some fucking flowers."

"Chocolate is always nice, or candy," Alex adds. "Unless she's feeling bad about her body; then chocolate is a bad idea."

"Charlene never feels bad about her body."

"Not that she's mentioned to you," Alex grumbles and slams his locker closed. "What's her favorite color?"

"I like her in purple."

"No, dickweed, not *your* favorite color on her, *her* favorite color. What color does she like the most?"

When she's the one picking the lingerie for the evening, she tends to go for dark and dangerous, even though she's anything but. "Black or silver, I guess."

"Jesus Christ, Westinghouse, if there was a boyfriend test, you'd be failing like a motherfucker," Randy laughs.

"Why?"

"Because you and Charlene have been together for two years, and you don't even know what her favorite color is. Think about the clothes she wears when you're with her—the color of her purse, her favorite mug, her goddamn fucking shoes," Alex snaps.

"Oh. Yellow?"

"Why are you asking me? Is it or isn't it yellow?" Alex asks.

"I think it's yellow. Or maybe it's peach. I could ask her." I pull up her contact on my phone, but Alex smacks my hand.

"For fuck's sake, don't ask her." Alex angrily thumb-types a message on his own phone.

"Are you asking Charlene?"

He gives me a look. "No, I'm asking my wife because she's your girlfriend's best friend, and girls know this kind of stuff about each other."

"Oh. Right. That makes sense. What's Violet's favorite color?"

"Red, most of the time." His phone buzzes. "Yellow is the correct answer for Charlene, so what you need to do is buy her some yellow flowers." He thumb-types another question as he speaks, and Violet answers right away. "She also likes mint and chocolate-covered candied ginger, so I'd get her some of that, too. Then go over to your girlfriend's house and make sure she's okay. All of your friends saw her naked yesterday, surrounded by a bunch of whacked-out sex toys. She might need some emotional support that extends beyond last night."

"I can do that. I can buy her flowers and chocolate and provide her with emotional support if she needs it."

Alex rubs the back of his neck. "I don't know whether to pat you on the back or punch you in the face."

I'm not sure which I deserve more at the moment.

THE BEST
BOYFRIEND
AWARD GOES TO ...

DARREN

I drop Alex off at his place. Before he gets out, he programs a flower shop into my GPS. "You don't have to get all yellow flowers."

"What?"

"The flowers—when you buy them for Charlene, they don't all have to be yellow. And, stay away from yellow roses. They mean friendship."

"How do you know this?"

"Google."

"Maybe you should come with me."

Alex claps me on the shoulder. "You can buy flowers for your girlfriend, Darren. Just tell the sales girl what you're looking for, and she'll be able to help you out."

"So tell her my girlfriend's favorite color is yellow?"

"And that you want to convey you like her for more than her ability to be a jizz depository." I'm not sure what my expression must be, but he tacks on. "Don't say that last part to the sales girl."

"I'm relationship-stunted, not a social idiot."

"Just making sure. There's a Godiva store down the street. You'll be able to get everything you need. And under no circumstances are you to stop at a lingerie store."

"But—"

"No buts. Do not buy her something you plan to take off her body. You need to show Charlene that you think about her beyond just sex."

"But I'd like to have sex with her tonight. We have away games."

Alex punches me in the shoulder. "Christ, Darren, how the hell have we been friends this long and I had no idea you were this relationship challenged?"

I roll my shoulder. "Because I've never had an actual girlfriend before Charlene."

"How is that even possible?"

"I don't know. Usually there's an NDA and lot of rules."

"Because of the freaky sex shit?"

"No, because I'm trying to protect myself and them from all the media bullshit."

"Did Charlene sign an NDA?"

"No. She promised we would keep our sex life private." I wanted to date her more than I needed an NDA.

"Look, I don't care what your sex life looks like. I mean, thanks to Charlene I've gained Area 51 access. It's limited, but more than Violet would probably allow otherwise."

"You have what?"

Alex waves me off. "Never mind. I'm just saying, as long as it's consensual and everyone's enjoying themselves, I don't give a shit what you two do. But if you want to take this relationship to the next level, and I'm pretty sure you do, then you need to make it clear it's not limited to orgasms. So let Charlene initiate."

"She only does that when she's wearing leather."

Alex blows out a breath. "I did not need that information. I'm getting out of the car. Go buy your girlfriend some flowers and chocolate."

"Okay." I pop the trunk as he gets out of the car. "Alex?"

"Yeah."

"Thanks."

"For what?"

"Helping me."

"All you need to do is ask, Darren."

I wait until he's closed the trunk before I follow the directions to the flower shop. The girl helps me pick flowers for Charlene, which is something I decide I'm going to do more often. Flowers are a lot like lingerie, full of beauty in different forms and textures. Some are lacy, silky, frilly, soft and pale, dark and heavy. It takes me nearly an hour before I have a complete bouquet, which costs almost as much as lingerie and contains everything from purple night lilies to yellow dahlias with petals that look like the tips have been dipped in red ink.

I stop at the Godiva store and fight the urge to browse the lingerie shop next to that. Alex is right. Buying lingerie for Charlene will give the message that I would like sex. Which is true. However, as soon as I choose lingerie for Charlene, she also believes I'm choosing how things will happen in the bedroom. Sometimes it's fun, but I would like to avoid that tonight.

I fire off a text to Charlene before I get in my car, but she doesn't respond right away, so I drive over, hoping I'm right and she'll be home. I can leave the presents for her if she's not, but it defeats the purpose.

My palms are sweaty as I pull in to her driveway. Her car is here, which means she should be home. Christ, I'm nervous, which is ridiculous considering I'm just bringing her flowers and chocolate. It's not like I'm asking her to marry me.

I contemplate that, the idea of marriage. Would I marry Charlene? The institution as a whole doesn't mean much to me. It's one's actions that dictate devotion. Words mean nothing if there's no conviction behind them.

Do I think Charlene would want to marry me? I don't know. But I'm not here to ask Charlene to marry me. I'm here to show her that I can be a normalish boyfriend. I can be thoughtful and buy her unnecessary and frivolous things.

It's with that in mind that I get out of the car, bouquet and chocolate in hand. I check my phone before I slip it in my pocket, noting that she still hasn't responded to my messages from earlier.

Her front walk is lined with pretty flowers in a variety of colors, but yellow seems to dominate, along with some purple and white, so the ones I've chosen should go over well. I hope.

Maybe she's in the bath. That would be nice. I like Charlene fresh from the bath. She'll be relaxed. I could let myself in since I have a key, but I rarely come to Charlene. My house is more convenient, and my bedroom is much better equipped for sex and sleepovers. And since I'm surprising her, I figure it's a good idea to knock and wait to be let in, setting a precedent and all.

Charlene opens the door the requisite three inches the chain latch allows. Her hazel eye widens. "Darren? What're you doing here?"

"I wanted to see you."

"Oh." Her hand flutters to her throat.

Hmm. I expected a slightly different reaction. "Can I come in? Have I caught you at a bad time?"

"What? Oh! No. Yes, I mean. You can come in. Just a sec." The door closes and the sound of the latch disengaging follows. A few seconds later she opens it again and steps back to allow me inside.

"This is a surprise." She pulls at the bottom of her shirt with one hand and pats her hair again with the other.

"That was my intention."

I look her over. She's wearing a pair of teal leggings covered in a donut print and a pale purple tank with a donut on the front holding a cup of coffee. Her hair is piled on top of her head in a messy bun, and her face is free of makeup. She's not wearing socks. Her toes are naked apart from the big one on the right foot, which is painted the same shade of purple as her tank. I don't believe she's wearing a bra based on her perky nipples.

Her gaze darts down where my hands are tucked behind my back in an attempt to conceal the massive bouquet of flowers and the box of chocolates. Actually, there are two boxes of chocolates since ginger chocolate and mint chocolate should be separated, according to the lady who assisted me.

I reveal the bouquet of flowers first.

Charlene blinks several times, eyes darting from the flowers to my face and back again. "You brought me flowers?"

"I did." I'm not sure what kind of response I expected, but again, this isn't quite it. She seems shocked. "Should I not have?"

"What? Oh! I, uh . . . they're just . . ." She traces the satiny petals. "So beautiful."

"Yes. Like you."

A soft smile lights up her face. I wonder at her sweetly unguarded surprise. I'm certain I tell her she's beautiful all the time. I know I think it every single time I see her. Maybe the words get stuck in my head and never actually make it out of my mouth.

"You can take them. They're for you."

Charlene's bun flops around as she gives her head a little shake and takes the bouquet. "Oh, wow, this is heavy." She buries her nose in the blossoms and inhales deeply. I want to frame the image.

"I brought you something else as well." I hold out the Godiva bag.

Charlene's expression shifts to childlike excitement. "You brought me flowers *and* chocolate?"

"I did." I smile. "And based on the samples the saleswoman

provided, I will attest that they're delicious—just like you, as well."

My smile widens at her blush.

"This is really sweet of you, and very unexpected," Charlene clutches the flowers and chocolates to her chest. "Um, I should go upstairs and change and then put these in some water." She makes a move toward the kitchen, which she'll have to pass through to get to her bedroom.

"No! I mean, I like you exactly as you are."

She glances down at her outfit.

"Please don't change on my account. I'm rather fond of this." I skim the strap of her tank and watch goose bumps rise along her arm. "Why don't I help you put the flowers in water, and you can try the chocolate? Unless you have plans this evening?"

"I don't have any plans."

"So it would be okay for me to stay and spend some time with you." I shake my head at how awkward I sound. "That was meant to be a question."

Charlene bites her bottom lip. "You can stay and spend some time with me, if you want."

"Yes. I want." I nod, then realize I haven't completed the thought. "To spend time with you."

I retrieve a vase from Charlene's pantry and help her arrange the flowers. She has trouble deciding where she wants them, and eventually settles on the kitchen table, which she can see from the living room and the front door.

Charlene's house is small, as one might expect for a single woman living on her own. She makes good money as an accountant for sports professionals, but she's still managing all of her costs on a single income, which is why I insisted on giving her a credit card to make special purchases.

She adjusts the vase, turning it half an inch to the right and then to the left, determining placement. Her ass looks fantastic in leggings, and I decide I need to find out where she gets them so I can buy some for her, and she can wear them more often.

When she comes to my place, her visits are always arranged in advance, which means her makeup is flawless and she's impeccably dressed. But I like this version of her as well. She looks relaxed and comfortable, something I would like to experience more of.

"What do you want to do now?" she asks.

"What were you doing before I arrived?"

"Just watching TV."

"Well, we could do that together."

"Uh, we can, but I was watching bad reality TV."

"That's okay." I'm likely going to be watching Charlene and not the TV, so the content is basically irrelevant.

I follow her to the living room, which is cozy, like the rest of her house. It looks like she was sitting on the couch, curled up with a blanket. I drop down at the end that's blanket free and adjust the pillow behind me.

Charlene folds the blanket and drapes it neatly over the back of the couch, then takes a seat on the other end. She fidgets. Picks up her half-consumed hot chocolate and takes a sip while she unmutes the TV.

I glance at the screen. "What is this?"

"*Teen Baby Daddy.* I told you I was watching bad reality TV."

"Wow. So this is really a show?"

"I can change it." She reaches for the remote, her cheeks flushing.

I cover her hand with mine. "No. Don't do that. It's fine."

"Sometimes I like to watch reality TV because it reminds me how easy my life is in comparison. But we can do something else if you want." She sets her hot chocolate on the side table and shifts closer. She looks shy and uncertain as she leans in, brushing her lips over the edge of my jaw. "Thank you, for the flowers and the chocolate. That was a nice surprise."

I have to fight with my body not to turn my head, slip my fingers in her hair and taste her mouth. I imagine she's sweet like chocolate right now. I remind myself that I have another purpose for being here that isn't supposed to be about sex. If it's offered, I don't want to say no, though, especially since I'm going to be away for a few days and all I'll have is my hand to keep me company.

"I wanted to make sure you were okay after last night and your afternoon with the girls."

She sits back, putting distance between us again. I don't like it. Maybe I should've sat in the middle of the couch, then she'd have to sit next to me. "Oh. Right, of course. Do you want to know what I told them?"

"Only if you want to tell me." I pick up the nail polish sitting on the coffee table and tap the end of her single, painted toe. "Don't you usually go to the spa for this?"

"I was going to make an appointment for when you're away."

"Would you like me to make one for you?" I shift and set her foot in my lap. "I could arrange to have Violet join you."

"You don't have to go to the trouble."

"It's no trouble. You could have a whole day at the spa if you'd like." I run my thumb along her instep. "In the meantime, I could paint these for you while you get your TV fix." I wiggle her big toe.

"Just as long as this isn't the beginning of a foot fetish, have at it," she says.

"I think you know all of my fetishes by now." I start to unscrew the cap but Charlene stops me.

"You have to shake it first."

"Like real paint."

"Exactly."

Charlene's feet are delicate, much like the rest of her. I definitely don't have a foot fetish, but I can appreciate that even her feet are pretty. While Charlene indulges in brain candy, I focus on the task of painting her toenails. It isn't exactly easy. I have to use a Q-Tip dipped in polish remover a couple of times when I mess up, since Charlene's toes are small, and my hands are not.

"I think Miller has a foot fetish," Charlene says as I finish the first coat. She's informed me already that they'll require two, which is fine with me. I'm touching her, and I'd like to continue doing so in a way that doesn't make it seem like I'm here just for sex.

"How do you know that?"

Charlene arches an eyebrow. "Sunny mentioned that he likes to paint her toenails."

"I'm painting your toenails, and I don't have a foot fetish."

"She also told us he likes to kiss her toes, and her face went completely red when she said that, so I have a feeling he might like to do more than that."

"You girls certainly like to share."

Her eyes stay fixed on her mug. "I keep it pretty vague. Violet always draws her own conclusions."

I wonder how much harm I've done her in asking to maintain such a high level of privacy. In doing so, I'm responsible, in part, for creating some of the distance in this relationship. My own secrets don't make it any better.

"And that's how you managed today?" I ask.

"No one made a big deal out of it. Except Violet and her Area 51 fears, but those are kind of justified, so . . ."

"Area 51?" Alex used the same term earlier. I have no idea what aliens have to do with sex.

"Anal invasion."

My smile is automatic and likely lecherous. "Ahh. Violet is opposed, then?"

"She's a little wary of Alex's size."

I've played hockey with Alex for years. There's a lot of time spent in the locker room showering and getting changed when you're on an NHL team. You get used to seeing a lot more of people than you would in most professions.

Charlene must read my confusion. "He's a grower, not a shower."

"And you know this how?"

"I accidentally got a peek in Vegas when we had to pry Violet away from Alex for the wedding. You would not be granted access if you were packing a cannon like that."

I'm not sure if I should be offended or not. "I'm above average." I know this because I've read the articles and taken the necessary measurements.

"Trust me, I'm very aware of how above average you are. But Alex is scary huge."

"Huh. Well that's . . . interesting." I accepted a long time ago that Alex is the better player on the ice, but I always thought I had a leg up—proverbially speaking—in this department. As a competitive person, I'm displeased to find out he's winning in that area, too. So far he's more accomplished in hockey, relationships, cock size, and who the fuck knows what else.

"How were the guys today? I'm sure they had all kinds of things to say." Charlene bites her lip and dips a finger in her hot chocolate before slipping it in her mouth. I'm not sure if it's meant to be intentionally sexual or not. I choose to pretend it didn't happen rather than offer her something significantly larger to dip in there.

"Randy wanted to know who wore the ball gag."

Charlene's eyes widen. "What did you say?"

"Why does it matter?"

"I don't know. Just curious, I suppose."

"I told them no one wears it."

"That's it?"

"And that you don't like the way it tastes."

She traces the edge of the donut on her knee. "I could try it again if you want."

Would I like to see Charlene wearing a ball gag? I mean, I wouldn't be opposed. But is it something I need? Absolutely not.

"I don't ever want you to do anything you don't one-hundred percent enjoy. My concern today is that you weren't overwhelmed by questions, or a sense of responsibility or ownership for what happened. I don't want you to feel as though you have to tell me anything you talked to the girls about today, but I hope if there's something that isn't working between us, you would come to me so I could try to fix it."

She tips her head to the side, eyes locked on mine. "I like how we are together. And I like that you're here now."

"As do I."

She takes another sip of her drink, licking away the marshmallow foam that sticks to her lip. She manages to leave a little behind.

"You missed some." I rub my thumb over the spot.

I'm not disappointed when Charlene's fingers wrap around my wrist and her lips close over my thumb, swirling slowly, eyes locked on mine. These kinds of real conversations aren't always easy with Charlene because we're both so guarded. But we can communicate incredibly well in other ways.

When she releases my thumb, I replace it with my lips. I didn't kiss Charlene last night, except for maybe once or twice. Which drives her crazy.

Charlene loves making out. She would kiss until her lips are raw if I let her. Sometimes I deny her, so the next time we're together I can capitalize on how much she seems to love the simple act of kissing.

I stroke inside her mouth on a leisurely sweep. Charlene moans, low and sweet, fingertips dragging softly down my cheek as she opens wider, inviting me deeper. Which is the exact moment I disengage and retreat to the other side of the couch.

"Your toes should be dry now. I can put on a second coat."

She's still clutching her mug in one hand. Her eyes dart down, and she exhales a shaky breath.

I take my time with the nail polish, making sure each toe is perfect before moving on to the next. I know Charlene is still trying to figure out what's going on here. My being here, unannounced, bringing her flowers and chocolate, painting her toenails for fuck's sake—I've never done any of this before. Not in two years. And I'm starting to see very clearly how that needs to change. Because tonight I've realized something very important. Up until now, I've only seen the side of Charlene she thinks I want.

And while I adore that she likes to try new things and experiment with sex positions and ridiculous toys, I think I might enjoy this just as much.

Once I'm done, I clean up the discarded Q-tips and tissues and take them all to the kitchen. I toss everything in the garbage and wash my hands, then root around in Charlene's cupboards for a snack. She has an odd balance between holistic stuff and junk food. I hit the jackpot when I find a bag of Cool Ranch Doritos stuffed in the back of the cupboard. I check the fridge for beer, but Charlene isn't big on it, so I'm unsurprised to come up empty handed. She has ginger ale and lots of milk. She also has a container of onion dip, which will go perfectly with the Doritos. I snatch the Godiva bag from the counter and bring it with me to the living room.

Charlene's expression goes from hopeful to crestfallen. "What're you doing?"

"I thought you might want a snack."

"Doritos and onion dip? Why did you even come here if you're going to eat that?" Charlene seems annoyed, angry even.

"Would you like me to find something else?"

She throws her hands up in the air. "Yes! You ruin making out when you have Dorito breath."

"I didn't come here to make out. I came here to spend time with you."

Her brows pull down. "Why can't we do both? Why does it have to be one or the other? Or do you not . . . want me like this? Do you need me to change?" She motions to her attire, her confusion endearing, and painfully understandable.

I drop the snacks on the coffee table and sit down beside her. "I always want you, Charlene."

"So why the Doritos? I don't get it. You come here with gifts, paint my toenails, tease me with that kiss, and then pull out

73

gross-breath snacks like it all makes some kind of sense. What the hell?"

She's definitely angry, which seems to defeat the entire purpose of me showing her I want more than sex. "You know that I care about you, don't you?"

She purses her lips, eyes roaming over my face as if she'll find some kind of explanation there. "Yes. I know that."

"How?"

"What?"

"How do you know?" I ask, because I want to understand what I do to make her see that, since I honestly don't know.

"You take care of my needs before your own. You understand when I take things farther then I mean to, and you always know where my limit is. You'll let me try new things even if it's not always something you're keen on. And you bring me flowers and chocolate because you think that's what I need based on someone else's idea of what constitutes normal. That's how I know."

It doesn't escape me that most of these references apply to our sex life, except for the last part, which only serves to reinforce how change is necessary, but it may need to be a bit more gradual. I have until the end of June, which should give me lots of time to make Charlene see that we're supposed to be more.

That way, if I'm traded at the end of the season, asking her to come with me won't be something she'll balk at. Broaching that subject now doesn't make sense, not when flowers and chocolate cause this kind of reaction.

"Darren? Did I say something wrong?"

I realize I've been staring at her, saying nothing in response. I smile in what I hope is reassurance. "No, firefly, you didn't say anything wrong."

She skims my knuckles and scoots a little closer. "This morning you threatened to kiss me for hours the next time we were together."

"I did say that, didn't I?" I drag a single finger along the column of her throat. "Would you like me to make good on that now?"

"Mmm. I would like that very much."

I shift until I'm in the center of the couch and move Charlene to straddle me. I press the softest kiss to her lips, then trail my fingers along her throat. I don't go back to her mouth like she wants me to. Instead I start at her fingertips, kissing each one, working my way over her knuckles, following the vein on the inside of her wrist all the way to her elbow. I keep going, up the inside of her arm, over her shoulder, across her collarbone, along the side of her neck and the edge of her jaw to her chin.

The entire time Charlene grinds over me, rubbing herself on my erection through the barrier of clothing. If we were naked, I'd be inside her already. For some reason, restraint is difficult to find and hold on to tonight. Maybe because everything is shifting for me, and I want it to be the same for Charlene.

I'm about to continue the kiss torture, starting with the neglected fingertips of the other hand, but Charlene grabs my chin to keep me from moving away. She doesn't try to kiss me. Instead her eyes meet mine, uncertainty flickering there. "Stay here for a minute, please."

I lean in and kiss the corner of her mouth before I brush my lips over hers. I curve my finger around the shell of her ear and ease my thumb along her throat until I reach the soft spot under her chin. Her pulse hammers there, hard and steady with untended need.

I angle her head slightly and tip my own in the opposite direction. Breathing in the warmth of her shaky exhale, I taste chocolate and marshmallow before our mouths are even connected. I press my lips to hers, reveling in the softness before I stroke along the seam. She tastes sweet, as she always does, and that little buzz of lightning always follows, much like the shock of light that appears in the sky when a firefly makes its presence known.

I don't stay for a minute. I linger at her lips, sweeping inside her mouth over and over, slow and languorous, as if there is no other place to be, and we're speaking through kisses that never end.

I have no idea how long we make out, but Charlene's lips are swollen and her chin is red from stubble burn by the time I disengage.

"Should we go upstairs? Do you want me to change now?" she asks on a breathless whisper.

I skim her bottom lip with a fingertip and shake my head. "I want to stay right here." I brush her nipple through her tank. "But I'd like to see more of you, if that would be all right."

She nods. "Please."

I find the hem and tug it up, exposing first her decorated navel, then the gentle curve of her belly to the swell of her breasts. I sigh when I reach her nipples. I had the barbells custom made for her. They boast the Chicago logo and my number on the little balls that hold them in place. She had them pierced a few months after we started dating. Avoiding them during the healing time was a torture worth enduring for both of us.

Charlene lifts her arms, and I pull the tank over her head.

"You're so beautiful." I meet her heavy, needy gaze. There's something else there, not the anxiety and anticipation that comes with wondering what's next, but a different kind of wanting.

A small smile curves her pouty lips. "So are you."

"I think only to you," I mutter, then dip down to pepper kisses along her jaw and neck and then lower until I reach the swell of her breast. I capture her nipple between my lips, tonguing the barbell before I tug it between my teeth.

Charlene arches and moans, that delicate sound sending a bolt of heat down my spine. The ache in my balls is damn near violent, but I'm accustomed to delayed gratification and determined to make good on this morning's promise.

I lick and suck and kiss one nipple and then the other, moving back and forth between them until Charlene's fingers are fisted in my hair and she's grinding aggressively, fighting her way toward an orgasm. I wrap my hands around her waist and lift so she can't achieve friction.

She whines my name.

"I'm pretty sure I said I was going to kiss you for hours before I let you come."

"It's been long enough, don't you think?" she pleads.

I glance at the clock on the wall, ticking away our evening. We've been making out for far longer than I realized. I pull her closer and kiss the space below her navel, and along the waistband of her leggings. I plan to kiss every inch of her body—eventually—but I'd like to play with her a little longer.

I settle her ass on my thighs again, but away from my erection so she can't rub on me. Her expression is pained, desperate, her need for release overwhelming. I keep one hand on her hip but slide the other palm up her stomach, between her breasts, until my fingers drift over her throat, tracing the edge of the pearls. Moving higher, I curl a finger along the shell of her ear and follow the curve of her jaw with my thumb.

As soon as I release her hip, Charlene tries to slide forward. I tip my head to the side, and she stops.

I follow the waistband of her leggings with a single finger. "I like these. Why don't you wear them more often?"

"I wear them all the time," she says breathlessly.

"I would like it if you wore them for me."

"Okay. I can do that."

I trace the outline of a donut that ends conveniently at the apex of her thighs. She sucks in a raspy breath as I run my knuckle over the bump of steel piercing her hood.

"I bet I can make you come like this."

"I'm sure you can."

I find the steel with my thumb and press gently. Charlene's grip on my knees tightens, and she rolls her hips. I decide this is how I want her tonight: in my lap, close like this, so I can see every emotion as it crosses her perfect, expressive face.

77

I keep circling the piercing, slow and gentle, aware that softness pushes Charlene to the edge the fastest, and that the lack of direct contact is going to make her even needier.

And just as I predict, she comes, body shaking hard, nails digging into my knees through my jeans. Her elbows give out, and I have to tighten my grip on the back of her neck to keep her in place as she rides out the waves of pleasure, her soft moans growing louder as the orgasm drags her under.

When she's over the crest I pull her close again. She's drunk on her orgasm, uncoordinated and fumbling as brings our mouths back together.

"Thank you," she mumbles, tongue already in my mouth.

She grabs the hem of my shirt and pulls it roughly over my head. Her satin fingertips drift down the sides of my neck to my chest. Charlene comes back to suck on my bottom lip as she circles my nipples, but when she attempts to go lower, I stop her. At her questioning expression, I grip her by the waist and lay her out on the couch.

"I want to taste how much you need me," I explain.

I drag her leggings down and toss them to the floor, then pause when I hook my fingers in her underwear. Most of them are some combination of lace, satin or leather. Sometimes it's all three, and occasionally there are buckles and chains and metal clasps—those are her choice, not mine.

But her panties tonight are different and nothing I've ever seen on her before. They're cotton—that boy short style I've never been particularly fond of. Until now. These are lace trimmed at the waist, with tiny polka dots. Sweet and sexy, just like Charlene.

"Do you have a lot of these?"

"A few pairs." Her cheeks flush.

"I can buy you more," I offer.

"They're not expensive. I get five pairs for twenty-five dollars." She lifts her hips, possibly encouraging me to remove them.

"We could shop for them together. Do they come in different patterns and styles?"

"They do. I can show you my other ones after."

I shimmy them over her hips and drop my head, pressing my lips to the crest of her pubic bone before I remove them and drop them on the coffee table.

I shoulder my way between her legs and make her come with my mouth. She smells like need and tastes like want. By the time I'm done, the ache in my stomach is damn near killing me. I let Charlene pop the button on my jeans and drag the zipper down. I shove my jeans and boxers over my hips and down my thighs. Charlene stands between my legs and pulls them off the rest of the way, then pushes the coffee table back and sinks to her knees between my parted thighs.

My erection is pretty much pulsing. Even the air hurts at this point. The head is an angry shade of purple usually reserved for eggplant emojis, and the tip is weeping.

"Oh God, Darren." Charlene runs her hands up my thighs, tongue sweeping across her bottom lip.

I cover her hands with mine before she can put them on me. "No hands, no mouth." Jesus. I can't even form sentences that make sense anymore. "Stand, please."

She braces her palms on my knees and rises. Then she starts to turn.

I grab her hips to keep her facing me, then slide my palm down the outside of her thighs until I reach the back of her knees. When I tug her forward she has no choice but to brace her hands on my shoulders and straddle my lap.

I meet her confused gaze, which is understandable. Usually sex is an elaborate event for Charlene. "Should we go upstairs now? I could—"

"I want you like this, please." In two years, we've never had sex like this: on her couch, the TV still droning in the background.

"Okay." Her eyes are glassy with the same need I feel. "I can take you now?"

I smile at her phrasing and grit out a *yes*.

Charlene's palms rest on my shoulders and she shifts forward, lining us up without touching me. I position my thumb at the base and angle it toward her. When her hood piercing skims the tip, I groan.

Charlene's eyes dart to mine and then back down as the head nudges at her entrance.

"Slowly, please. I want to savor the feeling of you surrounding me."

She places a gentle palm on the side of my neck. Every part of me is burning with need so extreme I feel as if my nerve endings are on fire. She eases down, legs trembling as I disappear inside her.

I let my head drop back against the cushions, eyes still on her, and take a moment to absorb the sensation. It's different tonight. Like it's weighted with something new.

I could come right now, without even moving, but that would be embarrassing as hell, so I hold her hips to keep her steady, close my eyes to block out the sight and just breathe. Charlene's fingertips brush along the edge of my jaw, and I have to tell her to stop.

I open my eyes and find hers. "Everything is magnified right now. Give me a few moments."

"Okay."

Recognizing how much I need her, all the versions of her, even the ones she might not want me to see, makes this experience so much more intense than usual. While I battle my response to being inside her like this, I trace the delicate lines of her body, distracting myself with the way her skin dampens under my touch and her muscles flex and tighten when I hit a sensitive spot. All of it threatens to push me over the edge, despite not having moved at all. I drop a hand between her thighs and draw tight circles, shifting under her just enough to make her come and keep myself balanced on the painful edge.

As soon as the orgasm tips her into bliss, I move to the edge of the couch, wrap her legs around my waist and pull her close until our chests meet. I rock her over me, the ache in my balls bitingly vicious as it expands, shooting down my legs and forcing its way up my spine.

"Ah, fuck." I press my face into her neck, sucking on the skin, nipping my way up to her mouth. I kiss her, fighting to stay gentle, but need takes over and our teeth clash. I pull back, and Charlene's nails bite into the back of my neck.

Her eyes are soft but her words are not. "You gave, now take."

I hold her hips, lift and lower, over and over, faster, harder until I come—the whole world a wash of white and stars, the fusion of pleasure and pain so violent I nearly black out.

Charlene runs her fingers through my hair, the rhythmic action soothing. Eventually I lift my head from the crook of her neck.

"Hi." Her voice is hoarse.

"Hey."

"Feel better?"

"Mmm." I kiss her tenderly. She'll need lip balm for days after this. I make a note to do some research and have some sent to her while I'm away. "You?"

"Mmm. Better times four, I think."

"I would like to spend the night, if that's all right with you."

Her eyes flare with surprise, and her smile makes my chest tight.

"That's all right with me."

CHARLENE'S BED IS A DOUBLE, so it means we spoon most of the night. My sleep might not have been the greatest, but the night was excellent, so I consider it a fair trade.

We sleep in late and have lazy morning sex. I'd like to spend the entire day with her, but apparently she has yoga with the girls this afternoon. We shower together, which turns into another round of sex, the slippery kind. Afterward, I watch her get dressed. She wears black yoga pants and a sports tank, her long auburn hair pulled into a ponytail. Like last night, her face is makeup free. She's always stunning, but I've decided I like her best like this. I want her without the mask.

I fold a hand behind my head as she slips on pair of flip flops. "What are your plans after yoga?"

"We usually go out for shakes afterwards. Would you like me to cancel?"

The answer to that is yes. I would very much like her to cancel, but I'm also aware it might be pushing Charlene too much, too quickly.

"I don't want to interfere with your plans. We fly out early tomorrow, so it's best if I get ready this afternoon and get a good night's sleep." I don't like that the first two playoff games of the series are away, but there's nothing we can do about it, other than come in prepared.

I throw the covers off and swing my feet over the edge of the bed. Crooking a finger I beckon her over. When she reaches me, I pull her between my legs and run my hands down her arms. Even with all the fabric in the way, she shivers.

"I'd like to speak with you tonight, if that's all right."

"Speak with me? About what?"

A furrow creases her brow, so I smooth it out with my thumbs.

"To find out how your day was. To hear your voice."

"Oh." The furrow returns.

"Is that okay?"

"Of course it's okay."

"Great." I take her face between my palms and kiss her until she has to push away and rush out the door for fear of being late.

I flop back down on the mattress. I could upgrade it for her. Get her something better and bigger, but I don't want to make her place more comfortable.

I meet up with Alex for an afternoon workout since I have nothing else to do and then head home. As I pack a bag for tomorrow's flight, I check my messages and frown when I note a voicemail from my grandparents. My good mood is dunked in a bucket of shit when I find out my parents are supposed to be in town this week for some kind of conference. I never hear from them directly. Technically I don't consider them my parents at all since my grandparents officially adopted me when I was four. At least I won't be in Chicago at the same time they are, so that's a relief.

I want to brush it off as meaningless, but it shines a dark light on the progress I made with Charlene last night. Because as much as I want things to change, one thing I want to keep her away from is my family, and I'm not sure I'll be able to do that forever.

Which is exactly how long I want to keep Charlene.

MOMMA DOMME

CHARLENE

Tonight the girls are coming over to watch the hockey game. I tidy up the living room, having passed out on the couch last night. I'll blame it on lack of sleep prior to Darren going away and the *Hoarders* marathon. The whole him showing up unannounced, flowers and chocolate thing was a shock, not to mention the normal-people sex and the all-night spooning. But I'll admit, I enjoyed every moment of it, and I'm not opposed to a repeat.

I go about setting out all the snacks—the Doritos and onion dip are perfect since the boys are away—and make sure I have wine and sparkling juice for Sunny and Violet. The doorbell rings in the middle of setting up. It's only five-thirty, and the girls aren't supposed to arrive until closer to seven, but Violet often shows up early, bestie privileges and all.

I open the door, ready for the shenanigans to begin, and Violet's snide comments about pearl necklaces and anal. Except it's not my bestie.

"Mom?"

"Char-char!" She drops her bag and throws her arms around me, enveloping me in a tight, painful hug.

I pat her back, glancing over her shoulder. Laverne, the old lady next door is busy tending her garden—or was. She's currently staring slack jawed in our direction. It takes me a moment to realize why. My mom is dressed in her work gear.

"Why don't you come in?" I maintain the hug while dragging her inside the house and away from the neighbor's eyes. I hope Laverne's pacemaker is working these days, because she looks like she might be going into shock.

I grab my mom's bag from the front porch, give Laverne a quick wave, and disappear inside.

"I didn't realize you were arriving today." My voice has that high-pitched quality to it, much like a prepubescent boy who's accidentally zipped up his man noodle.

My mom is decked out in a black leather corset, complete with buckles and chains—hence the painfulness of the hug. Her skirt is short and barely covers her butt, and she's wearing fishnets and huge heeled boots with buckles that end mid-calf. Her makeup can only be described as *goth*, or maybe *emo*. Her hair has been dyed jet black, and her lipstick is the color of a rich cabernet sauvignon.

"Oh! Did I forget to tell you I was coming in today? I swore I left a voicemail for you, or maybe that was in my head. I thought it might be nicer to stay with you than at a hotel. We can catch up and have some real quality mother-daughter bonding time!"

"Right. Sure. I have a spare bedroom. How long are you going to be in town?" I'm beyond relieved that Darren has already left Chicago for a variety of reasons.

"Just three days, so I want to make the most of it. It's been so long since I've seen you. You look . . ." She seems to struggle to find the right descriptive word and finally settles on "Good." Her pinched expression tells me she does not, in fact, think I look good.

I would describe my outfit as cute. As soon as I arrived home from work, I changed into my Westinghouse jersey and a pair of black and red leggings boasting the Chicago logo.

My mom flits around the kitchen, adjusting the dishcloth draped over the edge of the sink. "Anyway, tonight's a bit of a rush. I have a client meeting at eight that will probably take a few hours, depending—" She's interrupted by another knock.

Shit. It's still too early for the girls to be here.

"Oh! That's for me." My mother struts to the door.

"Did you invite your client here?" I choke the words out, mortified by the possibility.

She throws a look over her shoulder. "Of course not, Charchar. I'll explain it all. Just give me a moment."

She throws open the door and a swarm of people flood my kitchen. With video cameras. And there's some guy wearing one of those latex face masks with only eyeholes and a mouth hole, dressed in leather chaps, his entire ass on display. Thankfully his penis isn't hanging out.

"Mom?" There's that high pitch again.

She turns and claps her hands excitedly. "They're casting for a reality show this weekend. It's called *Momma Domme*! Isn't that cute? Anyway, I thought it was a great opportunity. This is my audition video. It's so much classier to film it in a house, you know? It'll only take half an hour."

And this, right here, is one of the many reasons I have never introduced Darren to my mother.

I pull her aside. "Is that a good idea, Mom? Being on a reality show? I mean, you'll be putting your face out there for everyone to see."

"I'll be wearing a mask, so it'll be fine. Plus, I dyed my hair for the show. You worry too much." She pats my cheek.

This coming from a woman who cut a hole in a barbed-wire fence, taught me how to hotwire a car, and drove me across continental middle America to escape a whole pile of crazy. Then she legally changed our names—not the best names, and not the best changes, but then, my mom doesn't always think things through. Who willingly chooses the last name Hoar?

"I have friends coming over soon," I tell her.

"Don't worry, Char-char. They'll be in and out within the hour."

I sure as hell hope so. Explaining my sex life with Darren is one thing, but explaining my mother is another entirely.

I make myself tea as the crew takes over the kitchen and starts moving furniture out of the way. The chair from my living room is relocated to where the table once was. A footstool is brought in while my mother opens her bag and sets out a vast array of sex toys, many of which I'm familiar with since she likes to send me every new prototype she gets her hands on.

"Nice place," Mask Guy says. He's doing that head-nod thing people do when they're uncomfortable and don't know what else to say. He also hitches his thumbs in his chaps, probably wishing he had pockets.

"Uh, thanks."

"So that's your mom, huh?" He inclines his head in her direction. She's using eyelash glue to attach a mask to her face. All it covers is the area around her eyes, so it's not particularly great at concealing her identity. I'd like to point this detail out to her, but there are currently too many people here.

"Yup." I bring my mug to my lips and blow. Later I'm drinking wine, or shots. Right now I'm trying to calm myself with chamomile.

"Do you ever tag team?"

I choke on a mouthful of hot tea and cough, trying to clear my airway. I set my mug on the counter as Mask Guy slaps me on the back. But when I keep coughing, he starts the Heimlich on me, and several flashes go off.

"Stop! Please don't touch me," I yell at both the photographer and the mask guy as I smack at his hands. He releases me and drops to all fours.

"I'm prepared to accept my punishment, mistress daughter."

I flail around. "Mom! Can you come deal with this?"

This is way more than any daughter should have to handle when her mom comes for a visit.

My mom steps in and slaps Mask Guy on the ass a couple of times. She gives me a patient smile while she pats his head like he's a dog, not a person.

"I brought you fresh candies. They're in my bag. Why don't you have one and relax, sweetie? I also brought you presents, but we can open them together if you want to wait."

I grab my mom's bag and take it to the living room, where there is no camera crew. I find the bag of candies in one of the side pockets—which is the only place I check because going through my mom's overnight bag isn't for the faint of heart, and I'm sure I'll find a few things I'd rather not see.

As promised, the camera crew is able to wrap things up within the hour. But of course, Mom has to chat them up, so they're on their way out the door when Violet and Poppy arrive.

Mask Guy pulls it up over his head on his way out the door. His hair is wet from being encased in latex for the past hour, and his face is red. He might be okay looking, but I'm too distracted by Laverne sitting on her front porch, witnessing the porn parade exit my house.

"If you ever get into the biz, and you need someone to practice on, I'd love to bottom for you," maskless Mask Guy says.

"I have a boyfriend."

"Of course you do." He slips his hand down the front of his assless chaps and withdraws a baggie. Inside are his business cards. "Here's my card, should that change."

"Uh, thanks."

Violet and Poppy stand at the edge of my garden as the porn parade disperses. They both check out maskless Mask Guy's ass as he passes. It's a pretty nice ass; I'll give him that. I glance the card—apparently his name is Rodney Steele. Of course. Steel rod, how clever.

Violet and Poppy give each other a look before they rush up the walkway and I usher them into the house. "Uh, you wanna explain that?" Vi asks as I close the door behind them.

"Hi girls! You must be Char-char's friends! I'm Whensday! Her mom!"

When we changed our identities, my mom wanted to make sure our names were easy to remember. Her real name is Wendy, so she decided on Whensday, spelled incorrectly—W-H-E-N-S-D-A-Y. Although she says it was on purpose. My life was a lot weird. Clearly it still is.

Poppy flashes one of her sweet smiles and extends a hand. "It's so nice to meet you."

"Mom, this is Poppy, and you remember Violet."

"Oh, yes, of course! And you're both flowers! How fun is that?" My mom is still wearing her fetish gear. The last time Violet met my mom she was wearing normal-people clothes, so this is a bit of a shocker, I think.

"Um, are you planning to change now that the camera crew is gone, or . . ." I let it hang, hoping she'll take the hint.

"I have to leave soon to meet with a client, so I'll change when I get back. What're you girls doing tonight?"

"We're watching the hockey playoffs."

The doorbell rings again, forcing me to leave my mother unsupervised with my friends.

Sunny and Lily are standing on my front porch. They look like a couple of bag ladies with all the stuff they're carrying, including a sleeping Logan strapped into his car seat. He could be a professional napper. When he isn't bumbling around being super cute, he's sleeping on any available surface: chairs, couches, laps, the floor, Lily's wiener dog's dog bed.

"Look, girls, I need to tell you some—"

Before I can finish the sentence, my mom makes her presence known. She appears behind me, holding a box of wine—the kind with the spout. "Hi, girls! Oh! This is so fun! Char-char, you have so many friends!"

"Lily, Sunny, this is my mom." I'm not sure if this is much better than when the guys saw me naked surrounded by crazy sex toys.

Sunny's eyes go wide, and her mouth forms an "o". Lily nudges her, and Sunny clamps her mouth shut. Her bag-laden arm shoots out toward my mom. "It's so nice to meet you, Ms. Hoar." Like Gertrude, she forgets that the H is silent.

Lily chokes back a cough, but my mom doesn't so much as flinch. "It's Whensday, darling."

Sunny's brow pulls down. "I thought it was Friday."

My mom throws her head back and cackles. She sounds like a crow being eaten alive. "Aren't you adorable? My *name* is Whensday."

"Like the Addams' Family girl?" Lily supplies.

"Almost! Except it's spelled like 'when are we going to go to the party', not Wed-ness. Anyway, *The Addams Family* is my favorite movie in the entire world!"

Sunny looks appropriately confused by this explanation.

My mom claps her hands and looks to me. "We should have a movie night while I'm here and watch it together!"

"Sure, Mom." Better than Dominatrix training videos, I guess.

I need to pull my mother aside and make sure she doesn't say anything to my friends about my childhood, because that's not something I'd like to explain. To anyone. Ever. I don't think she'll mention it, as we've spent the past decade pretending it never happened, but her behavior today is concerning, so I'm unsure what to expect.

"I wish I could hang out with you girls, but I have a client meeting, and I still have to figure out how to get there." My mom waves her hand in the air, like the life of a Dominatrix is painfully trying. "Maybe you'll all still be here when I get back." She taps her lip. "Although, this client is a bit difficult, so I might be several hours."

My mom sashays across the kitchen and grabs her bag. "I'll give you your presents now, Char-char."

"That's okay, Mom. They can wait."

She waves me off. "It's so much more fun to open presents when you're with friends, though, isn't it? And I think your friends will get a kick out of this. We're all adults here!"

"Sure are," Violet's expression is gleefully malevolent.

Usually when Darren buys me things, they're professionally wrapped, or they come in a pretty bag with nice curly ribbon. Not gifts from my mom. They come in nondescript plastic bags.

I reluctantly peek inside the bag. Oh yeah, this is going to be . . . stranger than usual. I should've gotten out the tequila in preparation. I reach inside and pull out the least offensive item.

"What is that?" Sunny tips her head to the side.

"It's a vibrating cockring. Watch." My mom plucks it from my hand and puts it in Sunny's palm before she turns it on.

Sunny's face turns an even brighter shade of red. "Oh. That would feel . . ."

"Great, right?"

Sunny nods uncertainly.

"Go ahead. There's more." My mom motions for me to keep going. When I'm not fast enough, she grabs the bag from me and dumps it on the table.

I sigh as I stare at the weirdness in front of me.

Violet screams and hides behind me. "What the fuck are those?" She points from her place over my shoulder.

"You mean these, or this?" My mom holds up two separate items, both of which are equally freaky.

Violet makes a gagging sound from behind me. "Either, both? Is that real?"

"These are Ben Wa balls, and this a Spidergasm. They're

prototypes for this year's Halloween Dominatrix party in Vegas! Fun, aren't they?"

That's not quite the way I would describe them. The Ben Wa balls—weighted balls that hang out in your vag for pre-sex stimulation—look like actual eyeballs, the kind you find on those creepy dolls, and the Spidergasm looks like a black widow spider.

Violet shudders. "So fun. Can we put those away now?"

"Are you afraid of spiders? This might help you get over your fear."

"I'm fine. It's okay." Violet uses me as a shield.

"No really, you should try it out."

"I can do it." Lily steps forward.

We all look at her like maybe she's lost her mind, but she smiles and holds her hand palm up.

"Okay. So imagine this is your clitoris." My mom turns on her sexy Dominatrix voice and runs one of her talon nails along the length of Lily's middle finger.

Lily shivers, but nods, eyes darting questioningly to me. I can't save her now.

My mom picks up the black widow and makes it pretend crawl across Lily's palm and up her finger—yes, it's creepy.

"And this little spider is about to fire off all eight thousand of those nerve endings!" My mom wraps the little spider around the end of Lily's finger and taps the butt.

Lily shouts her surprise, and then her jaw clamps shut. "Does it . . . bite?"

"Yes! And it vibrates. Research tests are showing that it takes the average woman four minutes to achieve an orgasm through the Black Widow Spidergasm model. That's one minute faster than their previous model." My mom maintains her Dominatrix sex sales voice through the entire spiel.

"Huh. That's—"

"—incredible, right?"

"This explains a lot," Violet whispers in my ear, still clutching my shoulder.

"I know," I mumble.

Thankfully my mom's phone alarm chimes. She pulls her pouty face. "Duty calls. That's too bad. I would've loved to chill with you girls tonight." She grabs my arm. "I know! Maybe you and all your girlfriends would like to come to the convention tomorrow."

"Convention?" Lily asks. The spider is still attached to her finger. She keeps pushing on its butt, increasing and then decreasing the vibrations.

"Sexapalooza! It's a great convention. I can get you all free tickets since I'm a presenter." She puffs out her chest, clearly proud of this accomplishment.

"Will there be more stuff like this?" Lily holds up her spider finger.

"Oh yes! If it has to do with sex, it's there." My mom roots around in her purse and pulls out a handful of tickets. "Charchar will fill you in. I must be on my way." She kisses me on the cheek. "I'll be back later. You girls have fun!"

And with that she's out the door.

Sunny raises her hand as soon as she's gone. "Um, what does your mom do for a living?"

Usually I say she's in the entertainment business, which is kind of true. "She's a Dominatrix."

"So what does she do, exactly?" Sunny wraps her hair around her finger.

"Basically she bosses men around until they have an orgasm." That's not totally accurate, but for the sake of simplicity, it works.

"Oh."

"I'm going to have a glass of wine. Anyone else feel like a glass of wine? Or some shots? We could do shots."

Poppy helps with the wine, and Lily pours sparkling juice

into champagne flutes so Sunny and Vi don't feel left out. I do two shots of Patron, and Lily joins me, because shots.

Once we all have drinks, we head for the living room. Lily still has the black widow spider attached to her finger, so Violet sits as far away from her as she possibly can. The game has already started, but the score is still zero on both sides.

Lily's only half paying attention, still fascinated with the clit-biting spider. "We're going to the convention tomorrow, right? Randy's been talking about lingerie shopping and ball gags so . . ."

"You'll be able to get your very own ball gag there for sure. And lingerie." I mean it to be snarky, but based on their expressions, I don't think anyone takes it that way.

Violet raises a brow. "I can't wait to see your mom in action. She makes mine look like a dream."

"I think your mom is interesting," Sunny offers.

"Will they have these at the sex show?" Lily wiggles her spider finger in the air.

"Probably, but you can have that one if you want it."

"Really?" Her eyes light up. I know Lily and Randy get it on, like, every five minutes or whatever, but I didn't realize they were into the freak-a-leak business. Or it's possible Lily is just now discovering her inner freak. It'd be nice to have a friend who's freakier than me. Violet believes Vagazzling makes her adventurous.

"Sure." I gulp my wine. "But I should warn you, it's probably been used."

Lily's elation deflates like a balloon. "Seriously?"

"Yeah, like once or something? Especially if it's a prototype," I explain.

"Prototype?"

"Yeah. Sometimes my mom tests out products before they hit the market."

"So your mom might've used this?" Lily peels it off her finger and drops it on the coffee table.

"Uh, it's possible? I mean, it could've come out of the package, but I have no way of knowing, unless you want me to ask her."

"That's okay. If they have them at the sex show, I'll buy one there."

"I don't think Miller would like that very much," Sunny says, thoughtfully. "He's not a fan of spiders."

"Understandable, really." Violet smiles behind her glass.

"Ever since he had his scrotum drained after that spider bite, he makes me get rid of all the eight-legged creatures. I don't kill them, though. I always take them outside when he's not looking."

"Whoa, Miller had his—" Poppy motions to her groin area. "—*drained*?"

"Oh my God! I forgot that was pre-Poppy days! So when Miller and I were still trying to figure things out, he went up to a Canadian hockey camp with Randy and they volunteered to train with the kids. It's so sweet, and special, really. But Miller was bitten by a spider, and he had an allergic reaction."

"His balls were the size of my boobs." Violet motions to her girls.

"Well, not quite that big, but there's a picture somewhere out there. They were very swollen. So he had to have them drained," Sunny explains.

"That's just . . . awful."

"It was. Poor baby. Anyway. His balls are fine now, obviously." Sunny pats her belly.

We half pay attention to the game while the girls exchange stories about the beginnings of their relationships. Which are a lot different than the way Darren and I started.

Chicago wins the first game. We all pick up our phones and send congratulatory messages that won't be seen for a while yet. Half an hour later, phones chime around us with replies. Sunny excuses herself to take a call from Miller. Lily gets a message from Randy asking if she's alone. Violet and Poppy both field short calls, and I sit with my phone in my hand, waiting for something, anything.

Eventually I get a message. It's simple. Short. A *thank you*. I remind myself that Darren doesn't engage in extensive texting, and any response is a good one. Most of the time it's enough, but in this moment it makes me feel a little too different, like I don't quite fit and maybe never will. I used to be fine with that. Tonight it makes my heart ache.

MEET THE 'RENTS

CHARLENE

The following afternoon, Lily picks me and Violet up at my place since she stayed the night.

I follow Violet outside and hit the lock button on the door—Darren didn't feel my previous lock set was sufficient, so he had a keypad installed with a code and an alarm system. It's another way I know he cares and wants to keep me safe. Although my neighborhood is pretty quiet. It's mostly older couples and a few young families.

I start down the front walk and scream at the sight of a mini Winnebago—the kind one pulls behind a car—parked in my driveway. "Holy fuck!" I rush back to the door and punch the keypad, but I'm too frantic to get it right, so it squawks at me in protest.

"Oh shit—" Violet mutters. "I should've warned you, but I figured you already knew it was here.

I shield my eyes. "Where did that come from? Why is it here? Who's in it?"

"I think it's your mom's?"

I stop freaking out. "What?"

"It was here when I came over yesterday, and the SUV it was hooked up to is gone, so it's just a guess. But I'm thinking it's a pretty solid one. Are you going to be okay?"

"What?" It feels a lot like I can't breathe properly. "Oh. Oh yeah. I'm fine."

"Should we go?"

"Yeah. Yeah. Sure." I've taken two shuffly, unsteady steps down the walkway when the alarm goes off in the house. "Shit. Hold on."

By the time I get the door unlocked, the alarm company is calling. I explain that I accidently hit the wrong code, give them all the personal details they require to ensure someone hasn't broken into my house and taken me hostage, and lock up a second time.

I keep my eyes averted as I speed walk to Lily's truck—well, technically it's Randy's truck, but she always drives it when he's out of town—and throw myself into the backseat.

"I didn't know you were a camper," Sunny says from the front seat.

"I actually hate camping."

"What's with the camping trailer, then?" Lily asks.

"It's her mom's," Violet supplies when all I do is sit there, dry mouthed and anxious.

"Oh, did you have a bad experience? When Lily and I went tree planting, it was awful." Even Sunny's frown is cute.

"I think it might've been the people we went with," Lily replies. "But it can be fun. If you're with the right people."

I don't say anything, because my experience with RVing is probably not like most people's.

Less than two minutes after getting into the truck, my phone rings. I'm surprised to see it's Darren. We don't have a lot of phone conversations when he's away. I bring the phone to my ear.

"Charlene? Is everything okay? Are you all right?"

His concern is even more surprising than the out-of-the-blue phone call. "I'm fine. Why?"

"Oh. Okay." He exhales a long breath. "Okay. That's good. I received a message from the alarm company that was . . . concerning. I wanted to make sure nothing happened and you were safe."

I hadn't realized Darren would be contacted if my house alarm went off.

"I'm fine. I put in the wrong code one too many times, and it went off. Sorry if I worried you."

"As long as you're safe, that's all that matters. It sounds like you're in a car. Are you driving?"

"I'm with the girls, and I'm not driving."

"Ah. That's good. Okay. Well, I won't keep you, then. Maybe, uh, we could talk later? Or I'll text if that isn't convenient for you."

My stomach flips. Darren doesn't usually suggest phone calls unless we're making a plan to see each other and texting will take too long. "I'd love to talk. I can message when I'm home and see if you're around?"

"That would be perfect. Have a fun day with your friends."

I finger my pearls, smiling at how formal and awkward he can be when he's unsure how to approach a subject. It's endearing. "Okay. I will."

"But not as much fun as you'd have with me."

I laugh. "Of course not."

I end the call with a smile.

"Everything okay?" Violet asks.

"Oh yeah. Darren got the message from the alarm company and wanted to make sure I'm okay."

"He gets alerts when your house alarm goes off?" Lily asks.

"He's the one who had it installed, so yeah. I guess he wanted to make sure I'm safe."

"That's sweet, isn't it?" Sunny smiles. "That he wants to make sure you're taken care of when he can't be with you."

"Yeah." I roll the pearls over my lips. "It is."

IT TAKES HALF an hour to get to the convention center, and another twenty minutes to find parking. Violet is absolutely shocked when Lily manages to back into a spot without hitting anything. Most of the time when we go out as a group we don't allow Violet to drive because she's so bad at it. She can manage to drive in a straight line, but parking, backing out, and turning all seem to be a challenge for her.

We hand our tickets over and head inside. I've been to plenty of sex shops to buy lingerie, and sometimes toys and fun stuff. But in the past I've tried to avoid these kinds of sex conventions because of my mom's job, so it's new, even for me.

Lily meanders from display to display, checking everything out. Poppy's face is an interesting shade of perma-red, and Sunny, well, I think this whole experience is going to scar my poor friend for life. At least I tried to shield her from it, which is more than I can say for the rest of them.

Violet is . . . Violet. She stops at a table with strap-ons and picks one up. "Can I test this out?" she asks the guy manning the booth. He looks like he probably watches a lot of internet porn and doesn't often see the light of day.

"Uh, test it out how?" he asks.

"Like, can I try it on? See if it fits?"

"Oh, yeah. For sure." He nods at her boobs. Although to be fair, she is wearing a v-neck Chicago shirt with the logo stretched across her chest. On the back is Alex's last name and jersey number. She has a lot of Alex-inspired gear.

She tosses one at me. "You should try this on, too."

I snort and roll my eyes. "I'm good."

"Oh come on! Aren't we in your favorite playground right now? Have a little fun!"

Before I can protest, Lily grabs it from me.

I think the guy manning the booth is going to have a coronary watching the two of them fasten each other with strap-ons. In fact, pretty much every guy in the general vicinity has stopped what they're doing to watch.

"You really can't take Violet anywhere, can you?" Poppy asks with a smile on her still-red face.

"Not really, but she's definitely entertaining."

As soon as Violet has Lily's strap-on in place, they have a dick sword fight, which draws more attention—the kind where people take pictures on the sly that are for sure going to end up on social media.

I drag Vi behind a display of dildos suctioned to the wall, and Poppy does the same with Lily.

"People are taking pictures," I scold. "Take off your dongs and act normal for once."

Violet's face is red from laughing and exertion. "But I like my dong."

"Pictures are probably going to be posted all over the place, and you're wearing an Alex shirt. He's going to get tagged, and then he's going to see you and Lily having a strap-on sword fight."

Her smile drops and she cringes, the red spots on her chest grow progressively blotchier. "Shitballs." She tries to unharness herself, but she's too frantic to manage it. "I can't get my dong off!"

"Here, let me help." I free her quickly while Lily unbuckles her own.

"You're awfully good with the buckles and stuff," Vi observes.

"Don't even go there," I tell her. "If it wasn't for you and the rest of the girls, I wouldn't be here."

"It's fun though, and it demystifies a lot of the stuff we read about in BDSM, right? Besides, this one is loving all the porny stuff." She thumbs over her shoulder at Lily, who shrugs and grins.

We come back out from behind the wall of dildos, thank the guy who's probably going to be blue balling it for the rest of the day, and go in search of Sunny. Which is when we run into Skye, Violet's mom, and Daisy, who is Alex and Sunny's mother.

"Shit!" Violet tries to pull me behind a display of latex-body-suit-wearing mannequins.

"Vi! Charlene! Girls!" Skye shouts.

Violet cringes and drops her head in defeat. "Hey, Mom. Daisy, what are you doing here?" She peeks inside the stroller Daisy's pushing. "With Logan?"

Skye wraps her arm around Violet's shoulder and gives her a big hug. "Sunny mentioned you were going to this 'palooza thing today, so Daisy and I looked it up and thought it would be fun if we came, too!"

"With a baby?" Violet asks.

"Logan is too little to remember any of it, so it's fine. Isn't that right, my favorite little chubbie-wubbie?" Daisy gets all up in little Logan's face and tickles his feet. He giggles and swipes at her swinging hair.

"You should've told us about this! We could've made it a whole mother-daughter bonding experience!" Skye flails around excitedly.

"Yeah, 'cause shopping for sex toys with my mom is exactly what I want to do on a Saturday afternoon."

"Oh, come on, Vi! We had so much fun when we went in Vegas, didn't we?"

"I think they have a maternity sex section," Daisy tells Sunny, who's finally wandered over. She looks a little disturbed to find her mother here. At least hers is just shopping and not part of the event.

This day keeps getting better and better. Especially when we finally stumble upon my mom, performing a Dominatrix demonstration. There's a different masked, assless chaps guy following her around on all fours wearing a leash. I know it's a different guy because this one has a massive back tattoo, and the guy from yesterday did not.

Thankfully, we arrive at the tail end of the demonstration.

Skye does her dejected-four-year-old flaily thing. "Too bad we missed that. It looked like fun. I wonder if Sidney would like those kinds of pants." She turns to Daisy. "I bet we'd look hot in that leather business. That woman looks to be about our age." She gestures to my mom.

It's then that my mother notices me and starts waving. She struts—she's actually incredibly adept at the whole strut deal—over to us. "Char-char! Are you and the girls having fun?"

I slip my hand into my pocket, feeling around for my candies. I'm a little worried about introducing Skye to my mom. Individually they're embarrassing enough, but together, the humiliation could be epic.

"Oh my God!" Skye shrieks like a teeny bopper at a boy band concert. "You two know each other?" Skye's hand shoots out, and my mom takes it. "I'm Skye, Violet's mother."

"I'm Whensday, Charlene's mother!" my mom replies with exactly the same level of enthusiasm. "But my stage name is Climaxica."

Maybe I can sneak away while this happens. My mom threads her arm through mine and hugs me to her, killing that idea.

"I was mentioning to Daisy how amazing you look in this ensemble!" Skye motions beside her. Daisy's still in charge of the stroller.

My mom runs her hands over her leather corset. "I have half

an hour between performances. I'd be happy to show you around and take you to a few of the BDSM-wear booths."

Daisy pats her hair. It used to be more helmet-like, but since Violet's wedding, it's moved into the twenty-first century. Her clothes are a slower transition out of the eighties, but at least she's not wearing shoulder pads anymore. "I'm not sure leather would work with my complexion."

"Are you kidding me? Blond hair and black leather are a lethal combination." My mom threads her arm through Skye's as well, and the girls follow her as she woman-swaggers through the crowd, waving hello to the other vendors and performers. She air kisses about twenty people and stops at one booth to paddle some random guy's ass.

As I observe my mother in her element, I recognize how she and I are very much polar opposites. Where she's spent the years since leaving The Ranch flitting from town to town, putting men in their place, I've put down roots, found stability, and tried to build a somewhat normal relationship. I'm not so sure I'm ever destined to be successful at the last part, but I'm certainly trying. I created a non-traditional family of my own so I wouldn't have to be alone.

We stop at a boutique called Leather & Laces and browse for a while. Lily takes an armful of outfits and disappears into a changing room. They have all sorts of sexy leather corsets and fun stuff. Darren prefers pretty and lacy. It's not that he doesn't like the leather, he clearly does—the peen doesn't lie—but his eyes light up in a different way when I'm in lace or satin. I always end up the recipient of an insane number of orgasms on those occasions.

The curtain beside us sweeps open a bit, and Lily's head pops out. "I need an opinion."

"What's going on in there?" I try to peek around her, but she's holding it like she's in *The Shining*, wearing the same creepy smile.

"You have to come in."

We've all been in various stages of nakedness on multiple occasions with each other, so it's not a big deal. I slip through the curtain, and Violet follows. The changing room is cramped with three bodies.

Vi's eyes go wide. "Holy shit."

"Is that good holy shit or a bad holy shit?" Lily tugs at the collar around her neck. "Is this overkill?"

I actually have almost the exact same corset ensemble. I've worn it a couple of times for Darren. I'm a big fan of the collar with the metal ring at the throat. There's something empowering about letting someone you care about deeply take control of your body and cater to your needs. And this outfit screams submission and trust.

"There's only one way to find out, isn't there?" I cock a brow.

"Uhh . . ." Lily glances from me to Violet and back again.

"Send a picture to Balls and see what he has to say?" Violet asks.

Lily chews on her lip and then hands me her phone. "Okay."

She strikes sexy poses while I snap a bunch of pictures. We scroll through them and comment on how it makes her cleavage look great before she picks one to send to Randy.

It takes all of thirty seconds before he responds.

> 1. Where the fuck are you?
> 2. Buy that if you haven't already.
> 3. Who took that picture and am I going to prison for murder?

Lily grins as she types her reply, and Violet and I leave her to change back into normal clothes. Skye is already at the register with her own purchase.

"I gotta say, I'm super glad I don't live in my parents' pool house anymore," Violet says.

"Right?"

We find Poppy and Sunny huddled with sleeping baby Logan over by the sweeter sexy things in pinks and greens and florals. I glance around, wondering how soon we can get out of here now that I've seen my mom. I note a couple in the porn star area. There are actual stars signing posters and old school DVDs, and even some VHS tapes for the serious diehard fans. Which is kind of sad.

"Hey." Violet elbows me and points to the right. "Doesn't that guy look like an older version of Darren?"

I follow her gaze and note the couple, probably in their fifties, posing for pictures. The woman is outfitted in a silver mini-dress and has definitely had her boobs done, and likely a lot of other things, including her face, but she still looks mostly human. The guy is tall, wearing only black leather pants with a zebra stripe down the side. He's still rocking a pretty decent body for being older, complete with four pack, even if it's the tiniest bit saggy.

I scan all the way to his face and take in his dark, slicked-back hair. "Huh. That's weird. He does look a lot like him."

"You need to take a picture with that guy. Tell Darren you found his future self—and he's a porn star! The resemblance is uncanny, isn't it?" Violet turns to Poppy and Sunny, who both nod their agreement.

I give in and let her drag me over. My mom seems to know them personally, so she flits on over and introduces us. "Rod and Cherry, this is my daughter, Charlene. She needs a photo with you!" Rod and Cherry. I guess subtlety isn't their thing. My mom squeezes me between them and snaps a million pictures.

I send one to Darren with a laughing emoji and the caption: *Your next profession could be a porn stunt double for this guy.*

"So you're a Chicago hockey fan, Charlene?" Rod's smile is blindingly white and eerily like Darren's.

"I am."

Rod leans in closer. "Can you keep a secret?"

It's starting to creep me out how much he looks like Darren.

His voice is even deep like Darren's, and he has the same icy eyes.

"Uh, sure?" I'm hit by an odd sense of foreboding.

"My boy plays hockey in Chicago." Rod's grin grows even wider as he looks over my shoulder. "And you're wearing his name on your back."

MOM'S APPROVAL

DARREN

I typically sleep on the flight home, but this time all I can do is tap on the armrest and count down the minutes until we land.

My worries revolve around Charlene. After the picture and caption, I fired back a message telling her not to talk to them. I tried to follow it up with a phone call, but it went right to voicemail. In my panic, I made some irrational demands, to which she responded that this certainly wasn't a phone conversation, let alone one to be had over text messages.

I honestly never thought there would be a reason to tell her about my birth parents since they had almost no hand in raising me.

I go directly to her place from the airport, even though it's unlikely that she's home from work so we can have a discussion. The Uber drops me off in front of her house. I have my hockey gear with me, which is somewhat inconvenient, but I didn't want to stop at home first. Charlene's car is missing from her driveway, and in its place is a mini red Winnebago hooked up to a small SUV.

The Winnebago is a shock, mostly because Charlene has a thing about RVs, regardless of size. I know this because once on our way to Alex's cottage we stopped at a gas station and she nearly had a panic attack when one pulled into the bay next to us. She refused to let me get out of the car until it left.

When I tried to pry more information out of her, she mumbled something about where she grew up and how she associated RVs with bad men. At that point I knew little about her upbringing, but I'd never seen her in such a state of panic.

So seeing this Winnebago in her driveway brings up all sorts of questions. Ones I'd like some answers to. I run my sweaty hands down my thighs and gather myself before I finally ring the bell. When it swings open, I'm face to face with a woman dressed in a black leather corset and a pair of heels that could double as murder weapons.

She slides her hand up the doorframe and the other one goes to her hip, which she juts out. Her brow arches and a grin forms on her wine red lips. "Well, hello there. If you're trying to get me to go to your church, I'm afraid I'm far too sinful for that. Would you like a demonstration?"

I look down at myself. I'm wearing dress pants and a button-down shirt. I suppose I can see how she might mistake me for a church type, but...did she just proposition me? I slip my hands in my pockets and glance over her shoulder, trying to see past her, but she takes up most of the doorway.

"I'll have to pass on that. I'm here to see Charlene."

Her smile falters as she inspects me in a new way. "Oh? Is that right? And who might you be?"

"I'm . . . uh . . . her boyfriend?" For some reason it comes out as a question.

"Oh! Yes, of course! Char-char can be so secretive about stuff like that." She gives me a conspiratorial wink.

Char-char? "I guess?"

She motions for me to come inside. "She should be home soon. Would you like to come in?"

"Sure. Thank you." When I enter the kitchen, I freeze. The counter is covered in sex toys. More specifically, the kind I typically find in Charlene's *I thought I might like it but I changed my mind* trunk. What the hell is going on here? "May I ask how you know Charlene?"

"I'm so sorry. I'm so distracted. I haven't even introduced myself properly. I'm Whensday, Char-char's mother." She extends a hand.

"Oh! I didn't realize you were visiting Charlene. It's nice to meet you."

I'd tell her mom I've heard a lot about her, but the truth is, I haven't. I know the basics. That she's a Dominatrix, and has been since Charlene was a teenager. Before that they lived in a rural community, and Charlene's father wasn't a good man, so they left. Aside from those details, I know little about Charlene's family or her early life. Neither of us is particularly keen to talk about our childhoods, so we don't.

"It's always nice to meet Char-char's friends. A mother worries, you know."

"I'm sure you do."

I agree even though I wouldn't know what that's like. My parents gave zero fucks about me. I'm fairly certain that hasn't changed in the past decade. And my grandparents, who did raise me, are about as warm as ice.

Charlene's mom crosses to the counter where a plethora of dildos and other sex toys are laid out on dishtowels. I make a mental note to throw out every dishtowel in the house.

"It's such a small world, isn't it? Char-char had quite the

adventure meeting your parents this weekend! The resemblance between you and your father is actually rather uncanny. So smart that they went into directing since porn stars have such a short shelf life. No one wants to watch boobs flop around when they're trying to get off, do they? And don't get me started on old balls, am I right?"

I'm not sure if she honestly expects me to respond. I'm also suddenly very aware that as fucked up as I might think I am, based on what I'm seeing and hearing, Charlene is just as much a mess. It doesn't appear that her mother sheltered her in any way from her chosen profession. It makes me want to protect Charlene from all the bad things in this world, myself excluded.

"So how long have you been dating Charlene, exactly?"

I go with vague. "We've been together for a while."

"Really? Hmm. . . Well, enjoy her while you can."

What the hell does that mean? "I'm sorry?"

"Char-char doesn't often let people get too close to her. Well, apart from her girlfriends, anyway."

My mouth is suddenly dry. I contemplate how well I really know Charlene, because there's some truth in what her mother has said. Charlene has always been the one to pull back in our relationship. I've allowed it because I don't want to risk losing her by pushing her, but we're two years into this, and I don't have the sense of security I'd like to.

"It's been nice visiting her. She has such fun friends. They all enjoyed themselves at the convention. You know, I tried to raise Charlene in a very sex-positive, shame-free lifestyle, at least once it was just the two of us."

"That's important." I'm not sure what else to say to that.

"It really is, but sometimes I think it might have been better for Char-char if she'd had a more normal childhood. She was always so sweet, and smart as a whip! My God, she could recite her times tables up to twelve by the time she was four. It's no surprise she works with numbers. If I'd had her smarts, maybe I would've made better choices." She gives me a rueful smile.

"I'd always thought maybe one day Char-char might want to travel the world with me, but she seems settled and happy here."

"She is happy, and very much settled." Her house is homey, her life has a routine and comfort in it, and I'm part of that.

She tips her head. "You play professional hockey, yes?"

"I do."

"That means you travel often?"

"During the season, yes."

"Mmm. . ." She says something that sounds like *close but not too close*. "That must make relationships challenging."

"I'm in Chicago during the off-season, and Charlene is very independent, as I'm sure you know." I force a smile, aware that even if she doesn't have the most conventional job, she's still a mother making sure her daughter is taken care of. "She also has good friends who are always here when I'm away."

"Those girls she spends her time with seem like a family," Whensday observes.

"They're very much like sisters," I agree.

"That's good. She needs that. She was always surrounded by a lot of—"

The door slams before Whensday can finish that thought. "Mom? I'm home!"

Charlene's voice is the balm I've needed since the plane landed, even if her words aren't directed at me. I'm simultaneously calm and anxious. I wonder if this is how Charlene feels on a regular basis when I return from away games.

She comes to a halt as soon as she sees me. Her eyes dart to Whensday, then to the sex toys in the drying rack before they swing back to me. "What're you doing here?"

I guess we're ignoring all the awkward. "I wanted to see you. I thought we should talk."

She arches a brow. "You could've called first."

Her mom seems to be oblivious to the sudden tension. "Darren and I were talking about professions. We have a lot in common with all the traveling we do, don't we?" She looks to me for confirmation.

It's really the only thing we have in common apart from Charlene. "I suppose—"

Charlene directs a withering glare at her mother. "Well, that's nice. I don't like living out of a suitcase, so I guess that makes me the odd one out." She motions to the sex toys in the drying rack, refusing to look my way as her cheeks flush. "Why is this stuff sitting out like this? Can't you put it away?"

"I couldn't pack them wet. And honestly, Char-char, it's not as if Darren hasn't seen it all before." Whensday turns her bright smile on me.

How would she know what I've seen and what I haven't? And suddenly it all clicks. Charlene wanting to try new things and then deciding against it. Charlene's box of *I thought I might* toys. They were never her idea; I just didn't realize that until now.

With her mother's traveling sex shop lying all over the kitchen, I can see exactly how Charlene came to believe this is normal, expected even. Prior to this moment, it hadn't occurred to that her mother might influence those choices, mainly because I'd believed she and her mom weren't all that close. This alters my perception of the antics she often pulls, and I have to wonder if she only suggests half the things she does because she's been brainwashed to believe I won't want to have sex with her otherwise.

A phone buzzes from somewhere amid the sex toys on the counter, and Whensday moves things around until she finds it. "Oh my! I didn't realize it was so late. I have to get going!"

Charlene helps transfer the toys into Ziplock bags, which her mom dumps into a small suitcase. I don't offer my assistance until everything is packed up since this whole situation is uncomfortable enough as it is. I carry the suitcases out to the little RV. Charlene is extra skittish once we're outside, close to the Winnebago. I might need to push for more information about the whole RV thing considering the way she keeps pulling at the collar of her shirt as I load her mom's bags. Once I'm finished, I get a hug from her mother and head back inside so they can say their goodbyes.

I pace the kitchen for a minute, then peruse her fridge for something to drink. Charlene has wine, but it's in a box. I'm not sure I've ever consumed wine in such a fashion, but I believe the conversation we're about to have requires alcohol, so I retrieve two glasses from the cupboard and fill them. Generously.

A minute later Charlene returns. Her back is to me, so she hasn't noticed me yet.

I don't say anything as she stands there, facing the door, fingers flexing on the knob, the other hand at her throat. Eventually she turns, working the buttons of her blouse free.

"Shit!" she yells when she sees me standing on the other side of the kitchen, leaning against the counter.

"I didn't mean to startle you." I hold out the glass. "Would you like some wine?"

Her lips flatten into a thin line, but she crosses the kitchen and grabs the glass. Some of the wine sloshes over the edge and lands on my foot, soaking my sock. She either doesn't notice or doesn't care. She tips her head back and chugs the contents. A dribble of wine spills down her chin, and she swipes it away with the back of her hand.

"Your mother seems . . . nice." Based on the glare I get, I'm not sure that was the best conversation starter.

"Really, Darren? That's what you're going with? My mom seems *nice*?" She steps around me and heads for the fridge. Wrenching it open, she pulls out the box of wine and slams it on the counter beside me. There's a fine sheen of sweat on her brow and her neck. Her hands shake as she fills her glass and drains it, again.

As she fills it a third time, I would like to point out that it typically only takes her three glasses of wine to get a buzz, but I don't want to make her more upset.

"I'm sorry."

Charlene freezes with the glass halfway to her mouth. "What are you sorry about? That my mom is a lunatic? That you lied about your parents? That you tried to boss me around over text messages?"

I'm not sorry about meeting her mother. If anything, it gives me a much better idea of who Charlene is. But I'm also uncertain if I can explain fully what I am sorry about, so I address the parts of that question that I can. "I didn't lie, and I was concerned."

"Really? Because I've seen a picture of you with your parents, and neither of them looked like Cherry or Rod."

"Rod and Cherry may have created me, but they didn't raise me. My grandparents did. They actually adopted me."

Her defiant, suspicious glare changes to confusion. "I don't understand. You told me you were raised in a strict house that lacked affection, and privacy was not permitted. Those were your exact words."

"And that is very much the truth."

"Why didn't you tell me you were raised by your grand-parents?"

"I didn't think it was necessary." I swallow down the panic that comes with being forthcoming about my family history. I've never told anyone about this. Not even Alex knows. Well, I'm sure he does now, but I've kept this terrible secret my entire life. Because it's very much the reason I'm as fucked up as I am. And the reason for the NDA agreements. "Please come sit with me so I can explain."

She exhales a shaky breath, but allows me to take her hand and lead her to the living room. She waits until I sit on the couch before moving to the love seat. I'm disappointed but unsur-prised that she wants space.

I sip my wine and try not to allow the displeasure to appear on my face. I make a mental note to have a couple cases of good wine delivered to her house so she doesn't feel compelled to drink this shit. Running my hand up and down my thigh a few times, I take a deep breath. "I've never shared this with anyone, Charlene. I had hoped I would never have to."

I take her in, noting the protective way she cups the bowl of the glass in her palms, warming the white. When I reach her throat, I note her missing pearls and my chest constricts. Charlene always wears them, and the significance of their absence is like a razorblade slice across my heart. Her expression and her posture are both guarded. I hope I haven't lost all my gains because of this.

I hate my parents so much for making me feel secrecy is necessary.

"I was raised by my mother's parents."

"Because your parents are porn stars."

"Yes."

She doesn't ask for more information, but silence will only widen the gap between us. She wants me to tell her without having to prod.

"My parents started dating in their last year of high school. They were eighteen and careless."

"And your mom got pregnant," Charlene says softly.

In a lot of ways our stories are similar. Young adults making mistakes and having kids—us—way before they were ready. "She did. And because of my grandparents' beliefs, she kept me. They agreed to support her *if* she broke it off with my father."

"But she didn't."

"She did not. They ran away together—such a romantic notion, isn't it?" I smile at the irony and glance at Charlene, who looks sad. "They learned very quickly how difficult it is to afford a child with no education and no support from family, so they found a way to make money. And they made a lot. But with certain professions, there's a lifestyle." I look down at my hands and a disjointed series of memories that never made much sense until I was older flicker like an old movie behind my eyes. "At a young age I was exposed to things I shouldn't have been."

Charlene's teeth press into her lip as she puts together what I mean. "Oh," she breathes.

"It was . . . damaging in more ways than I can count, which is why I don't like to talk about it. Most of the memories are vague and indistinct, like wisps of a dream I can't quite catch and hold."

She nods. "I understand that. Sometimes I feel the same about my childhood, like it's shrouded in a fog I can't sift through."

"Exactly." I worry what telling her this will do to us. I worry more that we're too cumulatively messed up to be good for each other. "When I was four, I was removed from my parents' home and sent to live with my grandparents. I was raised in two very extreme households. The first was expressly permissive and overly sexual. The second was suffocatingly oppressive. There were restrictions put on me that weren't always reasonable."

"What kind of restrictions?" Her voice is a whisper.

I consider how much I want to tell her and decide I might as well let her in all the way. "As soon as puberty hit, the door to my room was removed."

She frowns. "Why?"

"My grandparents wanted to eradicate the perversion out of me."

"And they thought they could do that by taking away your privacy?"

"Mmm."

"God, you must've had to take a lot of long showers."

I give her a rueful smile. "They put a timer on the thermostat in the shower. The hot water shut off after five minutes."

"How did you even manage?"

"I lived and breathed hockey. I spent hours at the rink every single day, and I became very accustomed to being uncomfortable. Thankfully I was drafted at eighteen. But sometimes, when you've been oppressed for so long, freedom causes more pain. I think you might understand that."

Charlene nods, and her fingers drift up her throat, but stop when she doesn't come in contact with her pearls. I want to ask where they are since they rarely come off.

"It's hard to trust," she murmurs.

I edge closer to her, my knee nearly touching hers. "Yes. That's it exactly. The only people I could safely place faith in were my teammates."

Charlene drops her head, her fingers dragging down the side of her glass. "Is it like that still?"

Charlene is just as broken as I am. Someone whole would be better for her, but I don't think I'm selfless enough to let her go if she's damaged enough to want to stay.

"I covet privacy because it was something I was never permitted. I didn't tell you about my parents because I never anticipated you would have the misfortune of meeting them. I took my grandparents' last name because it separated me from them and removed the threat of association. They didn't want people to know, and frankly, neither did I."

I exhale slowly, hating the tightness in my chest, wishing I could control it. "I'm not normal, Charlene. I don't feel things the same way other people do. Relationships are difficult for me because I genuinely struggle to understand where the boundaries should be. Mine were always too close or too far away. Real intimacy is unfamiliar and terrifying because I have not allowed it. Until you."

She startles when I trace the edge of her jaw without making physical contact.

"And I'm beginning to see I haven't done a very good job at conveying that, or making it easier for either of us with all of this secrecy," I say.

"I understand the need for secrets."

"I know you do." I skim the back of her hand, a whisper of touch that helps calm me. "The only good thing about my childhood was hockey. I learned very quickly that people like to use my past for their own personal gain, hence the NDAs and the lack of relationships."

"I understand that a lot better now." She flips her palm over, the ends of our fingers meeting.

"My childhood fucked me up, Charlene, and I would like very much if it didn't have the same impact on what we have. I didn't tell you because I didn't want to drive you away."

"Well, if you haven't noticed, my childhood was pretty fucked up too, so I guess our broken parts sort of fit together, don't they?"

"They seem to." I stroke along her throat, where her pearls should be.

She covers my hand with hers. "I was fidgety today, and I couldn't stop playing with my necklace. I worried I was going to break it again, so I took them off." Reaching into the pocket of her skirt, she withdraws the pearls. "Will you help me put them back on?"

"Of course."

She drops them in my palm.

Charlene gives me her back as she piles up her hair and bows her head, exposing the gentle slope of her neck. I clasp them around her throat and place a kiss just above where they lay. "I'm sorry if my secrecy hurt you, Charlene. I'll try my very best not to do that to you again."

LOVE GAMES

CHARLENE

Who knew finding out your boyfriend's parents are porn stars could take a relationship to the next level? Not this woman, that's for damn sure. It's been three weeks since Darren met my mom, and he hasn't decided my crazy is too much for him. In fact, for the past three weeks, I've seen more of him than usual. We've had more sleepovers in the past couple of weeks than we had in the two months before that. It's weird. I like it. But it also makes me nervous.

Because I still have a secret, and Darren doesn't anymore. I've considered telling him about The Ranch, but I don't want to upset this new balance. I'll tell him eventually—maybe after the playoffs are over and the expansion draft is out of the way.

I pull into the underground parking lot at Stroker and Cobb

Financial Management and groan as I hoist myself out of the driver's seat. My legs ache. So do my arms. Actually, my entire body hurts thanks to the marathon of sex Darren and I engaged in. Chicago lost last night's game, and Darren needed a way to get out some of that pent-up negative energy. Obviously I offered to help. Hence I'm underslept and achy, but sated.

I take the elevator to the third floor. Six months ago I was offered a senior accounting position. Aside from Violet, I'm one of the youngest on staff in a senior position. Jimmy and Dean, who were hired around the same time as me and Violet, weren't all that happy about it, and for a couple of weeks they were real dicks, but things have settled down. Mostly.

One of the perks of my promotion is that it came with a sweet office instead of a shitty cubicle and an extra forty grand a year. While I may only make a fraction of Darren's salary, I'm doing pretty damn good for an almost twenty-six year old.

I drop my purse beside my desk and turn on my monitor so I can check emails. I've just finished logging in when Violet peeks her head in the door. "Do you have any snacks? I'm so freaking hungry this morning."

"I should have something in this drawer." I tap my desk and motion her inside while I pull up my emails. My mother has sent me a million. She still hasn't figured out that she can text me pictures and doesn't have to send them individually by email. "I didn't know you were coming in today."

"I wasn't, but Alex wants me to come to Toronto this weekend if they go to game seven of the series, so I'm shuffling days around, just in case." Violet only comes in to the office two or three times a week at most. The rest of the time she works from home. As awesome as it is for her, I miss having my best friend around every day. Jimmy and Dean can be fun, but they're not Violet.

She digs around in the drawer, tossing items on my desk. "What is all this shit? Why don't you have any good candy?"

"Probably because you ate it all the last time you were here."

"It looks like I have to settle for this." She sighs and unwraps a chocolate-coated granola bar. Taking a huge bite, she makes a face. "The oats totally ruin this. We should hit the Thai buffet for lunch."

"Sure. Sounds good. I have a meeting from ten to eleven. Other than that I'm catching up on emails and reviewing accounts." I click on an email from my mom. I assume it's another picture from the sex convention.

Violet choke coughs at the image on the screen.

"Darren can never see this," I say.

It's an action shot of the masked dude administering the Heimlich maneuver when my mother auditioned for the reality show thing. It looks like he's trying to hump me from behind. Darren would break the guy's knees with his hockey stick for putting his hands on me. It's worrying that the idea makes me a little excited in the pants.

"Yeah. You should tell your mom to delete that, and then you should delete it, too. Forever."

"Yeah." I move on to the next email, cringing as I open it. This time it's a video of the dude giving me the Heimlich, but there's no sound, so it really does look like he's trying to hump me fully dressed. I rub my forehead. "I don't know why she insists on sending these to my work email."

Violet pats my shoulder. "Two days ago Skye told me she wore that fetish gear for Sidney. She also told me she slipped him a Viagra and his hard-on lasted so long they had to go to the emergency room. You're welcome for that horrifying visual."

"Is Sidney okay?"

"I think so? Skye was pretty proud of herself, so there must not be any lasting damage."

We're interrupted by a knock on the door. I quickly close my browser, expecting maybe Jimmy, Dean, or my boss, Mr. Stroker, but it's none of them, and I can't see the person on account of the huge bouquet of flowers.

"Delivery for Charlene . . . Hoar?"

"The H is silent," Violet says with a grin.

The delivery guy lowers the bouquet enough so he can see us. "Sorry 'bout that. Where would you like these?"

"Oh, right here would be great." I clear some papers from the corner of my desk, and he sets them on the edge.

I nearly choke on his cologne. It smells like he dumped the entire bottle on himself. My eyes are watering.

Violet coughs into her arm. "Fred?"

He adjusts his baseball cap, which sends another waft of cologne in our direction. "Violet?"

He seems familiar, but I can't place him.

"Hey! How are you?" She coughs again.

"Good, good. Still delivering flowers. Still single." He shoves his hands in his pockets and rocks back on his heels. "I, uh, saw in the news that you married Alex Waters a while ago, so, uh . . . congratulations, I guess."

Well, this is awkward.

"Thanks."

"That offer to take you to the movies doesn't have an expiration date, so if you ever get divorced, you can always look me up."

"I'm taking my wedding vows pretty seriously—the whole 'til death do us part thing. Besides, he's got a huge dick, so you know, lots of incentive to stick around." Violet cringes, likely because she's gone too far with her sharing.

"Right. Yeah. The, uh, condom endorsements made that pretty obvious. I guess if you're looking to downsize to something more average, I could be your man." He takes a step back, toward the door.

"I'll keep that in mind."

Fred's pager goes off, and he blows out a breath. "It was really nice to see you, Violet. Hopefully I'll deliver flowers again here soon." He continues to back out of the office, knocking his elbow against the doorjamb. He frees one of his hands from his pockets so he can wave and disappears down the hall.

Before I can say anything, he peeks his head in the office again. "Oh, those flowers should be in direct sunlight. They'll last longer that way."

"Thanks, Fred."

"Okay. Well, bye." He disappears again.

Violet waits a few seconds before she tiptoes across my office, but she's wearing heels, so she's not stealthy or coordinated about it. She almost trips and falls into the hallway. She manages to catch the doorjamb before she goes down and sticks her head into the hall.

"Coast is clear, but the hallway smells like an entire high school of teenage boys doused themselves in cologne at the same time." She smacks her lips together as we open all the windows in my office. "I'm probably going to taste that for the rest of the day."

It's not particularly warm out, but I'd rather freeze my nipples off than continue huffing cologne. I suck in several lungfuls of fresh air. "I think my olfactory senses are destroyed. Who the hell was that guy?"

"He used to deliver Alex's flowers when I lived in the pool house."

"Oh my God! I remember him! Didn't he ask you out right after you told him you'd had Alex's dick in your mouth?"

"That's the one."

"I don't remember his cologne problem being that bad before." I have to dab under my eyes to wipe away the tears since they're still stinging.

"Maybe it's gotten worse over time, like prolonged exposure to the flowers has made him incapable of smelling things." Violet motions to the bouquet. "Are those from Darren?"

"I don't know. Maybe?" I pluck the card from the bouquet, which is almost entirely comprised of yellow flowers with a few pinks and oranges thrown in. It's like a sunrise. I dab my eyes again, telling myself it's because they still sting from the cologne.

I slip the card out of its tiny yellow envelope. Darren's neat writing fills the space.

> A little something beautiful for my beautiful someone.

Violet's chin rests on my shoulder. "Wow. That's super sweet."

"It really is." And not like anything he's ever done before. I mean, the flowers, yes. He surprised me with that bouquet and candy before, just never at work.

"Did you let him in your backdoor last night or something?"

"Seriously?" I elbow her and accidentally get her in the boob.

"Ow!" She staggers back, gripping it in both hands. "That really fucking hurt, Char!"

I roll my eyes. "Oh, come on."

She keeps kneading her boob. "No, really. It feels like you tried to shave off my nipple with your pointy-ass elbow." She looks down her shirt, as if she's checking to make sure her nipple is indeed still attached to her body. "Remember how sore your boobs were when you were a teenager and they were just busting out?"

I shrug. "I guess."

"It's like that, but worse. They've been like this all week. Alex is getting frustrated that he can't slide his dick between them." She's still kneading her boob with one hand and fingering the petals of a dahlia with the other. "I have a meeting in twenty, but

I expect to hear all about what you did to inspire those flowers at lunch." She nabs another granola bar from my desk and leaves me to it.

Darren calls before I have a chance to reach out and thank him for the flowers.

"I was about to message you," I tell him.

"Were you now?"

I can almost see him smiling, and it makes my heart flutter.

"Someone sent me something beautiful."

"Is that right? What kind of something beautiful?"

"Some very stunning flowers. They look like a sunrise."

"So you like them?"

"I love them. They're gorgeous. I'm not sure what I did to warrant them, but they're certainly appreciated." Why are there butterflies suddenly flitting around in my stomach?

"You don't need to do anything to warrant something nice. If it was reasonable, I'd send you flowers every day." He clears his throat, and I can hear water running in the background. "I wanted to check in with you before I head out this afternoon. Would it be okay for me to call you later tonight, once I'm settled in Toronto?"

"Of course."

"And when I'm home, you'll stay over again? If you're not busy?"

"I'm available whenever you need me."

"That would be always, Charlene. I'll touch base when I'm in Toronto. Enjoy the flowers."

"I will. Bye, Darren."

He never ends a call with goodbye. I don't know why. I stare at my phone for several long seconds as I roll what he said around in my head. *"That would be always."*

With the recent revelation about his family, I've come to a few new realizations. Darren was essentially starved of affection as a child, and likely for his entire life, so his asking for my time is him trying to restrain his neediness. All those nights spent in his bed with him lying like Dracula was as much about giving me space as it was about being afraid to seek intimacy and be denied. It isn't control he's seeking, so much as a way to let go of the restraints placed on him.

Part of me loves being needed by him like this, but the other part worries that need turns into dependency, and that's when things get dicey. Until now I've never allowed myself to get involved with someone to the point of needing them so acutely.

I don't have time to fixate on it, though. My morning meeting and deleting my mom's emails keep me too busy to be able to obsess. At noon, Violet peeks in my door and declares it's lunchtime and she needs to eat all the Thai food because she's starving to death.

I shoulder my purse. "Should we invite Jimmy and Dean?"

She gives me her cringy face. "Only if we run into them on the way out?"

"Sure."

We're barely seated at a table before Violet is beelining it to the buffet, loading her plate with things she normally wouldn't. She barely utters a word as she shovels food into her mouth.

Violet slows down about halfway through her plate. "Okay, I think I got a little overexcited." She slumps back in her seat and rubs her tummy. "I hope Chicago doesn't shit the bed this game."

I pause with my fork half an inch from my mouth. "Vi! You can't say things like that. You're pretty much ensuring they lose with that kind of talk."

"Toronto has been solid this season, and they're fighting to win, you know? They haven't seen the Cup in more than half a century. Besides that, and you can't repeat this to anyone, but Alex hasn't been on top of his game. That injury last season has slowed him down, and the only reason he's been managing is because Darren is picking up the slack. Everyone knows that. All the guys, and Darren I'm sure, but none of them will say anything."

"Alex has been playing well," I counter. But even as I say it, I know it's a half-truth. Normally Alex is one of the top players in the league, but this year has been different. His stats have taken a serious hit, and he hasn't been playing as well as usual, whereas Darren's stats have been on the rise, particularly his assists. It's like he's handing goals to Alex instead of taking them for his own. Which says a lot about him as a person.

"Well, in the general sense of the word, but not like he used to. Promise me this conversation stays between us."

"Of course. I promise."

"You can't tell Darren."

Violet has been my best friend for almost a decade, so when she asks me to keep a secret, it's usually a no brainer. But since Darren and I just dealt with the fallout of one of his secrets, I hesitate for a second before I respond.

"I won't tell Darren."

I hold out my pinkie and Violet grips it with hers. "Imagine if you unzipped a pair of pants and found a dick this small inside. How sad would you be?"

"So sad."

"Darren seriously hasn't said anything about Alex's performance this season?"

I consider what she's asking, and weigh it with how freely I should share my private conversations with Darren. "He mentioned that recovery can be slow and Alex was playing his best."

Violet nods and pushes her food around on her plate. "He really is. But he's also aware that his shoulder doesn't feel the way it used to. He doesn't want to wreck his body. He's been thinking about the future a lot, about what he sees for himself after the NHL, so when his contract is up with Chicago, he's considering retirement."

"What if Chicago wants to renew again?" I ask.

"We'll see, but it really depends. I don't think he wants to go out with tanked stats, you know? He's been at the top of his game for a long time, and it's hard for him to put in so much extra work and not see the payoff."

"What will he do when he retires?" Darren's plan once his hockey career ends isn't something we've discussed.

"He's talked about sportscasting or coaching. I'm hoping for the former since he'll probably be able to get on in Chicago, and then I won't have to quit my job."

"You're serious about this, aren't you?" This makes me intensely aware of how different my relationship is with Darren. We don't plan past next weekend, let alone next year. That he asked me to be available when he returns from the away game in Toronto is a big deal.

"The concussion last season scared him. He still has holes in his memory, Char. Sometimes he has difficultly remembering simple things, and he gets flustered. It's not anything really worrying, but it's there. He doesn't want to take the risk anymore, especially now that he's actively trying to knock me up. He doesn't want to compromise his family for his career."

"I can understand that, but retirement? It seems so final."

I have to wonder what that's like to have someone love you so much that they weigh choices in favor of who, not what they love.

There's a pit in my stomach, and every time we have one of these heavy conversations, it gets a little deeper. Everyone else is settling down, creating their own microcosm of family, and here I am getting excited over Darren wanting time with me next week.

Violet folds her napkin until it sort of resembles a diaper. "I know, but Alex wants to be involved, and traveling would made that hard. Besides, Alex doesn't want to leave Chicago, and I know Buck has plans to settle here once his career is over."

She smiles wistfully. "It'd be nice if our kids could all grow up together, wouldn't it? I can kind of see what the future would be like if all of us stayed here. Wouldn't it be awesome if we both had girls and they were best friends like we are?"

I don't even know if Darren is going to be in Chicago next year, let alone if we're still going to be together, and already Violet is planning our kids' futures.

Violet wipes under her eyes and stares down at the wetness as if she can't understand how it got there. "Oh my God, I'm not even pregnant yet, and I'm already crying about everything."

I hand her a clean napkin, and she blots under her eyes. "Are you sure you're not pregnant? I mean, you're eating like you're trying to win some kind of competition. And the breast tenderness . . ."

I mean it as a joke, but she pulls out her phone and flips through her calendar. "Oh shit."

My stomach does a little flip.

"I should've gotten my period five days ago." Violet's eyes are huge. She grips the edge of the table. "What if I'm pregnant?"

"Isn't that what you want?"

"Well, yeah, I mean, I guess that's the whole point. I figured it would take a while—like, more than a couple of months, you know? I thought I'd be able to have a glass of wine this weekend. If I am preggers, it's going to be a year before I do that again."

"At least you'll have Sunny to keep you company?" It's meant as reassurance for her, but it causes a twinge of jealousy because it's another way I'm not like the rest of the girls.

"Yeah, there's that." Violet taps her lips. "You know what we should do?"

"Stop at a CVS on the way home and get one of those pee-stick tests to find out if you're knocked up?"

"No—well, yes, but that's not what I was going to say. If they go to game seven in this series, we should *all* go to Toronto. And if I'm not pregnant, I'm totally going to drink my face off."

"Either way, that would be fun." It would be nice to get away for a couple of days.

I feel bad that I'm almost hoping Violet isn't pregnant. I'd like to get smashed with my best friend.

"Right? We can start looking at flights. Maybe go in a day early and do some shopping? Stock up on all the mapley deliciousness."

"I'll ask Darren if he'd be okay with that."

Violet's eyes light up. "Or you could surprise him!"

"Uh . . . I'm not so sure that's a great idea, considering what happened the last time I did that." My face heats at the memory.

"This is different, though. You're not planning a BDSM bash. You'd just be coming to see him play hockey and ride his joy stick."

I give her a look. "I should still ask him first. Just to make sure."

"Why? I mean, he's going to want you there regardless, isn't he? If Chicago wins, they move on to the next round of the playoffs, and you get to have fuck-yeah sex." She pumps her fist almost like she's jerking off a pretend penis. "If they lose, you get to have condolence sex. You're the one who told me this back when Alex and I were doing our mating dance."

"I'll talk to Darren about it. In the meantime, let's find out if you'll be able to drink something other than ginger ale for the next nine months, unless you want to wait until Alex gets home and do it then."

"I can't wait until tomorrow. We're doing this now."

We stop at the CVS on the way back to the office. Violet makes me come into the private wheelchair bathroom with her while she pees on a stick. I face the wall while she does the honors, letting out a crazy squeal.

"Holy shit—are you pregnant?"

"No, I just peed on my hand!" After she's finished her business, she sets the stick on the edge of the sink and washes her hands three times, breathing like she's practicing Lamaze. "Has it been two minutes yet? Jesus, I'm so nervous. You look for me." She closes her eyes and thrusts the stick at me.

I look at the little window and swallow down the lump in my throat. "It's a plus sign."

Her eyes pop open. "What does that mean? Does that mean I'm preggers?"

I nod and show her the test, smiling softly at my best friend even though a part of me is so very sad.

She grabs the test and stares down at it, slack jawed. "Look at how blue that is. I went off the pill two freaking months ago. Alex is going to be so proud of his magic sperm. Fuck. Shit. I'm pregnant, Char. What if I make a terrible mother? What if I'm like Skye and I embarrass the fuck out of my kid? What if it hates me, and we become estranged, and it writes a tell-all book about how horrible I am—"

"You're an amazing best friend, Vi. You're going to make an even more amazing mother."

She throws her arms around me, hugging me hard. "I don't know if I'm ready for this," she mumbles into my shoulder.

"You've got this. You're going to be fabulous."

She steps back, holding my shoulders, maybe for balance or support. "I'm going to get so fat, and my boobs are going to be huge."

I laugh, but tears threaten to spill over. "Alex is going to love that."

She cups her hands over her mouth. "Oh my God, he's going to be so excited."

"Are you going to call him?"

"I don't know. I mean, he'll be home tomorrow. Maybe I should wait and tell him in person. I should wait. I want to see his face. And I don't know if I want to tell anyone else yet. It's still so early, so much can happen." She takes my hands in hers. "Can we keep this between the two of us for now? I'll tell Alex tomorrow, and we'll figure out when we want to tell everyone else. But for now, it'll just be us who know, okay?"

"Of course."

"Oh my God, Char. I'm going to be a mom, and you're going

to be an aunt, because let's face it, you're as close to a sister as I'm ever going to get."

She hugs me hard again, and I let the tears fall, because as happy as I am for her, I'm a little sad for me and how this is going to change things.

11

SHIFT

CHARLENE

Chicago ends up losing the game in Toronto, which means they're coming home to play game six in the series. If they lose again, Toronto moves on to the next round, and they're out of the playoffs. If they win, they go back to Toronto to play game seven.

The second Darren lands in Chicago, he calls to make sure I'm still coming over after work, which is good, because I need a distraction from Violet's not so little secret.

That anxious feeling settles in my stomach and moves lower. Too bad sneaking off to the bathroom at work to get myself off is frowned upon. "If you still want me to, yes."

"Definitely. Yes. I want you." There's a short pause before he continues. It sounds like he's opening and closing drawers. "To come over after work."

"What are you doing? You sound distracted."

"I can't find any of your clothes in my dresser. I mean, apart from lingerie. You must have a few articles in here somewhere," he says.

"Oh, uh, I always bring my things home with me after I spend the night."

"Oh." He exhales heavily. "I didn't realize that. You should leave things here for the nights you plan to stay."

"Okay. I can do that."

"Good. Great. I'd like that. You'll stay tonight, then?"

"You have a game tomorrow night; you need your rest. You know I'm an active sleeper." I can't be responsible for interfering with his game when Chicago is so close to making the finals again.

"I suppose I'll just have to wear you out so you don't pose a threat to my sleep."

I laugh at that. "Are you sure?"

"Positive. I would like more rather than less of you, and you staying the night solves that problem."

"I'll stop at home before I come to you after work and pick up some things, then."

"I can do that. I have errands to run so I'll be out anyway. I could stop by your place and pick up a suit and whatever else you need, That way you can come straight to me—if that works for you, of course."

"Are you sure? It's kind of out of your way, isn't it?"

"Not at all, and it means you'll be at my place that much sooner. We'll order dinner in." He almost sounds giddy.

"Sure. That sounds great."

"Perfect. I'll see you soon."

I leave work promptly at five, my body humming with nervous excitement as I head to the parking garage. I need

Darren tonight as much as he seems to need me. Violet's pregnancy news is hitting me harder than I expected. It's another thing she and Sunny will have in common, and another way our relationships are just so different. I wonder how Violet's doing. I'm sure I'll get a message from her tonight at some point, or maybe she'll be too busy celebrating.

In my head I'm already filtering through the lingerie drawer at his place. Since they lost the last game, I'm thinking Darren will want sweetly sexy tonight. Something soft to distract him from a hard loss. I imagine I'll end up in pale purple.

Before I leave the garage, I decide it would be a good idea to let Darren know I'm on my way. Normally he's quick to respond, but I don't get anything from him between getting in the car and arriving at the security of his gated community. The guard lets me in, and I pull into Darren's driveway. It's empty, but he often keeps his cars in the garage, so it's not out of the ordinary. I check my appearance in the visor and take a deep breath. The pinging ramps up in my lady bits as I cut the engine and grab my purse from the passenger seat.

I ring the doorbell and wait, but after a minute, there's still no answer. I check my messages again and find I have a new one from Darren. My stomach drops at the possibility that he might be canceling, but as I scan the text, I smile.

> Had to run out. Make yourself comfortable. I'll be back soon.

He gave me the code to his house a long time ago, but since most of our dates are planned, I've never needed to use it. It feels odd to let myself in, but I punch the numbers and open the door. The first thing that catches my attention is the massive bouquet of flowers on the side table to the right. Flowers aren't a typical decoration for Darren. In fact, knickknacks and decorations in general aren't Darren's thing.

His house is pretty much on the extreme side of minimalist. There's generally no evidence of clutter, or that he even lives here, apart from the occasional mug in the sink or a pair of boxers that missed the laundry basket in his walk-in closet.

Much like the ones that arrived in my office several days ago, this bouquet seems to be keeping with the sunrise theme. It's filled with pale and vibrant yellows, soft peaches, pinks, and purples. There's a card beside the vase with my name written neatly on the front. I flip it open and smile at the note inside.

Charlene,
I'm sorry I'm not here.
Upstairs you'll find
something more comfortable
to change into.

The restless pinging down below ratchets up a few notches as I consider what exactly his something more comfortable might consist of. Taking the note with me, I head upstairs to his bedroom, which is where I'm assuming the something more comfortable will be.

I bark out a quiet, shocked laugh when I step inside his bedroom and turn on the light. The very first thing I notice is a second bouquet of flowers, which contrasts perfectly with the one downstairs. Instead of a sunrise, this is more sunset with a cascade of yellow, darkening to vibrant peach and nearly black purple lilies and dahlias at the base.

The flowers aren't the only addition to the room, though.

Laid across the end of the bed are several clothing options. I expected lace or satin, or possibly some combination of the two. But that's not what I'm looking at.

It appears Darren has done some shopping at my favorite legging store. There are five new pairs. Two of them are ridiculously adorable and firefly themed, and the others are covered in fun pastel prints reflective of the season. He's also gone to the trouble of buying matching tanks and shirts, and a vast array of new cheekies in every color, pattern, and fabric available.

In addition to those, there's a black gift bag tied with a bow. I'm not sure if I'm supposed to open that now or wait, so I leave it and pick a pair of leggings, a shirt, and a pair of panties to change into. They're freshly washed, as evidenced by the distinct smell of Darren's fabric softener.

I head back downstairs to wait for him and find yet another surprise in the living room. Set up on the table beside the reading chair he bought for me is a bucket with a bottle of white wine chilling and a glass waiting to be filled. Several books are stacked on the seat of the chair, their spines creased from my excessive reading and pages folded over. Sometimes, when I love a book I'll earmark certain chapters or passages so I can find them easily and read them over.

Darren must have scooped them from my nightstand and brought them here for me. I press my fingers to my lips, my chest light and heavy at the same time. His attentiveness is endearing, and while part of me loves it, the other part worries about what it means. So many things are changing, and I don't know quite how to handle it. The neat lines we'd drawn seem to be erasing themselves, and I don't know how to do this without them. It makes me feel unsteady.

With shaking hands, I pull the cork free and pour myself a glass of wine. I take a small sip and moan. This is way better than that boxed stuff my mom brought with her. I actually considered tossing the rest of it, but figured it was too much of a waste, so I mixed it with ginger ale and juice. Then it wasn't so bad.

I grab my phone and my ear buds, because I might as well enjoy the lengths Darren has gone to for me.

Moving the books to the table, I relax into the chair, cover myself with the throw, and sigh contentedly. On the next inhale, I note the faint scent of Darren's cologne clinging to the fabric. I turn my head and press my nose against the backrest. I'm not sure if I'm imagining things, but I swear it smells like his shampoo, which means he's been using the chair when I'm not here.

I slip in my ear buds, pick a playlist, and settle in with a book, flipping to one of my many favorite chapters. I like to read romance, maybe because my childhood was such a mess and the kind of relationships I witnessed weren't normal. I like the smutty ones as much as the sweet ones, but my favorite stories have the most broken characters. Even though it's fiction, it gives me hope that even the most messed up people can find someone to love them.

I'm on my second glass of wine, rereading my second favorite chapter when a shadow passes over my book. I startle as I look up to find Darren standing in front of me, and I nearly douse myself in wine.

He grabs the glass before I dump it in my lap, a wry smile forming as he tugs my ear buds free.

"I didn't hear you come in." I look him over. He's wearing black jeans, and a T-shirt that hugs his biceps and stretches tight across his chest.

"I gathered that from your reaction. You look cozy." He takes a sip from my glass.

"So cozy." I close my book and set it on the table.

"Can I see which ones you picked?" He tugs at the end of the blanket so it slips down a few inches.

"You went a little overboard, but thank you." I pull the throw off, and Darren's grin widens.

I grip the arms of the chair to push myself up.

He raises a hand. "No, no. Stay right here."

"Okay?" I draw the word out as I drop back down.

He drags a finger from my ankle to my knee. "This is nice— you right here, looking like it's where you belong."

I shift over and pat the seat cushion. "Why don't you join me? There's plenty of room." The chair is huge, and round. There's more than enough room for two bodies, even if one of them belongs to a huge hockey player.

"Let me get a glass."

"Or we could share mine?"

"We could definitely do that." He adjusts my legs so they're draped over his and stretches one arm across the back. Sliding his palm up my thigh, he runs his nose along my neck and follows with his lips. "I like you being here when I get home."

I laugh and then sigh as his lips trail along the edge of my jaw and across my cheek. When he reaches the corner of my mouth I turn toward him, our lips brushing.

His rough fingers glide gently up my arm and thread into the hair at the nape of my neck. The kiss starts slow, the warm soft drag of his tongue becoming a sweet tangle. I have no idea how long we kiss, but eventually Darren pulls back, his thumb sweeping back and forth across my bottom lip, his breath coming hard.

"How was your day?" he grinds out.

I laugh and twist in his grip so I can straddle his thighs. "Long." Knowing he was back in Chicago but having to wait to see him made the day pass more slowly than usual.

"Same." He settles his palms on my hips. "But this makes it worth it."

"Making out in my reading chair?" I reach for the glass of wine and take a sip.

"Just you being here period. But the making out is nice too." He watches as I take another sip. "I'd like some of that."

I raise the glass, expecting him to take it, but he doesn't. Instead he parts his lips and cocks one sinister eyebrow.

"I might spill it on you," I warn.

"It's white. I'll take the risk."

I tip the glass up until the wine reaches the edge, wetting his lips. My tongue is caught between my teeth, my smile wide as I lift the tiniest bit too high and it trickles out of the edge of the glass and down his chin.

"Told you." I set the glass on the side table, nearly missing since I'm paying more attention to Darren's mouth than what I'm actually doing. I catch the drip with my tongue, then kiss the wine away, but when I get to his lips I pull back.

Darren's apparently not having it, because I suddenly find myself airborne. I land on my back on the chair, Darren's mouth on mine as he parts my legs with his knee and sinks his hips into mine.

Half an hour later, I've had three orgasms and I'm back in my spot on the chair with my legs thrown over his, except now we're both mostly naked. Well, I'm totally naked, but Darren put his boxers back on. He tucks the blanket around me. "I'd planned to take you upstairs before I got inside you."

"So I could dress up in whatever's in that black bag on the bed?"

His brow pulls down. "Haven't you opened it?"

"Was I supposed to? I thought since it was wrapped I would wait until you were here."

"You can open it before we go to sleep since that's when it'll come in handy." He reaches over and picks up the single wine glass, offering it to me before he takes a sip.

I run my fingers through his hair and his head drops back, eyes falling closed. When he's like this, unguarded and at ease, he looks much less severe. "How are you feeling about the game tomorrow night?"

He runs one hand slowly up and down my thigh. "Truthfully?"

"Unless you feel like you need to lie to me about it to make yourself feel better."

He cracks a lid and a smile, then lifts his head. His smile disappears and his eyes seem to trace over my face. "Worried."

"You played really well last night."

"Not well enough." He blows out another breath.

"You can only be as good as your teammates allow, though." I drag my nails down the back of his scalp and goose bumps flash across his arms.

"It's not *my* game I'm worried about."

"Alex is struggling." It's not a question. I've seen it during the games, and then there's the conversation Violet and I had.

Darren chews on the inside of his lip for a few seconds before he gives me a reluctant nod. He's incredibly loyal, and even though it's the truth, I know all Darren wants to do is protect him.

"He needs to go into this game with a positive frame of mind, and my biggest concern at the moment is that he's beating himself up over the loss."

"Home ice advantage should help, shouldn't it?"

"Theoretically, yes. We have a great team, and Randy is an excellent front line player. Rookie is pulling his weight, and Miller and Lance are holding defense, but Alex has always been the best for scoring, and he's just not making the shots the way he used to." Darren drops his head and mutters a quiet *fuck.*

"Hey." I take his face between my hands and force him to look at me. His expression is pained, and I want to take that away for him. "It's okay to talk to me like this. You're not being disloyal for saying what's true. I'm sure he knows this and it's eating at him that you're the one picking up the slack. I know it's hard to separate your friendship from the welfare of the team and Alex's ego, but you might need to start taking some of the shots you've been passing."

"It's not that simple, Charlene."

"I know Alex likes to be the best at everything, but surely he must see how it would be better for the team—"

"It's not Alex; it's me."

"That's untrue. You've been incredible out there. I realize I'm biased—"

He presses his lips to mine to stop me. "You don't understand. Alex doesn't want me to pass to him. He knows he's not playing like he used to, and it's killing him because he feels like he's letting down his team. He wants me to take the shots, but I've been passing anyway, so it's my fault we lost last night, not his."

"Why would you pass to him if he asked you not to?"

"Goals get more points than assists," he says.

As if I don't know this. "And that matters why?"

He mumbles something else.

"I'm sorry, I didn't catch that."

"Can we just drop this? It's a real fucking downer, and that's not what I wanted tonight to be." His jaw tics and his throat bobs, fingers tightening on my thigh briefly before they skim up and in. I twist away from his wandering hand and cross my legs so he can't get between them.

He purses his lips, and I mirror the expression. His sigh is heavy as he trails his fingers down the side of my neck, pushing away the blanket. "Please, Charlene. Not tonight. Any other night." He drops his head, lips finding the place his fingers just were and gliding up to my ear. "I just want to get lost in you."

There's such vulnerability in his words and his tone. I pull back, wanting to see his face, trying to understand the sudden shift, the shutting down when we're finally making progress.

"I need you to let this go tonight. We can come back to it." His pained eyes search mine. "But for now, I need this. You. Please."

"Okay, Darren." I press a palm to his cheek. "If that's what you need."

He kisses me, softly at first, and then greedily. It's late when we finally make it upstairs to bed. I don't flail in my sleep. I can't with Darren wrapped around me like a human blanket.

We're shifting again, and I worry too much change too fast is dangerous. It creates fault lines and cracks. The kind I'll get lost in and won't find my way back out of.

12

SISTERHOOD

CHARLENE

Chicago wins the game against Toronto with Darren scoring the winning goal. He should be happy about it, but he's stoic instead. I want to chalk it up to game seven being in Toronto, but I'm sure it has to do with Alex.

We're sitting at the bar after the game, and Darren has me tucked into his side, one arm thrown over my shoulder. He's been quiet, smiling when people pat him on the back, but not saying much else. Which isn't unusual. What is unusual is the number of times he tucks my hair behind my ear, or leans in to kiss my neck.

"So we're all going to Toronto to cheer our boys on, right?" Violet says from across the table.

She told Alex last night that she's pregnant, but she wants to keep it quiet until she's through the first trimester. Considering how many weeks away that is, and how much he's fawning over her like she's an injured bird, I'm not sure the secret is destined to be kept.

I find out how right I am about five seconds later. "We can celebrate the end of the series and the fact that I'm going to be a dad!" Alex shouts. He's a few beers into the night, so it's hard to hold him too accountable.

Violet slaps his chest. "Alex!"

He cringes, then turns to her. "Sorry. Shit. I'm just so fucking excited. You're going to be the sexiest pregnant woman in this history of the universe."

There's a flurry of excitement, and I stand, along with Darren. His mouth is at my ear. "Did you know?"

"I was with her when she took the test. Violet didn't want me to say anything until she told Alex." I feel as if I should apologize.

He squeezes my hand and nudges me forward. "You don't have to explain. Alex told me this morning."

I look into icy eyes that seem somehow soft and warm. "You're not upset that I didn't tell you?"

"She's your best friend. You keep her confidence, as you should." He strokes my cheek and presses a gentle kiss to my lips.

A moment later I'm swallowed up in Alex's bear hug while Darren gives Violet a much gentler version of the same affectionate congratulations. I step back to let a teary Sunny hug her brother.

Darren slips his fingers between mine and pulls me into him. "It's a weekend game; can you get an extra day off? I want the time with you."

It's as if he knows that this good thing is in some ways bad— like it separates us from them in yet another way.

"I can talk to my boss tomorrow," I tell him.

"He'll say yes."

He's not being cocky, not really. Our firm represents a number of Chicago players. Violet is married to the top earner on the team, and only two other players in the league have bigger contracts than Alex. Darren isn't a slouch either, and Stroker handles his account directly. He'll let us go.

By ten the following morning, we have the green light from Stroker, much to Jimmy and Dean's dismay, and our plane tickets are booked. Darren wanted me on his flight, but I have to work on Friday, as do most of the girls, so we're leaving in the evening, which means we'll have all day Saturday to do fun girl things before the game.

When we arrive Friday night, the boys swarm the lobby and claim their significant others, leaving only the parents—of course Skye and Sidney came along, and Daisy and Robbie drove out from Guelph to be here—at the bar. It's late, but Darren needs some release before I force him to go to sleep.

I check my phone around midnight to see what the rest of the girls are up to. Looks like I'm the last one to be done putting my hockey man to bed. I slip out from beneath the covers, find my clothes, and tiptoe to the bathroom so I can change without disturbing Darren.

It's after two by the time I come back to the room. Lily and I drank too many cocktails while we talked lingerie. Skye and Daisy were far more sauced than us though, having been in the bar all evening. I'm not as quiet or coordinated as I'd like to be as I strip down. I try to find my pajamas, but it's too dark, and I don't want to risk waking Darren, who's curled around my pillow.

I pull his discarded shirt over my head and slip between the sheets as stealthily as possible. He shifts as soon as I'm under the covers, but he's still hugging the pillow, so it bars his way. Darren grunts his displeasure, groggy and only half aware as he struggles to get near me.

I turn to face him, settling a gentle palm on his cheek. "Let me help."

He hums and his limbs go lax, eyes fluttering open for a second before falling closed again as I replace the pillow with myself. Darren sighs and buries his nose in my hair. His arm comes around me, fingers splayed across my stomach. They travel up, between my breasts, skimming my collarbones until he reaches the pearls. He follows the strand, curling his fingers around my shoulder, thumb resting in the hollow of my throat.

I close my eyes and relax into his warmth. I want to hold onto this protected feeling, but it's terrifying. I crave this closeness with him, and when he's sleeping it feels safer, because it's unconscious on his part. I don't have to face it the way I do in the waking hours.

I fall asleep wishing I could erase my past so I could be a better version of myself, one that didn't have her innocence blown apart at the age of fourteen when I learned my life had been a fucked-up lie in a fucked-up world.

I wake up to Darren's hard-on pressed against my hip and his lips at my ear asking to get inside me. There's no chance I'm saying no to him, so we follow morning sex with room service while he gets ready for his pre-game skate, and I prepare to explore Toronto with the girls until game time.

He's quiet, which isn't unusual for Darren, but he's tense and restless, even after the morning orgasm.

"You okay?" I smooth his shower-damp hair away from his face.

"Mmm." He sits on the edge of the bed, pulls me between his legs, and tucks his head under my chin.

"That's not really an answer," I point out.

"Keep touching me, please."

"We're supposed to be downstairs in two minutes."

"I'm not asking for sex, Charlene. I just need you close to me."

"You're going to be amazing tonight."

His nose brushes my throat at his nod, and his fingers flex on my hips. His palms slide up my back, wrapping around my shoulders as he pulls me in tighter. He tips his head and his lips press against the side of my neck and part. The soft, wet touch of his tongue warms my body, and heat settles low in my stomach.

"Darren." It's warning twisted with desire.

He stands quickly, one palm curving around my nape. I tilt back as he looms over me, his gaze hot and needy.

"What—"

He cuts off the question with his mouth. His tongue pushes past my lips, and he finds his way under my shirt with his free hand. We need to be downstairs now. His team is leaving for their pre-game skate in minutes. We don't have time for another round of morning sex, and I don't want to be the reason he's off his game tonight.

I put my palms on his chest with the intention of pushing, but his fingers dip into the waistband of my leggings—it's pretty much all I packed for the weekend—and slide into my panties.

I gasp and grip his shirt when he finds the barbell piercing my hood and circles it roughly. He goes lower and thrusts two fingers inside me. Finding the magic spot, he curls fast and hard, making my knees buckle. His grip on the back of my neck tightens, preventing me from sinking to the floor.

He curls his fingers one more time before he withdraws to circle my clit again. It won't take much to make me come. Just a bit more friction and I'll go tumbling over the edge. But his hand disappears, and he wrenches his mouth away from mine.

I cry out at the loss of his touch and try to pull him back to me with his shirt. His name is a whine on my lips. My clit is throbbing, and my knees are weak.

"Please, Darren." The high pitch should be embarrassing, but dear God, the muscles are already clenching with the promise of an orgasm, if only he would touch me again.

His hot, almost angry gaze stays locked on mine as he lifts his hand, fingers glistening. I groan as he slips them into his mouth, sucking loudly.

Somewhere to the right a phone buzzes with a message.

One corner of his mouth tips up in a sinister smile as his fingers slide out of his mouth. He licks between the webbing, and my eyes roll up. I attempt to shove my own hand down my pants to finish what he started.

"No," he barks and grabs both my wrists. He spins me around until my knees hit the back of the bed and I drop to my ass. He straddles my legs, clamping them together as he hovers over me once again. "How do you feel right now, Charlene?"

The sound that comes out of me is somewhere between a whimper and a growl.

"That's not an answer, little firefly."

I fight against his hold on my wrists and swivel my hips.

He dips down until his face is an inch from mine. "Are you on the edge?"

"Yes."

"Are you angry?"

"No."

"No?" He quirks a brow.

"Yes!" This time it's a moan.

"Restless? Needy? Wanting? Desperate?"

I nod fervently. "All of those things."

"This is how I feel every time I'm away from you."

His eyes stay on mine, unblinking as he waits for me to process what he's just admitted. We don't talk feelings, and yet here he is, telling me more in these few words and actions than he has in the past two years.

"Don't make yourself come today. Whatever happens tonight, this is how I need you so we match when we're back together. Do you understand?" His voice is hard, but his expression is vulnerable.

"Yes, Darren. I understand."

His smile turns soft and his lips are softer still as they brush over mine. He releases my wrists and steps back, setting me free. I feel like I've been shot up with adrenaline and tranqued at the same time.

"Come on, baby. The girls are waiting for you, and I'm going to be in trouble with my team if we don't move our asses." He extends a hand and winks.

"You're an asshole," I gripe, but take his hand because I don't think I'm capable of standing on my own.

His chuckle is dark as he pulls me to my feet. I stumble and end up mashed against his chest. I might try to rub myself on him during that brief contact. He kisses my temple. "But I'm your asshole."

I snort, but he's right. He hands me my purse and phone, then pockets his own and grabs his bag. I'm less than coordinated as he opens the door and ushers me into the hall. I have to concentrate on putting one foot in front of the other rather than slamming him into a wall so I can hump him until I come.

He punches the elevator button, and I stare at the numbers as they rise. The churning in my stomach grows the closer it gets to our floor. I don't know what I want more—the elevator to be empty or full. If it's empty he's going to torment me, as he sometimes likes to do. I'm aware that this is tied to his stress level over the game tonight.

The elevator dings, and the doors slide open. *Shit*. It's empty.

"Come on, firefly." Darren links our pinkies and tugs. I stumble forward, my mouth dry. Expectation and anxiety make the ache between my legs flare. I catch a glimpse of my reflection in the mirrored walls. My eyes are wide and glassy, cheeks flushed, lips swollen from his kisses.

He presses the button that will take us to the lobby, and I watch as the doors slide closed. Darren drops his bag on the floor and crowds me into the corner, pressing his hips into mine.

I groan and let my head fall back against the glass, waiting for him to do something, anything. His lips find my neck and trail up to my ear. "Feeling trapped?"

I shake my head.

"Still needy?" Now his lips are on my cheek.

I exhale a shuddering breath and nod.

151

His smile makes the harsh angles of his face even more severe rather than softening them. "I bet your panties are already soaked through."

I swallow hard and clench my thighs harder. His knee presses against mine, and I open, letting him in. I glance up. We have thirty more floors, but the elevator could stop anytime to pick up people. He rolls his hips, his erection pressed against my stomach, his thigh providing the friction I'm so very desperate for.

The orgasm is like an aura in the air, the glitter of a sunrise on the water—close but not quite within reach.

"What are you waiting for? Chase it. See if you can catch it before it's too late."

I fist his shirt and grind shamelessly on his leg, not caring how desperate I must look and sound as I whimper and roll my hips while he stands immobile, one hand gripping the bar on either side of me, eyes fixed on mine. He's not helping, but he's giving me a chance to help myself.

I glance over his shoulder. *Shit.* Only fifteen more floors to go. I grind harder, moaning loudly as sensation builds and funnels, a tornado gaining momentum.

His gaze follows mine in the mirror. "Better hurry. Time is running out."

I'm right there—bliss a lit firecracker ready to explode in my clit—when the elevator dings. Darren covers my hand with his and steps back, even as I try to follow his thigh. He shakes his head, his expression almost remorseful, and he uncurls my fingers from his shirt and brings my knuckles to his lips. He kicks his bag to the wall and leans against it.

He's quick to wrap an arm around my shoulder and pull me into his side. He drops his head, lips finding my temple as he whispers, "Sorry, firefly, you almost had it."

The doors slide open and a family enters, giving us half smiles while their kids press their faces against the glass and the youngest one tries to push all the buttons. My knees feel weak all over again, and I want to cry. My clit is still singing "I was *that* close."

When the elevator finally reaches the lobby, Darren laces our fingers together and guides me to where his bus is waiting and the girls are huddled around their phones.

"Finally!" Violet holds up her phone, showing us the time. "They were about to leave without you." She thumbs over her shoulder to where Alex is standing outside. Darren's phone rings as Alex brings his to his ear.

"I gotta run. I'll see you tonight. Have fun today." Darren brushes his lips across mine in a very uncharacteristic public display of affection.

I stare after him as he heads for Alex, who throws his hand up in the air. All I catch is "What the fu—" before the doors close and cut him off.

Darren holds up a hand, probably telling him to settle down. He claps him on the back and Alex shakes his head, shoulders rolling as he turns and climbs onto the bus. Darren looks over his shoulder as he brings two fingers to his lips and holds them up in my direction.

I smile until I realize it's the fingers that were inside me not that long ago—the same ones that did not provide me with an orgasm. As my grin falls, his rises. And then he disappears onto the bus.

As soon as he's out of sight, I turn to the girls, ready to issue a somewhat insincere apology for holding them up. They're all staring at me, eyes wide.

"What?" I touch my face and pat my hair, making sure it's not all messed up.

"What the hell was that?" Violet makes wild hand gestures.

"What was what?" *Why are they all looking at me like I've grown another head*? I look down to make sure I'm not flashing a nipple or have a wet spot on my crotch.

"I didn't think Darren was big on PDAs," Violet says.

I shrug. "He usually isn't." Until now, I guess.

"Well, I think it's sweet," Sunny says, rubbing her bump. "Can we get something to eat before we go shopping? I'm starving."

I'm grateful that she takes the attention off me.

"I second that!" Violet says, and we pour out onto the Toronto street.

We stop at a breakfast place that has vegan options. Violet orders a full breakfast and a side of bacon and devours everything. We stroll down the street, stopping at a candy store, and then of course we find a sex shop, so it's imperative that we go inside, at least according to Violet and Skye.

Violet's eyes light up as she rummages through the penis-themed party favors. "Oh! Poppy, we need to start planning your bachelorette party!"

"I don't think that's necessary quite yet since we're not getting married for at least another year, maybe two, depending."

"Unless Lance knocks you up," Lily wags her brows.

Poppy rolls her eyes. "He's not going to knock me up. I'm on the pill."

Sunny raises her hand. "I was on the pill, and I got knocked up."

"Yeah, but you were on antibiotics and forgot that makes the pill ineffective," Lily reminds her.

"Oh, right. Oh well, at least this time around it was planned. Might as well have them all now so they can grow up together." She pats her tummy.

Lily smiles softly, but there's a sadness there, too. Her mom got pregnant by an NHL player when she was eighteen. He took zero responsibility and never paid a dime in child support. Randy's dad, a former NHL player, had a bad habit of sleeping with women who weren't his wife while he was on the road.

While Lily and Randy seem to have a great relationship, they're both a little skittish about marriage and kids. She's still young and not in a rush to start a family of her own, but I think part of her is sad that if she does end up having kids, they'll be much younger than Sunny's.

I can relate, I guess—not that I want to get married and have kids. I mean, I guess maybe I would eventually consider the kid part, but marriage seems a lot like a prison sentence from my experience growing up.

On the way back to the hotel, we're forced to stop again because Sunny needs more food. The game doesn't start until seven, but we arrive back at the hotel around four in the afternoon. It appears housekeeping has been by to tidy up, and Darren has come and gone. On the bed is huge black box tied with a red ribbon and a small black card with my name written on it in silver ink.

The ache between my legs that finally dulled into something tolerable this afternoon becomes sharp again as I consider the contents of the box.

I'd message Darren, but I don't like to distract him before games. I pick up the card and flip it open.

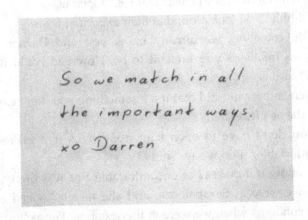

So we match in all
the important ways.
xo Darren

I shiver at the memory of what he said this morning when he left me hanging. It's been a long time since he's brought me to the edge like that—twice even—and kept me wanting all day. What if it's some kind of sex toy in there? How the hell am I going to make it through the rest of the night without an orgasm?

I'm still standing at the edge of the bed, staring at the box, when there's a knock at my door.

I glance through the peephole, thinking maybe he organized room service—which is totally something he would do—except it's Violet standing in the hall with the rest of the girls.

I flip the lock and open the door. "Hey, what's going on?"

"We're getting ready for the game, and you weren't answering your messages, so we all came to you," Violet replies.

They file into the room toting bags. Lily has champagne, and Sunny is carrying a bottle of that sparkling grape juice she's in love with.

All of them are already dressed and ready for the game, wearing their jerseys and leggings.

"Ooooh! You have a present!" Violet picks up the box and shakes it around. It doesn't make a sound, so clearly there's nothing metal in it. She thrusts it at me. "Open it!"

"Uhhhh . . ." I look around at their expectant faces.

"Oh, come on, we already know you and Darren aren't nearly as freaky as you pretend to be. How bad could it be?" Violet reasons.

"Remember you said that if it's something you don't expect." I take the box from her.

"You don't have to open it in front of us if it makes you uncomfortable," Poppy says softly.

I wonder if it makes her uncomfortable. She was pretty quiet when we were at Sexapalooza, and she mostly looked at the funny condoms when we were in the sex shop. For as horrible a reputation as Lance had with women, he's incredibly tender with Poppy. He treats her like she's a delicate flower, even though I think she's kind of a badass with the way she handles him.

I take a seat on the end of the bed and pull the red ribbon, then nervously flip open the box. I press my fingers to my lips and suppress a grin. Now the note card makes more sense.

Inside is a brand new jersey to replace the one I've had for nearly two years. There's also a pair of leggings covered in a team logo and WESTINGHOUSE 26 pattern. He even went so far as to get matching socks. But it's what I find under the jersey and leggings that makes me fight back a thick swell of foreign emotion. I'm not sure if I want to laugh or cry.

I pick up the small card sitting on top of the bra and panties set and flip it over.

> I'll probably be lynched for going against team colors, but I thought this suited you better.

I run my fingers over the pretty pale yellow cheekies, edged in lace and decorated with not only the Chicago logo, but a tiny firefly print. I have a feeling they might be glow in the dark. I flip them over and laugh. They read WESTINGHOUSE on the butt. The bra is the same fabric, minus the text.

"He really is sweet, isn't he?" Poppy says.

"He is," I agree.

He's always been big on gift giving. Mostly it's been lingerie and sometimes more practical things, like upgrading the alarm system in my house and buying me that reading chair. But these kinds of gifts are new. And I think I like it, even though it scares me. I should be bracing myself for the possibility that he's going to be traded at the end of the season, not holding on tighter.

"You look like you might need this." Lily hands me a glass of champagne, which I gladly accept.

I take a small sip at first, then a much larger one since it's so delicious, and she's right. I do need it. This whole coming to away games with Darren isn't new. I've been invited plenty of times. It's how the dynamics have changed that's freaking me out.

I've always come prepared and with a plan. Or Darren has mentioned specific lingerie or toys he'd like me to bring. This time he offered to pack the leggings and shirts he purchased and keeps at his place—in the third drawer he cleared out for me. The first and second contain all the lingerie he or I have purchased over the past two years.

I chug the rest of my champagne and head to the bathroom so I can freshen up a little and change before I start the whole makeup process. The bra and panty set are adorably perfect. If I'd brought my phone in with me I'd consider taking a selfie and sending it to Darren, but that's not something I've done before, and I'm not sure if he'd appreciate it or be put off by it. Besides, I have a feeling it will be more impactful if he sees this on me in person.

When I come out of the bathroom, fully dressed in my brand new, freshly washed outfit—I know this because the clothes smell like Darren's laundry detergent—Lily hands me another glass of champagne.

Violet and Sunny are arguing over what color eye shadow will look best on Poppy. Well, not arguing so much as holding up different color palettes and debating what will look more natural. Poppy doesn't need to wear makeup at all, and neither does Sunny. They have those natural, flawless faces that look best with a hint of lip gloss and maybe a coat of mascara.

I don't go crazy on the makeup, but pictures from the games often end up online, so I won't go out with a naked face, either. While my relationship with Darren got a lot of press and questions when we first started dating—which was unnerving for a lot of reasons—it was difficult to really qualify it since physical contact in public has never been our thing. It kept everyone guessing as to what was going on.

If Darren pulls another PDA like he did this afternoon, that could change things again. So of course I want to look decent if my picture ends up splashed on hockey sites for the bunnies to rip apart.

At six we meet Alex and Violet's parents in the hotel lobby and head to the arena. It's a short walk, but it's clear both Daisy and Skye have been drinking already—and possibly engaging in other activities that are legal in Canada.

The champagne has loosened me up a little, but I'm still nervous about the game. I root around in my purse for one of my mom's candies. I'm grateful when I find several at the bottom. I pop one in my mouth and sigh as the minty flavor coats my tongue. I know it's probably the placebo effect, but I immediately feel the tiniest bit better after a couple of sucks.

The stadium is full of blue and white jerseys, so we stick out like sore thumbs with our screaming red and black. Not that any of us gives a flying fuck. Violet figures Toronto would've picked Alex up—as a Canadian player—if they'd been on their game and realized what a formidable opponent he was going to be. Even with an injury he plays better than most, though he's been a lot more cautious recently, and I see that now in a way I wouldn't have before the conversation with Darren.

We have the kind of seats people want to shank you for. We file down our row, drinks in hand, and settle in while we wait for the teams to be announced. While the girls were in my room I'd almost forgotten about the discomfort between my thighs, but it's back with a vengeance. Part of it comes from knowing I'm wearing those pretty panties with his name on the ass.

I reach into my purse for another one of my calming candies.

"Are you coming down with something?" Lily asks from my right.

"Huh?" I pop the candy into my mouth and try not to groan

out loud as the minty taste coats my tongue for the second time in the past hour.

"Is that a cough drop?"

"No. Why? Do you need one? I might have some." I don't want to part with my mom's candies.

"I'm good. It probably won't taste great with my beer." She clinks her can against mine, and we both take a sip.

Yeah, it's not all that delicious when you combine mint and beer.

A few minutes later, the teams take the ice, first Toronto, then Chicago. The apprehension I've been holding on to all day drops from my stomach to settle lower, between my thighs, making the pervasive ache that much worse. It's going to be a long game.

We all wave as the boys skate past, warming up before they take the bench. Violet's knee is bouncing, and she chews on her thumbnail.

"You okay?" I ask.

She nods. "Just nervous. I want them to win."

"Me, too."

Alex and Darren have their heads together as they take the bench and wait for the ice to be cleaned, Darren's hand on his shoulder. I lift my pearls to my lips as Darren glances in my direction.

He raises two fingers, the hint of a smile appearing as he taps his lips. I drop the pearls and mirror the movement.

The buzzer sounds, and his smile fades. He puts on his helmet and gloves and takes the ice. The first period isn't great. Darren passes the puck instead of taking shots, and Alex can't seem to get it past the net. Toronto steals the puck from Alex more than once, and by the end of the first period, Chicago is down one.

In the second period, Alex narrowly avoids getting slammed into the boards by Cockburn, the same guy who took him out last season and nearly cost him his career.

Darren puts himself in the way and takes the hit for Alex. He and Cockburn crash into the boards, the sound echoing through the arena.

"Fucking Cockburn!" Violet jumps out of her seat and starts yelling at the ref to call the dirty play.

Darren shakes it off, and Toronto takes a penalty, giving Chicago a two-minute power play. They switch out Alex for Randy, and he takes control when the puck drops, barreling down the ice toward the net with Darren on his right. At the last second, Randy passes to Darren who takes the shot, sliding the puck past the net, tying the game.

He doesn't smile as his teammates pat his back, eyes on the scoreboard and the minutes counting down the second period.

"Holy shit." Lily nudges my arm and points to the screens above us. Darren and Randy's faces flashes across it. While Randy wears a cocky smirk in his picture, Darren's eyes are dark, mouth almost set in a scowl. Their stats flash across the screen. Darren's sitting just below Randy this season, which makes him an incredibly valuable player—the kind who is covetable despite his age.

It's the reason he's been passing when Alex has asked him not to. He hasn't wanted all the points because of the draft. It all makes sense now.

The heavy feeling I've been carrying all day grows as the game continues. Randy scores a goal in the top of the third period, giving Chicago the lead, but Toronto ties it again halfway through. Alex and Darren are back on the ice together with three minutes left in the game. I can barely breathe when Alex gains control of the puck and skates down the ice toward the net, Darren parallel to him.

I cross my fingers as Alex makes the shot, but it goes wide. Darren catches the puck as it glides past the net and skates around behind it. It looks like he's going to pass to Alex, but he takes the shot instead, scoring his second goal of the game.

Toronto fans give a collective groan as the Chicago fans go crazy. It's a matter of keeping the puck away from the net while the final seconds tick down, securing Chicago's place in the next round, bringing them that much closer to the finals again.

TV crews swarm the players once they're off the ice. Darren looks uncomfortable with cameras on him, especially when they start talking about how his stats are the best of his career and then ask questions about the expansion draft and trade possibilities. Alex plasters on a smile when they turn the mic on him, but there's tension in the set of his jaw. He's unhappy with his performance.

"Guess I better get the Epsom salts ready. Tonight's going to be hard on the beaver," Violet says as we file out of the arena and pour onto the street, heading for the hotel.

We go directly to the bar, aware that it'll be a while before the guys arrive. Daisy and Skye appear to be three sheets to the wind already, and they've ordered a round of shots. They're having an inappropriate conversation—not unusual for those two—about their husbands and their sexual prowess.

Violet turns to Sunny. "That could be us one day."

Sunny rubs her belly. "I wonder if this one will be another boy. I'm getting really big really fast this time."

Violet leans her head on Sunny's shoulder. "Wouldn't it be great if we both had a boy or a girl at the same time? They'll have so much fun together, and when they're older we can have the kind of conversations our moms have and embarrass them."

I watch their sisterly exchange and selfishly fear that this new bond they're forming is going to usurp all the years of friendship between me and Violet. They'll have so much more in common now that they're both pregnant, and Sunny will be able to give Violet new-mom advice. They'll have stories and experiences to share that I can't be part of.

She'll have new responsibilities. I've seen how motherhood has changed Sunny this past year, and I worry it will be the same for Violet. She'll settle into her new role, and I'll won't fit into her life quite the way I did before.

Poppy pulls me out of my personal pity party when she

hands me a drink.

Daisy and Skye's conversation seems to have moved away from doing the dirty to hockey, which is a little better.

"Robbie used to play hockey in college. I loved going to the games." Daisy sighs wistfully.

"I went out with a hockey player once," Skye blurts.

"Really?" Daisy perks up.

Violet rolls her eyes.

"Mmm. In my first year of college I used to waitress at this little bar. It was near the stadium, so sometimes we'd get fans and players in there." She waves a hand around in the air. "Anyway, this guy came in and sat in my section. He was a real hottie, and he played professional hockey—I think maybe for North Carolina? I can't remember now, but he was charming, and one thing led to another." Skye grimaces. "Sadly, he was terrible in the sack, and he had a tiny penis."

"I love your mom," I snicker.

"Wanna trade?" Violet grumbles. "Wait, it's pretty much the same thing, so never mind."

"Oh no!" Daisy puts a comforting hand on Skye's arm. "That's awful."

"It was such a disappointment. The condom slipped off in the middle, and I ended up having to fish it out after." Skye shudders, and Violet makes a gagging sound. "One good thing came from the experience, though." She turns to Violet and pats her on the cheek. "I got you."

Violet's mid-sip, so she spit-sprays ginger ale all over her mother's face and also gets my cheek. "What?"

Skye wraps her arm around Violet's shoulder. "I was almost five months along before I realized I was pregnant. In hindsight, I should've figured it out sooner, but sometimes things happen for a reason. I had zero interest in that hockey player, so I raised you on my own until I met Sidney and we fell in love."

"My dad was a professional hockey player?" Violet asks.

"He was. Not a very good one, mind you, but a hockey

player nonetheless."

"I can't believe this is the first time I'm hearing this! Why didn't you tell me before now? I always thought he was some random."

Skye gives Violet a patient smile. "He was a random, honey."

"Does this random have a name?"

"Of course he does."

"Do you remember it?"

Skye makes a face. "Well, yes."

Violet arches a brow. "Care to share?"

Skye sighs, maybe realizing she's not going to get out of this. "His name is Dick, which is kind of ironic really, considering his was so small and all."

"My father's name is Dick?" Violet looks unimpressed.

"Sidney is your father, Violet. He gave you away at your wedding. I think that trumps being a sperm donor."

"Agreed, but still—even if Dick is a dickless dick, he's my biological father, and I think I have a right to know who he is, Especially since he's contributed half of my DNA, and I'm pregnant, and who knows what effect his genetic bullshit will have on this kid." She motions to her stomach, eyes wide with horror. "What if we have a boy and he has a tiny little penis?"

"You're almost exactly like me, and nothing like your biological dad. I'm sure Alex's DNA will win out in this case."

"Still, it'd be good to know. Does dickless Dick have a last name?"

"Of course." Skye grimaces and mutters something.

"What was that?"

"His last name is Head."

Violet blinks. And blinks again. "Come again?"

"Head. His last name is Head."

"My dad's name is Dick Head?"

"Technically it's Richard, but yes." Skye takes a healthy gulp of her drink. "Maybe we should talk about this later."

"Richard Head? And he played for North Carolina?"

"Yes, honey. Are you okay? You're really pale." Skye gives me a worried look.

"Maybe you should sit down." I put a hand on Violet's shoulder and urge her to the closest stool. Something about this conversation is very familiar, and I can't place why that is.

Lily appears, having returned from the bathroom. "Is everything okay? What's wrong with Violet?"

"Skye just told her who her birth father is."

"What?" Lily's eyes go wide.

"She's pretty drunk," I say.

Lily frowns. "I thought Violet was pregnant."

"Oh, Violet's not drunk, Skye is."

"And I thought Butterson was a bad last name." Violet shakes her head. "I guess Head isn't the worst, unless you name your kid Richard, and even then, you could go by Rich, or Richie, Why go by Dick?" She looks like she's hovering between shock and horror. "You're just setting yourself up for a world of ridicule. What kind of person, other than a dickhead, goes by the name Dick Head? My fucking father, that's who."

Lily grabs her shoulders. "What did you just say?"

"My sperm donor's name is Richard Head, but he goes by Dick. Seriously, he must be the biggest asshole in the history of the world with a sad, tiny dick," Violet replies.

And then I remember why this conversation is so damn familiar; two New Year's ago, before Randy and Lily were super serious, we talked about Lily's biological father, and Violet couldn't get over his stupid name.

Both Violet and Lily's eyes go wide. "Oh my God!" they say in unison.

"Your bio dad's name is Richard Head?" Lily asks.

"And your deadbeat dad's name is Richard Head," Violet replies. "Did he play for North Carolina?"

Lily nods slowly.

"What are the chances . . ." Violet trails off. "Holy shit. Does this mean you're my half-sister?"

13

I GOT YOU

DARREN

I'm not sure if the cost of winning this game will be worth it. The only thing that's going to make me feel better is Charlene. I want to put the lid on her jar and never let her go.

I realize, very clearly, that I'm in a terrible frame of mind. I've kept her on edge all day and probably shouldn't have since she was already there to begin with. I'm also aware that having done this to her is fucked up, but it seemed better than telling her things she's not ready to hear, especially when I'm not sure if I'm ready to say them.

Alex is quiet and in a shit mood as we make our way to the bar. He's not angry that we won the game; it's *how* we won that he's upset about. It's not jealousy, it's bigger than that. It's about his worth to the team. It's the position he feels he's putting me in. It's knowing that my chances of being pulled in the expansion draft get higher the more I pick up the slack he can't manage. It's the nine-million-dollar-a-year salary he doesn't think he's worth anymore.

The bar is loud and busy. I look around for Charlene and the rest of the girls, but they're not easy to find since pretty much every female in the place is decked out in our team gear. Loud shrieking and jumping draws my attention.

"There they are." I point to where Violet and Lily are hugging.

"I'm glad Vi can't get wasted. I need in my wife tonight," Alex says.

I scan the area around them and finally find Charlene. Her pearls are at her lips, her expression reflecting none of the excitement Violet, Lily, and the other girls seem to be experiencing. Which makes me question what's going on.

We weave through the crowd slowly because of the volume of people. Thankfully, not many attempt to talk to me, probably because I don't come across as friendly, and I don't often engage in conversation with people I don't know.

I step up behind Charlene, who's still worrying her pearls against her lips, and drop my mouth to her ear. "What's happening here?"

She startles and nearly fumbles her drink as she spins around. She tips her head back as I straighten, eyes finding mine. Emotions flit across her face, pain floating around in there. I'm unsure if it's physical, emotional, or both, and I regret keeping her hanging all day.

"Violet and Lily just found out they have the same father," she says softly.

"Is this a joke?"

Her voice cracks, along with her forced smile. "I wish it was."

I want to ask her to explain, but Violet is jumping around, screaming at the top of her lungs. It's drawing a lot of attention. "Isn't this awesome? Both of our moms made terrible choices!"

Violet motions between herself and Lily. "Can you see the resemblance? Boobs aside, of course."

Lily rolls her eyes. "Maybe I should put on one of your bras and stuff it with socks so it's easier to see the resemblance."

Randy comes up to stand beside me, observing the spectacle. "Did I hear that right? Vi and Lily have the same dad?"

"Apparently."

He runs a hand over his beard, looking from one woman to the other. "I don't see it."

I shrug because neither do I. Apart from the fact that they're both female and on the petite side, that's all the similarity I can find. Violet is busty and curvy where Lily is narrow and lean. Lily also has a couple inches on Vi. "Does Lily look more like her mother?"

Randy nods. "Yeah, kind of like Vi looks like hers." He tips his head in Skye's direction. She really does look like Violet, plus about twenty years. She also dresses very much like her daughter.

I'm grateful for the soap-opera-style family drama, because it takes the focus off tonight's game. I should be happy that we're going to the next round, and for the team I am, but the call I received this afternoon before I went on the ice worries me. My agent let me know that Lucas, the owner of the Vegas team, had contacted him for the third time, wanting to talk numbers. There's been interest from other teams too, and I'm still unsure where Charlene and I are headed. I feel like I'm just figuring out how to do this new version of us right, and I don't want to screw that up.

It's another hour before I finally manage to get close to Charlene again. She's drunk, and based on the empty glasses scattered over the table, someone thought shots were a good idea. She's positioned herself at the end of the table, slightly apart from the other girls, quiet instead of engaged in the lively conversation. She reminds me of how I get when there are too many people and I feel exposed.

I bend so I'm at her ear and don't have to yell. "You want to go up to the room now so I can take care of you?"

I back up enough so I can see her face. Her expression is a mixture of relief and desperation, so intense that for a second I think she's going to burst into tears, which is very unlike Charlene. The only times I've seen her cry were when Alex had his accident last year and Violet was a mess, and when my teammates found her surrounded by sex toys.

Her lips move, forming the word *please*, but it's not accompanied by sound, and I'm uncertain if it's because she hasn't made any or because it's too loud to hear.

I straighten and pull her chair out, giving her space to stand up.

"You're going?" Violet frowns. "Come on! Just stay a little longer."

"I apologize, Violet, but I need her." Which is true. I very much need to get lost in her for a while, and I have a feeling Charlene needs the same.

Violet jumps up and rushes around the table so she can hug Charlene. I don't understand why women feel the need to hug each other all the time. It's not as if they won't see each other again soon, like in the morning.

When all the hugging is over, I link our fingers, marveling at how much softer and smaller her hand is than mine and how much I crave this innocuous contact. I keep her close as we weave through the bar. Alex holds up a hand when he sees us leaving. I nod but don't stop to talk. This whole thing with Violet tonight has taken his mind off of the game, but soon he'll want to sit down and figure out how to manage the next series.

We're not alone on the elevator ride up to the penthouse floor, so I simply keep our hands joined, sliding my thumb back and forth over her knuckles. Charlene's free hand is at her throat, fingering her pearls.

She exhales a shuddery breath when the last couple exits the elevator at the twentieth floor. When the doors close, I lift our twined hands and bring them to my lips. "Are you okay?"

She nods, but her bottom lip trembles, and her breath comes sharp and fast.

"You don't seem okay," I observe.

She opens her mouth to speak, but the doors slide open. A couple of women wearing Chicago jerseys fall into the elevator, giggling, clearly drunk. One of them pushes the button for the lobby while the other leans against the rails opposite us.

I'm annoyed at the interruption.

"Oh my God!" one of them shrieks. "You're Darren Westinghouse! You were incredible tonight!"

The high-pitched, exclamation-point-laden yelling makes me want to pull out a roll of duct tape, but instead I smile and tuck Charlene in tighter to my side. This is part of the reason I've never tried to be better than I am. Because it draws unwanted attention. Stay solidly average and out of the limelight, and people don't recognize you on the street. Play better than most, and people start to notice.

I've been content to be Alex's wingman for the past six years. He loves the accolades and thrives on it. He manages it better than I can. I don't want this overwhelming level of notice. I don't want these drunk screaming girls, looking for autographs. I don't want to be nice and open and friendly. I want privacy and Charlene. I want some semblance of normal in a life that's never been that way.

One of the girls roots around in her purse for a pen so I can sign something for her. Neither of them acknowledge Charlene. It's as if she doesn't even exist. So when one of them finally manages to find a pen and her game ticket, I tip Charlene's chin up and press an unexpected kiss to her lips.

"This will just take a moment," I murmur, lips still touching hers.

"Okay." It's more breath than word.

I just want to be alone with her. I want these fans and my

worries to disappear. I want to drown in her taste and her scent and her soft, sweet moans.

But first I need to sign some shit.

The women gawk unapologetically as I tuck a loose tendril of Charlene's hair behind her ear. It's unnecessary. Her hair is perfectly fine the way it is without me messing with it. I just want a reason to touch her, to indicate on some base level that she's mine, and I'm hers.

I sign their tickets, then sign the back of their jerseys, even though one has Ballistic and the other has Waters, which makes sense since they're the star players on the team. Thankfully the elevator chimes. I reach for Charlene's hand, tugging her along as I hit the close door button and slip out into the hall. I don't want them following us. When the door stays closed, I exhale a sigh of relief and walk quickly toward our room, rooting in my pocket for the key card, but Charlene is already prepared. She swipes it across the sensor, and I throw it open, ushering her inside.

The door barely has a chance to lock before Charlene launches herself at me. She forces me back against the wall—which is no easy feat considering I have a good six to eight inches on her and I outweigh her by a hundred pounds. I'm attributing it partly to her catching me off guard.

Her fingernails cut into my shoulders as her mouth connects with mine, and she tries to hoist herself up. I spin so she's against the wall and lift her by her ass, positioning her so my erection is finally where it's supposed to be, albeit covered by clothes. I plan to remedy that soon.

She rolls her hips and moans, head hitting the wall as she arches. Her nails bite my scalp, and her teeth sink into my bottom lip. Charlene is a lot of things in the bedroom—uncertain, curious, semi-adventurous, adorably sort-of commanding when she's decked out in leather—but she's rarely, if ever, aggressive like she is now, which tells me I've either pushed her too far, or something is wrong.

Possibly both.

I also think her prolonged anxious state means she needs to come, badly.

Pinning her against the wall with my hips, I press a palm to her chest and splay my fingers out to frame the pearl necklace.

"Darren, please." The words draw out on a plea.

This is about so much more than delayed gratification. She's not just wanting, she's desperate and sad and panicked, and I need to understand why. But first I need to take care of her, for both our sakes.

I run my free hand down her side and under the waistband of her leggings. "After I make you come, you're going to tell me why you're so upset."

"Whatever you want."

I slip my fingers into her panties, which are practically soaked through. All day I left her in this state—too many hours and too much uncertainty. It's my fault she's out of control, and I'm right there with her.

She jerks as soon as I find her clit. Her legs go lax, along with the rest of her, as if she's been dosed with Valium. I ease her down the wall, wishing I'd made it to the bed, but aware that stopping now would be an even worse kind of torment. So I push two fingers inside and curl forward, fluttering fast and hard.

Charlene is lost in all the sensations, chasing down bliss. My name is a guttural groan as she comes in waves, and I keep pushing her, dragging it out because I can, and she needs it.

She sags against me, hot breath fanning across my skin, and I kiss her temple. "Do you need me to keep going?"

She makes a noise, but I can't tell if it's a yes or a no. I skim her clit, and she sucks in a gasping breath, fingers tightening in my hair again. So I keep circling, light and slow, pulling her to the edge and pushing her over gently. This orgasm is much less violent, but no less intense.

I ease my hand out of her panties, grab her thighs and hoist her up, keeping her wrapped around me as I carry her to the bed. A stream of light from the bathroom cuts across the floor, illuminating the way.

"I won't do that to you again," I promise as I lay her out on the bed, kissing along her temple and down her cheek. "I won't leave you needing that long ever again."

She's shaky and clumsy as she tries to unbutton my shirt. I cover her hand. "Let me get it."

I kneel between her legs and shrug out of the suit jacket, unfasten the first three buttons and pull my shirt over my head, tossing it somewhere on the floor. Charlene's already managed to get her jersey over her head and her leggings off.

"Leave the rest for me, please." I unclasp my belt, pop the button on my pants and get my zipper halfway down before Charlene pushes them over my hips, taking my boxers with them.

My erection springs free, and Charlene wraps her soft, warm hand around the length. Her eyes flash up to mine, glassy and desperate as she leans forward and parts those gorgeous lips, engulfing the head.

I groan out a low *fuck* and close my eyes for a second, because seeing her like this is almost too much.

The head bumps the back of her throat as I shove my fingers into her hair. But I don't try to control her. I don't need to. She knows me well enough to anticipate what I want. She pulls back, sucks the head, and then draws me in, over and over, again and again, eyes locked on mine.

I trace her bottom lip. "If you take me deep one more time, I'm going to come down that pretty, sweet throat of yours." It's as much a warning as a promise.

As fun as it is to make a mess on her chest, I'd prefer not to do that tonight, mostly because I don't want to take the time to clean it up before I get into those pretty panties of hers with more than my fingers.

I'm right there, balls tightening, the ache merging with the promise of release. She sucks hard, her hot mouth surrounding every inch of me, and I let go, pulsing as she swallows. I fold forward, groaning her name, struggling not to thrust since I'm already as deep as I can go.

When I'm finished coming, I ease out gently and bend to brush my lips over hers. "I didn't deserve your mouth tonight."

"I didn't do it for you. I want you in me for a long as possible tonight, and this guarantees that."

I chuckle and kiss her softly. "Well, I'm going to need a few minutes before I can do that, and I have a really great idea about how to pass the time." Charlene smiles against my lips. I'd like to stay where I am for a while, but I've tortured her enough for one day, and there's little I love more than watching her unravel for me.

I drop a kiss between her breasts and one below her navel. The custom bra and matching panties are perfect on her gorgeous body. "I want to see the back of these," I murmur.

Charlene slides up the bed and flips onto her stomach, craning to look her over shoulder. Her lip is caught between her teeth. I run my hands down her sides to her hips.

"I don't know why it took me this long to come up with these, but they're my new favorites."

"I think Violet has a pair for every day of the week with Alex's name stamped on her butt."

As soon as I get home, I'm going to order them in every color combination, style, and pattern I can. Fuck lace and satin. Cotton boy shorts are where it's at.

I regret how I handled her this morning, because now I want to take my time, but I'm aware I can't. I open the clasp on her bra and kiss the space between her shoulder blades, then the dip in her spine before I pull the panties over her hips and bite the swell of her ass, smiling at her gasp. I drag my thumb along the divide, and she jolts and moans. Slipping my fingers between her thighs, I skim the length of her slit, passing her entrance to find the steel piercing her clit. Her hips lift as I circle once.

"On your back baby, I want to spend some time kissing you."

Charlene is quick to comply, flipping over and tossing her bra on the floor.

I stretch out between her legs, hooking my arms under her thighs and lick up the length of her pussy. Charlene writhes against my mouth when I take her clit ring between my teeth and tug. The first orgasm comes hard and fast, the second only minutes behind the first. And I keep going, pushing her higher so I can watch her spiral down, down, down.

I lose track after orgasm number three. And eventually I can't and don't want to wait any longer. It's not just about getting lost in her, which I admittedly want. But more than that, I need her. I need the closeness. I need to know she's mine and that no matter what happens at the end of the season, that's not going to change.

I prowl up her body, position myself at her entrance and ease in.

I drop my forehead against her neck and groan. "Only you make me feel this alive."

Charlene's knees press against my ribs, and links her hands behind my neck. "I felt empty all day," she whispers.

Her words make the hairs on my arms stand on end. Something about her tone tells me this isn't just about withholding orgasms. It's more.

I kiss my way up her neck and across her jaw. "And how do you feel now?" I push up on my arms so I can see her face.

"Like you're under my skin, but I can't get you deep enough."

I roll my hips, and she moans quietly. I don't know what's happening here, but I want to give her everything she needs. I want to be everything she needs.

I slip my fingers into the hair at the nape of her neck, cradling her head in my palm as I drop my lips to hers. I can still taste her on my tongue, so when she licks at my mouth and moans, I know it's because she can taste herself.

I kiss her the same way I move inside her. I'm in no rush for this to end, and somewhere inside my head, I fear what will happen when it does. Things between us are shifting again. And as close as I feel to her in this moment, I worry that outside of it, there will be distance I don't know how to bridge.

Charlene grabs my biceps, fingernails digging in while she moves with me. I pull back in time to see her eyes flutter open and meet mine as she starts to pulse around me.

Charlene spends a great deal of energy trying to make sex into some kind of event, as if she feels I need to be entertained to enjoy her. But nothing compares to this. There are no distractions, nothing to get in the way as I watch her light up under me. She lifts her hand and drags gentle fingers down my cheek.

I close my eyes for a second, absorbing the sensation before I catch and hold Charlene's gaze again. The orgasm is painfully intense as it burns through me. White spots blank out of my vision, taking away Charlene's perfect face for the briefest moment. It feels as if I'm drowning in pleasure so extreme the possibility of never having it again is agony.

I drop my head, nuzzling into her neck, breathing in the salty sweet scent of her skin. My body feels weighed down with satiety. I want this every day. I want to wake up to this, go to sleep to this, come home to this, and I'm not sure why it took this long for me to realize it. My limbs are heavy and uncoordinated as I ease out. I slip an arm under her and roll to the side, taking her with me.

Charlene tucks her head under my chin, a shiver ripping through her. At first I think it's the aftermath of such a powerful, drawn-out orgasm, or maybe she's cold. I try to shift away so I can tuck us under the covers, but she mumbles *no* against my neck and tightens her hold.

"Let me get a warm cloth so I can make you more comfortable," I murmur against her temple, once again trying to extricate myself.

She clings tighter and shakes her head, shuddering again.

I pull back enough so I can see her face, but she twists her head away, tucking her chin against her shoulder, eyes screwed up tight.

"Are you okay?" I stroke her cheek, hoping to calm her, but her lips twist as if she's fighting whatever emotions are swimming to the surface, ones she's clearly trying to hide.

"I'm fine," she whispers brokenly, still not looking at me.

"You seem the opposite of fine."

"I need a minute. Please."

I don't know what to make of this reaction, or the way she's clinging to me. This isn't typical Charlene behavior, and I don't know how to handle it.

A tiny whimper hums across my throat.

"Did I hurt you?" I don't think I did. I'm always extraordinarily careful with Charlene.

She shakes her head into my shoulder, which should be a relief, but the fact that she's breaking down emotionally after sex seems bad. The sound of her pain tears at my heart, her ache my own.

I want to be better at this, at caring for someone. A wave of emotion slams into me, the kind I've guarded against my entire life. I shift her body so I can sit up and keep her in my lap. She wraps her legs around my waist, arms locked around my shoulders with her face buried against the crook of my neck.

She feels like she could break apart in my arms, and I'm forced to finally accept the truth I've been hiding from: I'm in love with Charlene, and have been for a very long time.

Jesus. I'm so emotionally stunted by my fucked-up family, I couldn't even recognize love until it punched me in the face.

I rub circles on Charlene's back with one hand and smooth my free palm over the back of her head. "Breathe, baby," I murmur in her ear and press my lips to her temple. "Let me make it better."

She sucks in a high-pitched breath, and I worry I'm making it worse. Eventually she seems to calm, and then her lips find that sensitive space behind my ear. She trails kisses up my neck and along the edge of my jaw.

For a moment I'm confused, until I realize her mouth is meant to be a distraction. It almost works.

I cup her face in my hands and lift, forcing her to look at me. Charlene's eyes are red rimmed, her cheeks flushed, and her expression is pure panic.

"What's going on?"

"Nothing. I'm fine. I want you again." She tries to come back to my mouth, but I hold her still.

"What is this about?" I smooth away her tears.

"That was intense. Today was intense."

"And that's the only reason for the tears?" I press. "I need you to talk to me, Charlene."

"I waited all day for you." She sighs and lifts her gaze, vulnerability leaking through. "I know the game was stressful for you, and it's the same for me. You wanted me on edge, and I was. I was worried and anxious. It was a lot."

I still think she's leaving things out, purposely or not, so I try to pull them out of her however I can. "What exactly are you worried about?"

"I don't know. Everything? You? What you're not telling me."

I sigh. I'm going to have to give to get here. "My stats are too high, and I'm getting too much attention. I don't like it, and I don't want it. But I don't have a choice, and I won't tank our team because I dislike the press I'm getting."

She blinks a few times, maybe stunned that I'm being so forthcoming for once. It's about fucking time, I suppose. Buying her new clothes and nice things only goes so far. I have to let her into my head if I want her to let me into hers.

"Now can you tell me why you're so upset, other than the fact that I'm an asshole for having kept you on the edge all day?"

Her fingers go to her pearls. "Now I feel stupid."

"What? Why?"

"Because you're worried about your team, and I'm worried about myself."

I want to erase the sadness that pulls her mouth down. I want to take the ache away. "Trust me when I tell you it's not just my team I'm worried about, Charlene. I'm not that selfless."

"What else are you worried about?"

I shake my head, aware this is yet another diversion tactic. "Not understanding why you're so upset."

She runs her fingers through my hair, eyes fixed there, maybe so she doesn't have to look directly at me. "It feels like I'm losing things that are important to me."

"How do you mean?"

"Violet's always been my best friend. And maybe it's petty and stupid, but she's going to get closer to Sunny because they're both pregnant, and Sunny and Lily have always been close, and now Violet and Lily are *actual* sisters, and I feel like I'm on the outside with no way in. And then there's this whole expansion draft, and what if you're traded and I . . ." She sucks in a deep breath, trying to keep herself in check. "I don't want to lose all the people who mean the most to me."

I skim the hollow of her eyes, brushing away more tears. As much as I don't like to see her upset, I'm almost relieved we're on the same page, at least about not wanting to lose the people we care for. I can't control what's happening with Violet or Alex, but I can try to keep hold of what we have.

"Whatever happens with everyone else, I'm in this with you. We can be on the outside together."

She drags her fingers along the edge of my jaw, eyes sad. "Everything's changing, and I want it to stay the same. I need this to stay the same."

My stomach bottoms out. "This?"

"Us. How we are."

Is it a warning? Was tonight too much for her? The closeness is something I want more of. And it has to be gradual, something that happens so slowly she won't even recognize the change is happening at all. So I don't ask for clarification, because I don't want an answer I won't like. Instead I tell her what she needs to hear.

"It's always going to be me and you, Charlene. Whatever you need, I'll be that for you."

ALL GOOD THINGS

CHARLENE

Things seem to stabilize after we return to Chicago. My panic over losing my best friend because she now has a real half-sister wanes as I realize things haven't changed all that much. I mean sure, Violet and Lily might be a little closer because they literally share DNA, and she and Sunny can gripe about sore boobs, but it hasn't changed how much time Violet and I spend together. In fact, once we're home, Violet and I are together more, rather than less. Darren and I spend a lot of time in coupley situations with Vi and Alex, so I don't feel like my best friend position has been usurped.

Things between Darren and me are good—great even. He hasn't shifted from a quiet, introverted, sometimes guarded man to the kind of guy who shares all of his feelings and loves being

181

around lots of people. But there are shifts, and not all of them are subtle.

I now have a rack in his walk-in closet filled with brand new business wear, the kind I can't afford unless I switch careers and become a high paid escort who works every night of the week. The price tags are always missing, but I've done my research. I know what a Fendi suit costs—especially if it's this season and has been custom tailored to fit me.

One side of the bathroom vanity now houses duplicates of the stuff I keep at home.

Darren also purchased a second dresser to match his, which is where all of my lingerie, new leggings, sleep sets, and panties now reside. When he has home games, he requests that I stay with him almost every night. He's grown particularly fond of returning from a game or practice to find me snuggled up in my reading chair with either a book or account files I've brought home with me. Although admittedly, that chair ends up being used for sex almost as much as it is for reading.

Series three of the playoffs is intense, once again going to game seven, and putting Chicago into the finals. Darren's stats continue to rise, and with them his anxiety, *and* his requests for me to stay at his place. I can't and don't want to say no, but I worry, more than I let on, about what's going to happen at the end of the season when the expansion draft finally happens.

I'd like to believe he's not going to end up on the chopping block, but the truth is, his game keeps improving. Which tells me something incredibly important about Darren. He adapts to his environment and the people in it.

He played only as well as he needed to in order to keep Alex in the limelight. And now he's playing better to keep his team afloat. As I settle into this new us, I've begun to realize this is who he is and how he operates, whether consciously or not. He adjusts himself and his expectations based on someone else's need.

When his grandparents took away his privacy as a teenager,

he found ways to adapt—physically, mentally, emotionally. In his career, he always puts his team's needs in front of his own, and I believe, in a lot of ways, he does the same with me.

I'm the reason our relationship never progressed. I'm the reason we've stayed the same all this time. Whatever I wanted, Darren gave me. He never tried to open the doors I kept locked. Until recently.

He's always very careful and calculated in the way he manages me. Us. Except now we're transforming, and I don't know how to stop it—or if I can, or if I even want to.

Chicago wins the first two home games of the finals, but loses the first away game in Tampa. I worry this will be another seven-game series, making their off season that much shorter, when they could use the extra time to recuperate. I'm relieved when they win the second away game by one goal, and even more relieved when it's Alex who scores it, and Randy who handles the assist.

I'm already at Darren's place when he arrives home. For the first time in a long while, he picks out lingerie. I'm unsurprised when he chooses to dress me in lavender satin and lace. But when he opens the *I thought it would be fun but I changed my mind* toy box, my nervousness immediately skyrockets.

"What are you doing?"

It takes a few seconds before he finally shifts his attention away from the contents of the box. "Looking for something."

His expression is flat. I don't know how to read him tonight, and that nervous feeling drops low in my tummy and settles between my thighs.

He stops what he's doing and crosses to where I'm standing in the middle of the doorway. He caresses my cheek and bends to press his lips to my forehead. "Wait for me on the bed, please."

I search his face, but all I get is the tiniest hint of a smile before he turns me around, pats me on the butt, and sends me out of the closet.

I sit on the edge of the bed, nervously toying with my pearl necklace. Several minutes pass, or at least that's how long it feels, before he finally appears, carrying an armload of toys.

I swallow hard as I take in the items he's chosen, and the heaviness between my thighs expands with each toy he carefully places along the end of the bed on either side of me. I recognize several of them as items I'd foolishly surrounded myself with when his teammates walked in on me.

Darren comes to stand in front of me. I look up—taking in his dress shirt, the sleeves rolled up to his elbows, the top two buttons undone—until I reach his face.

He stares, unblinking as he taps my knee. "Open, please."

He tips his head to the side, eyes roaming over my body, pausing between my legs where everything is already tight and pulsing. He reaches out and skims my jaw, making every single muscle in my body clench and quiver.

"Are you nervous, firefly?"

"Yes."

He exhales slowly and runs his fingers up the inside of my thigh. I suck in a shallow breath when he slips one under the edge of my panties. If I wasn't wearing lingerie, I'm sure I'd be leaking all over his comforter.

I bite back a moan and eye the items on the bed.

"Tell me why," he whispers, voice low with gravel.

"You know why."

He shakes his head. "I don't think I do."

I look at the ball gag on the right and then that creepy face-mask with only a mouth hole on the left.

"Darren," I moan when he circles my clit.

"Why do we still have all of this if we're never going to use it?"

I'm not sure why he wants to have this conversation right now. I expected him to walk in the door and get me naked on my reading chair, as has been typical recently.

"Does that mean you want to use it?" I ask.

I have to admit, as unnerving as it's been to have Darren focused solely on me and not any of the stuff I usually bring into our sex games, I actually love sex without all the distractions. I thought maybe he did, too.

He withdraws his fingers, trailing them down the inside of my thigh, leaving a streak of wetness that makes me blush as he sinks to his knees front of me. "I'd like you to answer my question before you pose one of your own."

I don't know what's happening here. Or how I'm supposed to answer that because the truth is at odds with my actions over the past two years.

"I thought maybe one day I'd change my mind."

"Is that really true?" he asks.

I bite my lip and shake my head.

"So all of this serves what purpose?" He gestures to the array of toys. "Apart from being a distraction."

"I thought maybe it was what you wanted."

He skims the pearls at my throat. "And I thought I was showing you that you're more than enough. I will give you almost anything you want, but I only need you. *You* are all I want, Charlene."

I motion to the items surrounding me on the bed. "Do you want me to get rid of all this stuff?"

"That's entirely up to you. I'm just telling you I can take it or leave it. Could it be fun? Maybe. But only if it's what you want. Otherwise it's unnecessary." He runs his hands up my thighs. "Now, I've been without you for four days. I'd like spend some time enjoying all the things I missed."

THE NIGHT that follows could possibly end up being the championship game. I'm not as on edge as I was at the end of the last series, even though there's more at stake with this game. As usual we're all seated in close to the ice, behind the bench

Darren is as worried about winning as he is losing. The beginning of the game is rocky, with Tampa scoring twice in the first period, but Chicago evens it out by the end of the second. Alex scores a goal, which is good for his ego and team morale. Randy owns the second goal, with Darren as the assist for both, taking them into the final period tied. That doesn't last long, though.

They're less than five minutes into the third when Darren circles close to the net with the puck. He passes to Alex, who I'm sure is going to take the shot, but at the last second he fakes right and shifts the puck to Randy who scores another goal for Chicago.

They hold onto the lead through the third, and with less than three minutes left in the game, Darren gets hold of the puck and sprints down the ice on a breakaway, scoring again for Chicago.

Tampa is down two points with less than two minutes left in the game, and one of the players gets in Alex's face. The ref calls a roughing penalty, giving Chicago a power play for the final minute of the game, and of course they take the opportunity to score again, ending the game, and the season, with a 5-2 win for Chicago.

Chicago took the Cup home when Darren and I first started seeing each other, but this is different. Back then Darren had a no-trade clause, and we weren't as serious as we are now. So much is tied up in him, and our friends are interconnected, so this monumental win is both something to celebrate and fear.

Change is coming no matter what. Someone is going to Vegas at the end of the season, and hopefully it won't be Darren, whose stats are the best they've ever been.

Sunny passes Logan to Miller so he can skate him around the ice while they celebrate the win. The sports journalists clamor for interviews. Darren is never comfortable in front of the camera, unlike Randy and Alex. His answers are always short and to the point, almost as if he's annoyed. When one of the journalists asks him how he feels about the expansion draft, he mutters something about being at the end of his career and younger, better players being a safe bet. Then he turns around and stomps down the hall toward the locker room.

The journalist turns to Alex who defends Darren, saying they've been playing together for a long time, and any trade would be a big change.

Darren is quieter than usual at the bar, but he doesn't shy away from the celebration, maybe because it's possible this is the last time he'll get to do this with his Chicago teammates. I hope that's not the case.

The expansion draft won't happen for a few more weeks, so there will be unease while we wait for the outcome. Plus, losing one team member could have a domino effect. I try not to worry, but it's not easy.

We're all sitting around a long table in the back of the bar, chatter making it hard to focus on any one conversation. Also, Darren's hand is under the table, kneading my thigh and slowly moving higher.

"We need to have a party for your birthday this year, Char!" Violet shouts.

"Yes!" Lily agrees. "A real one since it's your champagne birthday!"

I shoot them both a look. Birthday parties have never been my thing. I don't like being the center of anyone's attention, except maybe Darren's.

"I've been thinking about your birthday," Darren says so only I can hear, in a tone that sends a shiver down my spine.

I wave Violet and Lily off. "It doesn't need to be a big deal."

"So how about a BBQ at our place? We can celebrate all the things! Your champagne birthday, winning the Cup, and the end of the season," Violet suggests.

Lily pulls up her calendar on her phone. "What about next weekend?"

"That's perfect!" Violet turns her smile on me. "Plus it's a holiday weekend, so a BBQ is essential anyway. We can eat burgers and lactose-free ice cream and cake and all the delicious things. And I need to wear a bikini and take pictures before this baby takes over my body!"

I don't have the heart or the desire to argue. Besides, with the trades still looming, I have no idea if this is the last birthday I'll get to celebrate with all of our friends. Will one of them will be somewhere else next year? I don't want to miss out on making memories, even if they might hurt in the future.

"Okay," I tell her. "Let's do it."

WHEN YOUR BEST friend is married to one of the top earners in the NHL, she can pull together a pretty damn sweet party in a very short span of time. Violet hires a caterer and buys all the decorations online.

Darren must ask me a million times, in a hundred different ways, what I want for my birthday. What I really want is for him to stay in Chicago and not be traded to Vegas, or anywhere else. But he doesn't have control over that, so I tell him I don't need anything and the party is enough.

My birthday begins with orgasms from Darren and a promise that he'll see me later. He leaves my bed, much to my dismay, just after ten in the morning and is replaced by Violet.

"I brought breakfast!" She wrinkles her nose as she takes a few steps into my bedroom. "It smells like Darren and sex. I vote we eat downstairs."

I roll out of bed, not caring about my messy hair or the discarded lingerie—I'm wearing one of my many shorts-and-tank sleep sets—as I follow her downstairs.

"You didn't have to go to all this trouble, especially since the party is at your place."

"Are you kidding? I wanted a couple of hours of you-and-me time before I have to go sharing you with all our friends. Remember when we used to eat pints of ice cream and have *Hoarder* marathons on your birthday?" She turns the bag over and two half-pints of Ben & Jerry's roll onto the counter. Her smile is questioning. "We don't have time for a marathon, but we could do an episode or two."

I don't know why I'm suddenly emotional, but I throw my arms around her.

When we finally release each other, Violet puts her hands on my shoulders. "I know a lot has changed recently, especially with me and Sunny both being pregnant, and then Lily and me finding out we're half-sisters—which is, like, so daytime soap opera, by the way. But there's only one you, Char. We've been best friends for almost a decade. We went through frosh week together and survived for Christ's sake."

I laugh at that. "You'd think we would've learned shots were bad back then."

"Academic intelligence isn't the same as social smarts. How the two of us made it through college without a criminal record is beyond me." Violet snort-laughs and then grows serious. "No one is ever going to replace you, Char. When we're old and saggy and we have to yell to hear each other, we'll still be best friends."

Of course that's the moment I burst into tears, because as much as I don't want to admit it, those are exactly the words I need to hear. And that sets off a whole chain reaction in which Violet starts crying, too. So we hug some more and cry a bunch like sappy idiots.

"I'm probably going to cry a hundred times today because my hormones are insane," Violet sniffles.

"At least you have an excuse."

Violet and I spend the next two hours eating crap and half-watching TV. It's good to have a little time with just her before the party.

My mom calls around noon to wish me a happy birthday, and she promises to visit soon. I'm a little disappointed, especially since she uses the reality show she auditioned for as the reason she's so busy. But then, we never made a big deal out of birthdays at The Ranch, likely for reasons I didn't understand at the time. Afterward, it sort of stayed that way, so the fact that I've agreed to a party at all is kind of a big thing.

Early in the afternoon, Lily and the rest of the girls come by to pick me and Violet up—apparently Alex dropped Vi off this morning. I don't need an overnight bag because I'm staying the night at Darren's, so all I bring is my beach bag with my bathing suit, sunscreen, and a hairbrush.

Lily is parked across the end of the driveway in Randy's huge Ford F-150. This one is new, and though I'm not all that big into cars, or trucks for that matter, even I can appreciate how cool it is with its chrome everything and grill guard on the front.

Violet bounces down the front walk for a few steps before she grimaces and holds on to her boobs. "Sweet Jesus, you'd think my bra was made of sandpaper with how sensitive my damn nipples are these days." She threads her arm through mine. "It's party time! You better do some shots for me tonight to make up for the fact that I'm incubating Alex's future hockey legacy."

I give her a side hug. "Shots are never a good idea, Vi. We both know this."

"Agreed. But there are Jell-O shooters, so you have to do at least one of those."

Violet makes a move to get in the backseat. I offer to help her in, because it's a long way up even with the running boards thanks to the huge tires on this truck, but she slaps my hand away. "I'm pregnant, not incompetent. I can do it myself."

Violet is uncoordinated at the best of times, but add height, her center of gravity being thrown off, and an additional cup size to her already huge boobs, and she's a walking disaster. Still, she somehow manages to get her ass in the backseat without damaging herself or anyone else.

"Happy birthday!" The girls call out as I drop into the passenger seat. They're all wearing birthday hats with a set of champagne glasses, my name, and the number twenty-six on them. Lily blows one of those birthday horns, and the thing that rolls out hits me just above the eye. It's followed by a burst of gold raining down on the front seat.

Lily's eyes go wide. "Vi! Not in the truck!"

The dash and the front seat are littered with gold glitter and tiny sequins. I cover my mouth with my palm, trying to decide if I should laugh or not, based on how horrified she looks.

Violet makes her apologetic face. "Sorry. I got excited and forgot."

"Randy's going to kill me!"

"We can stop by a car wash and vacuum it out," Poppy suggests.

"We don't have time. Everyone's supposed to arrive around two, and it's already one thirty. The birthday girl can't be late." Lily runs her finger along the dash. "Glitter is the worst. It never comes out. I'm pretty sure I still have glitter stuck to my vag from the last time Randy wanted to play figure skater," she says.

"Was that last night?" Violet asks.

"Last week." Lily puts the truck in gear. "Roll down your windows, girls, let's see how much gets sucked out the windows on the way to Vi's. And you're totally taking the heat for this. Randy can't get mad at a pregnant woman."

As Lily drives down the street, I spot an enormous RV parked not far down the road. I point and scream.

Lily puts on the brakes, maybe thinking she's accidentally almost run over my neighbor's cat, who has a terrible habit of playing chicken with cars. I swear he's maxed out his nine lives.

I unbuckle my seatbelt and try to tuck myself under the dash.

"What's wrong?" Lily asks.

"It's the RV, just keep going," Vi says.

Lily glances down at me uncertainly, but takes her foot off the brake and hits the gas. A cloud of glitter whirls in the air, and everyone sputters and waves their hands in front of their faces as they get pelted with it.

I cover my eyes with my palms as much to protect myself from the glitter as to hide from the RV. "Tell me when it's safe, Vi!"

We slow as we round a corner and then speed up again.

"Okay. You're good," Vi calls out.

"Are you sure?" My God. My heart feels like it's part of the backbeat to a techno track. It was bad enough when my mom parked her stupid mini Winnebago in my driveway for three days, but a full-sized RV is a whole different bag of no-fucking-way.

"I'm sure. We can't see it anymore."

I uncover my eyes and slowly pull myself back up, checking to make sure Violet isn't lying. The girls are looking at me like I've lost my mind.

"Are you okay?" Lily asks.

"Fine. Good. Sorry about that."

"Once when Lily and I were little, we went to the park and there was a guy in a white van with no windows and he offered us candy. Remember that, Lily?" Sunny asks.

Lily nods and shudders. "Sure do."

"Thankfully Alex was there playing hockey with some of the boys in the neighborhood. They started shooting their pucks at the van and broke the windshield." Sunny twirls her hair. "Ever since then, white windowless vans give me the willies."

"That's totally reasonable." I nod my agreement. "I feel the same way about RVs."

"Bad people are everywhere," Sunny says softly, still rubbing her belly. "I'm glad this one will have an older brother to protect him or her."

Violet and Sunny start talking about what it's like to have an older brother. Violet's experience is a lot different than Sunny's. Skye and Sidney married when Violet was a teenager, and she and Miller only had to go to the same high school for a year. But

Miller and Vi really do act like brother and sister, and always have, as far as I know.

We pull into Violet's driveway a few minutes later. There are yellow balloons tied to the trees with Happy Birthday written on them.

I give Violet the eye. "I thought this was going to be more like a Memorial Day Weekend party."

She shrugs. "We're celebrating all the things, and as your best friend, I reserve the right to make a big deal out of your birthday even if you won't. Plus, Darren can be pushy when he feels like talking and making demands."

"He's good at that, the making demands part," I agree.

The guys are already in the backyard, playing Frisbee in the pool.

"The birthday girl has arrived!" Violet yells.

Darren turns as Lance lets the Frisbee go and ends up getting clocked in the back of the head. He nabs it before Randy can and hurls it back at Lance.

"Aye, fucker! It's nae my fault yer no payin' attention!" Lance's usually mild Scottish accent grows thick, and he winks in my direction as Darren wades to the shallow end. He pulls himself out of the pool, wearing a sinister smile as he rushes me.

"Don't you dare! I don't even have my bathing suit on yet!"

"You should've been better prepared, firefly." His smile widens as he hauls me against him. My yellow sundress soaks through and I push on his chest, trying to get free, but it's impossible.

"You're not supposed to run on the pool deck!" I shriek as his lips find my neck, and then we're airborne. The water is warm, but still a shock when we go under.

Darren brushes my hair away from my face and bubbles burst out of his mouth as he laughs, possibly at my expression. He launches us skyward when our feet touch the bottom of the pool.

Before I can yell at him for ruining my hair and the only

outfit I brought with me, he grips the back of my neck and locks our mouths together. Someone whistles, and I'm pretty sure Randy tells us to get a room.

"You're a jerk," I mumble around his tongue.

He laughs and swims me to the shallow end. "I'm your jerk."

"You could've waited until I was wearing a bathing suit! I don't even have a change of clothes."

"Don't worry, I've got you more than covered." He grabs a towel from the edge of the pool. "Want some help changing out of your wet clothes?"

"From you? Nope." I push on his chest, biting back a grin as I climb out and wrap myself in the towel.

"We'll get him back for you later, Char," Miller calls after me.

"Oh, don't you worry. I'm more than capable of making him pay for his transgressions, and I'm sure my punishment will be far worse than anything any of you can dream up." I arch a brow at Darren and grab my bag, smiling at the chorus of laughter that follows me into the pool house.

Darren and I both know any kind of "punishment" I'll be doling out will be of the teasing variety, but they don't need to know that, and sometimes it's fun to keep them guessing.

It's a hot day in late May, and the air conditioning is on in the pool house. Goose bumps flash over my skin as I pad across the cold tile floor to the bathroom. On the counter is a yellow gift bag tied with a bow. My name is written on the little card in Darren's neat cursive.

Before I open the gift, I strip out of my clothes and wrap myself in the towel. I pull the satin ribbon, wondering if the whole dragging-me-into-the-pool business was an orchestrated move. I assume so. Darren doesn't do anything without plan or purpose. I remove the tissue paper, noting the firefly print.

Inside is a small package wrapped in more tissue paper; this time lavender. I pluck at it from the back and gently tear the paper.

A soft knock is followed by the twist of the doorknob. "Charlene?" I'm unsurprised that Darren has followed me. I'm curious as to what his plan is—whether it's going to be a delayed-gratification day, or the kind where we sneak off and satisfy our cravings for each other in short bursts of need and want. I'm banking on the latter since it's my birthday, and I should be able to call all the shots.

I clear my throat, my body already warming. "I'm getting changed."

"I came to assist with that."

I bite back a smile as I open the door and peek through the gap. Darren grips the doorjamb, eyes moving down my neck to where my pearls lie, then dipping lower to where I clutch the towel.

"What if I don't want your assistance?"

"I can just watch if you'd prefer." His smile is full of dirty promises as he pushes on the door, and I step back, allowing him in. He closes it and flips the lock. "It's your birthday. Whatever you want, you get."

"Whatever I want?" I tap my lips. "Hmm. You know, I've been looking at those new Teslas. I think I'd look pretty great in the driver's seat."

"We can go car shopping later."

"Haha."

I'm clearly joking. It's a two-hundred-thousand-dollar car. I would actually be terrified to drive it. Darren is quite sensible about his purchases. He has two vehicles—an SUV and a sweet sports car—neither of which cost an excessive amount of money. It's one of the many things I appreciate about him. His most frivolous purchases are usually lingerie related, or at least they were until a couple of months ago when he discovered his love of cotton panties that retail at five dollars a pair.

I turn back to the lavender tissue paper so I can finish unwrapping what I suspect is the first of many gifts. I find a brand new bikini in a soft, pale purple—one I've looked at more than once over the past month or so.

"This one is as much for me as it is for you, hence the color." He drops his head, lips finding my shoulder. "Are you sure you wouldn't like my assistance?"

"Everyone is going to know what's going on in here." I point out as he kisses up the side of my neck.

"I don't mind if they know I'm apologizing for throwing you in the pool." He untucks the edge of the towel, and it falls to the floor.

"Is that what you're doing? Apologizing?"

He skims the curves of my hips, making fresh goose bumps flash over my skin again. "You mentioned something about a punishment. I thought it might be a good idea to get that over with now." His lips lift against my cheek.

"You're welcome to serve your penance on your knees."

His mouth touches mine for the briefest moment before he drops to the bathmat.

Lifting me onto the vanity, he hooks my legs over his shoulders and shows me exactly how sorry he is with his mouth, and then again when he gets inside me.

It's a good half hour before we come out of the pool house. I'd be embarrassed, but this happens quite regularly with my group of friends—although usually it's Randy and Lily who make use of the various bathrooms. Hockey players have high sex drives, and watching their girlfriends or wives wander around in bikinis gets them excited. There are worse problems to have.

Lily passes me a glass of champagne as soon as I settle myself in one of the loungers.

"Oh! I like this!" She motions to my new bikini. "Do you know if they have the bandeau-style top?" Lily is modest in the chest department. She's incredibly lean and so fit she has a four pack.

"I think they might. I'll text you a link to the site."

Violet lowers herself into the lounger beside me. She adjusts her bikini top with a frown. "What the hell am I going to do if these get bigger? I'm already busting out of these tops as it is."

"Doesn't Alex buy you a new bikini every week?"

"I have some from my last pregnancy that might fit you," Sunny says from under her sunhat.

"Yeah, I might have to take you up on that. I'm constantly at risk of flashing a nipple here." Violet leans back in her chair, and then checks to make sure the movement hasn't exposed anything it shouldn't.

Lily, Poppy, and I drink champagne while Violet and Sunny drink fizzy grape juice with strawberries floating in the glass. I survey the pool, smiling as the guys play volleyball and Lily's and Sunny's dogs—Weiner, Titan, and Andy—run up and down the length of the pool, waiting for someone to throw them a ball or a Frisbee. As far as birthday celebrations go, this is my idea of perfect. I have almost all the people I care about right here.

About an hour later, commotion in the driveway draws my attention. Darren pulls himself out of the pool and heads for the gate. Robbie and Sidney appear, both carrying coolers, and behind them are Daisy and Skye.

When they move to the side, I shriek and jump out of my chair. "Mom?"

She grins and gives Darren a nervous smile before she does jazz hands. The best part is she's dressed like a normal person. "Surprise!"

I rush around the pool and throw myself into her arms. "I thought you were in the middle of filming."

"I might have fibbed a little. As if I could miss my baby girl's champagne birthday." She hugs me tight. "Darren called me last week and arranged to fly me out here."

He shoves his hands in his pockets and smiles. "I thought it would be a nice surprise."

After I'm finished hugging my mom, I launch myself at him. He catches me as I wrap my arm and legs around him. His smile grows, and he chuckles. "I did okay?"

"You did amazing. Thank you." Other words I want to say get trapped in my throat, so I kiss him instead.

The afternoon is full of appetizers, dips in the pool, crazy conversations between the moms about pregnancy, sex, and other things I've never wanted to know about Violet or Alex's moms, or mine. But I wouldn't trade the crazy for anything in the world.

We're in the middle of setting the table for dinner—I could use the food thanks to the amount of champagne I've consumed this afternoon—when another commotion at the gate draws my attention.

"What's going on over there?" I ask Violet, who's busy trying to attach pickled pearl onions to baby gherkins and wrap them in ham so they resemble mini Super MCs.

Violet looks over her shoulder and shrugs. "Maybe it's another delivery, courtesy of your boyfriend?"

"I'm going to check it out."

Darren has bought me a ridiculous number of gifts, and apparently there are more waiting at his place. I've unwrapped a new closet's worth of shirts and leggings this afternoon.

I tiptoe stealthily across the patio in hopes that I can catch a glimpse of whatever is being delivered.

"What the fuck is going on?" Darren mutters. "Why is this thing parked in your driveway? We need to get it gone before Charlene sees it."

Darren is standing shirtless with his arms folded across his chest, Alex beside him, adopting the same pose. I suppress a shudder when an RV comes into view. It's parked in the driveway. It looks eerily similar to the one that was parked on my street earlier today.

The door to the RV opens with an ominous creak. Anxiety ricochets awkwardly through my entire body as a man appears in the doorway.

I break into a cold sweat as memories I've spent the past decade trying to keep locked away and buried claw their way to the surface. I've never been more terrified of beige khakis with an elastic waistband and an off-white golf shirt. I feel like I'm being pulled into a nightmare. This can't be happening—not now when everything is so perfect. Not when I finally have all these good things in my life.

I fight for breath as he searches the faces of my friends, his combover lifting in the air like a hand waving. I take a step back, seeking cover, my knees wobbling perilously as his wild eyes land on me and a creepy-ass wonky-toothed smile spreads across his pale, doughy face.

"I knew the signs would lead me to you!" He spreads his arms as if he expects me to run into them. "I've come to bring you back into the fold!"

I'm pretty sure my scream can be heard all the way to Canada.

15

DADDY FRANK

DARREN

E verything awesome about today dies a horrible tragic
death when some pasty fucker steps out of the massive RV
parked in Alex's driveway and starts yelling about signs and
"the fold."

I question whether this is someone's idea of a practical joke,
and whether or not I'm going to have to kick some serious ass,
because it's sure as fuck not funny.

An ear-piercing scream startles us all, and I turn to find Charlene standing about ten feet away, eyes wide with terror, one
hand clutching her pearls, the other covering her mouth as she
continues to scream, and scream and scream some more.

I know she has some kind of RV-related PTSD, much like I
have a complete aversion to open doors—especially in the bath-

room—but this reaction is extreme. I'm also concerned she's going to pass out from lack of oxygen. I don't know how a person can scream that long or that loud without taking a breath.

"Charlotte! I've come to save you!" Khaki Man yells.

Who the hell is Charlotte?

Charlene lurches forward and squeezes between me and Alex. I reach out to stop her, but she pushes away, careening toward Khaki Man. She corrects herself, stumbling as if she's drunk. She grabs my arm, eyes bouncing around my face as she motions to the RV.

"Tell me this is a nightmare. Tell me this isn't happening."

"Are you okay? Do you know that man?" I try to wrap her up in my arms, but she pushes away again.

"No, no, no, no, no!" She grabs two fistfuls of hair, clutching hard as she shakes her head. "This isn't happening. This can't be happening." She spins around to face Khaki Guy. When she speaks her voice is clear, but shaky, "What the hell are you doing here, Frank? How did you find us?"

He makes some random hand gestures while waving around a cell phone. "I saw your mother on the devil's box, and I knew it was a sign to harvest again. I've been searching for you for so long. It's time to come home." He opens his arms wide. "Come give your Daddy Frank a hug."

"Daddy Frank? Is that Charlene's father?" Alex asks.

"I have no fucking clue," I reply.

Everyone from the backyard starts to trickle out in the driveway. "What the hell is going on?" Randy asks from somewhere behind me.

"Oh! Did Charlene's whole family come to celebrate her birthday?" Daisy asks.

This Frank guy claps his meaty hands twice and a woman appears at the door of the RV. She's wearing a white long-sleeve blouse buttoned all the way to her throat and at her wrists, despite it being eighty degrees today. She's also wearing a white bonnet, like she stepped off the set of *The*

Handmaid's Tale. It's one of the few shows I've watched recently.

She hesitates on the last step, but when he motions her forward, she hikes up her long beige skirt, revealing a pair of white Keds, and takes a tentative step down. She scans the crowd, eyes falling on Charlene, and her expression is a mixture of fear, sadness, and envy. "I thought I'd never see you again," the woman says softly.

"What the fuck is happening here?" Lance asks from the other side of Alex.

Charlene takes a halting step. "Carrie?"

"Come see your sisters. They've missed you, Char-char!" Frank the fucker claps his hands again, and several more women follow the first one off the RV.

I notice several things: they're all wearing the exact same outfit, as if it's a uniform, and the rest of them keep their eyes fixed on their white Keds. They all also have medium to light brown hair that falls to the middle of their backs, which makes them look eerily like Charlene.

"Do you want me to call the cops?" Miller asks. "I think this guy has a few screws loose."

Based on Charlene's horrified expression, I'm pretty sure Miller is right about that. I step up, because Charlene's welfare is my first priority and my responsibility. "You need to leave before we call the police."

Khaki Man turns his wide, freaky-ass smile on me. "I can't leave. The devil's box sent me a sign and brought me here to save my Char-char from a life of excess and corruption." He motions to Alex's house and all of us standing there in bathing suits, beach coverups, and swim shorts, and finally to Charlene, as if that's all the explanation he needs to give. "I knew it was too late for her mother when I saw that awful show." He turns to Charlene. "But I can still save you. Don't you see? It's fate that I've found you again. It's time for you to come home and take your rightful place in the co-op."

Charlene shakes her head furiously and side steps toward the house, away from him. "This has to be a nightmare," she mutters. "You can't be here. This isn't happening. This can't be real."

"Oh, shit." Charlene's mom pushes through the crowd holding a huge bowl of potato salad, which she hands off to Poppy, who looks confused and alarmed. She stomps across the interlocking stone toward Khaki Pimp Daddy. "Frank! What in the ever-loving fuck are you doing here?"

He puffs out his chest. "I've come to save Char-char from your poor choices!"

"Poor choices? For the love of Christ, falling for your bullshit was the poorest choice I made. Now get your pasty ass back in that RV and go back to your subpar greenhouse operation where you belong!" She nods at the women. "Carrie, Cassie, Clara, Clair, Cara, Caddie, so sorry, no offense."

"Production really took a dive when you left," one of the women says with a shrug. The rest of them nod in silent agreement.

"Enough!" Frank puts a hand out as if he's some kind of magician and can stop Charlene's mom from advancing on him. "Cendy, you're no longer welcome in the fold."

"My name was never Cendy, you crazy dickbag! It was Wendy, and I had to change it to keep your psycho ass from finding us! And newsflash, Frank, I don't want to be in your fold, and neither does Charlene. Now get the hell out of here, or I'm going to file a goddamn restraining order."

"I won't leave without Char-char! It's time to bring her home!"

Frank pushes Whensday, or Wendy, or whatever the hell her name is, out of the way and lunges at Charlene.

His rash, ill-thought-out move spurs a series of actions. Charlene flails and screams as he grabs for her elbow. The women from the RV let out a collective gasp of surprise, and one of them yells for Charlene to run.

Poppy, Violet, Sunny, and Lily all converge on Charlene as she stumbles back. She trips on an uneven stone and lands on her butt. The ping of something hitting the interlocking stone and rolling across the driveway barely registers.

"Poppy! Get away from that guy!" Lance yells.

It's followed by shouts from Randy, Alex, and Miller, but the only thing that resonates is Charlene's desperate shriek.

I stop thinking. Instead I react, launching myself at him. I take him to the ground before he can put his hands on anyone else. He's soft and doughy, and clearly not built for a fight. He lands on the ground with a loud *oomph*.

"Run, beige ladies! You're free! Run while you can!" Miller yells.

The first punch hits Khaki Man's soft middle, and he groans and tries to curl into a ball.

"She's not yours to touch—not fucking ever. Do you understand me?" I yell in his pale, now somewhat greenish face.

"She belongs with me! She belongs with the co-op!" He tries to shove me off. "We need you back to make us whole again, Char-char!"

"She's mine, motherfucker. You can't have her." This time I punch him in the mouth to shut him the hell up.

Before I can give him a black eye, several sets of hands latch onto me, pulling me up. I fight against the restraints, because all I want to do is destroy this fucking lunatic who's a threat to my girlfriend.

Alex's voice is in my ear. "You gotta calm down, Darren. You're scaring the shit out of Charlene, and everyone."

I glance at the terrified faces of the beige-clad women and then at the cluster of women huddled protectively around Charlene. Behind them is a semi-circle comprised of Alex and Violet's parents, while my teammates act as a barrier between me and them. I note the nervous, unsettled expressions that color every single one of their faces.

I look back at Frank the fucker whose nose is bleeding. He

struggles to sit up while holding his hand to his mouth. Blood streams down his chin and drips onto his pristine white shirt.

A few of the beige women gather around him and help him to his feet. They throw dirty looks over their shoulders at me as they usher him back in the RV. He starts it up and rolls down the window as he throws it into gear. "I'll be back for you, Charchar! I'll save you yet!"

"Come back and I'll run you over with your own goddamn RV!" I yell and try to rush the vehicle, but Lance and Randy grab me.

"I don't think you're helping the situation." Randy inclines his head to where Charlene sits on the driveway, trembling violently. Her knees are pulled up to her chest, clenched fists pressed to her lips. Violet wraps a towel around her, and Lily brushes her hair away from her face while Sunny tries to pry her hands from her mouth. Poppy picks something up off the ground. Multiple somethings.

I turn to Charlene's mom. "Can you tell me what just happened? Was that Charlene's father?"

"I suppose he functioned as one during her childhood, but no. That's my . . . ex for lack of better terminology, but it's a long story." She glances around and wrings her hands nervously. "One I'm assuming Charlene hasn't shared with any of you."

I shake my head, and there's a murmur of agreement from everyone else. I look to Violet, almost relieved that she seems to be similarly shocked, and swallow down the huge lump in my throat as I try to process what happened. I need to understand a lot of things right now, starting with what Charlene's childhood actually looked like, because the picture she painted for me wasn't *this*.

I make a move toward her, wanting to . . . I don't know, understand? Comfort her? I need something, anything to replace the strange state of disbelief I'm currently suspended in.

Alex puts a palm on my chest. "Look at your hands."

I cringe at the blood coating my knuckles. "Fuck."

"We'll get her inside and keep her safe until you've cleaned up and calmed down," Alex says.

Charlene's mom helps her up and wraps a protective arm around her, and all I can do is watch as the woman I'm in love with, but don't even know, walks away without looking back.

16

THE ANSWERS AREN'T ALWAYS IN YOUR FAVOR

DARREN

L ance looks at me, lips pressed into a thin line. He puts a hand on my shoulder, his expression almost piteous. "This makes our parents look like they should be up for family of the year award, aye?"

I don't know much about Lance's family situation, other than the fact that he doesn't have a relationship with his mother and he only sees his father once a year at most. But based on his history with women, I can certainly make an experienced guess. Porn star parents and being raised by grandparents who were determined to eradicate the inherited perversion out of me seems pretty decent in comparison to what I now suspect Charlene went through.

And now my mind is reeling out of control. I want to hunt

207

that fucker down and torture him in ways that would make horror movies look like they were produced by Disney.

I feel almost like I'm walking through a fog as Lance takes me to the pool house bathroom to wash up and throw on a shirt. I don't pay attention to much as I head for the house, feeling exposed and uneasy.

Violet meets me at the door, her face pale and eyes wide with the kind of disbelief that makes a stomach turn. "I had no idea. Not about any of this. I mean, I knew she grew up in a trailer park and it was bad, but I didn't realize it was this kind of bad."

"I don't know if that's supposed to make me feel better or not," I tell her.

"I'm sorry, Darren. If it's any consolation, we're all as shocked as you are."

"It isn't, but thanks."

"There's obviously a reason she didn't tell anyone, including you and me." Violet gives me a sad smile. "Alex and I are going to send everyone home. She's in the living room with her mom."

"Okay."

I don't know what to do with any of this. It explains everything and nothing at the same time. And even though I should probably be angry, all I am is sad that I wasn't safe enough to confide in.

Before I cross the threshold, her mom appears in the doorway.

"I need to ask you something before I talk to Charlene," I say in a hoarse whisper.

"Of course. I'll answer if I'm able, but this is Charlene's story to tell."

I nod and take a deep breath, my stomach rolling. "Did anyone ever—" I swallow down the bile. I don't know that I'll be able to refrain from killing Frank if the answer is yes. "Did Frank —was she ever in physical danger?"

"Oh, Darren." She settles a palm on my forearm and shakes

her head. "Her childhood was a lot of messed-up things, but it wasn't that. I got us out before she was ever at risk."

I pinch the bridge of my nose, fighting against the sting behind my eyes and the tightness in my throat. "Okay. That's good."

She hugs me, and I stiffen for a moment, not expecting the embrace. But I accept it anyway, because for some reason knowing Charlene's innocence was kept intact makes me feel marginally better.

Her mom steps back and looks up at me. For being as small as she is, she certainly has a dominating presence, so I can see how she ended up where she did. Sort of.

She tips her head to the side. "Does she know?"

I frown. "Know what?"

Her smile is soft. "That you love her."

"I'm afraid I'll push her away if I'm honest with her."

She pats my cheek. "You're quite perfect for each other, despite the odds."

I find Charlene curled up in the corner of the couch, having changed into one of the new outfits she unwrapped this afternoon. It's a Chicago T-shirt with her first name on the back, because I avoid using her last name whenever possible, and the number twenty-six, since it's her birthday. I like that it's also my number. Despite how warm it still is, she's also wearing leggings.

She looks up when I enter the room, her eyes wary and her bottom lip caught between her teeth. I guarantee it'll be chewed raw by the end of the day if it isn't already.

"Are you okay?" I ask, advancing slowly, as if I expect her to bolt. She certainly looks like she wants to.

She lifts her shoulder and lets it fall. "Are you?"

"Not particularly, no." I'm a lot of things at the moment, but okay is definitely not one of them.

She bows her head and raises her hand to her bare throat, but drops it right away when there's nothing to fidget with. "I'm sorry."

"For what?" I want to rewind time and make us both different, not two irreparably damaged people trying to figure out how to be together without imploding.

"I should've told you," she whispers.

"Were you ever planning to?" I let her into all my darkness, but it hasn't been willingly. She's had to drag it out, and now I'll have to do the same with her.

She sighs and focuses on her hands. She's holding something, rolling it between her palms. "I wanted to. I was going to, especially after I found out about your parents. But it seemed like too much all at once, and trying to explain . . . I thought I could wait until after playoffs were over, but then with the expansion draft still looming, there was always a reason to wait. I didn't want to risk it."

"Risk what?"

"Losing you before I had to."

"Why would you think you'd lose me?"

She looks up, her expression guarded. "Nothing about me is normal, Darren. My childhood was messy and fucked up."

"I'm just as messy and fucked up. I thought we'd already established that."

Charlene scrubs a hand over her face. "I know, but my mom's already so much crazy—I didn't know if you could handle any more. I mean, who raises their child in a commune and thinks it's okay? And not just any commune, but a batshit crazy one where women are treated like property. The whole thing is like a bad talk show episode."

"Did you think I wouldn't be able to handle it?"

She sighs. "It wasn't you specifically. I've never told anyone, ever. We never talked about it after we left. It was like . . ." She pauses, maybe searching for the words. "It was all a terrible nightmare. My mom told me not to say anything because we didn't want Frank to find us and bring us back there."

She runs her hands up and down her legs. "I remember the night we ran. My mom woke me up in the middle of the night, and we escaped through a hole in the barbed-wire fence."

"Barbed-wire fence?" It sounds more like prison than a home.

"Yeah, it was meant to keep the bad guys out. Anyway, there was a car waiting for us down the road. I had to hotwire it because she was too panicked to find the key. I didn't even know what we were running from at the time."

Her eyes are the kind of haunted I associate with old memories made new again.

"We drove for hours before we finally stopped at a little diner somewhere in Nebraska. I'd never been to a restaurant, never seen a TV before, never shopped in a grocery store, never even worn a pair of pants, Darren. It was such a shock to realize the world was so much bigger than what I knew. It was too much to process. I don't remember it clearly at all—more like it was some messed-up recurring dream. And reliving it, trying to explain it . . . My extremes were the opposite of yours, Darren. I went from isolation to inclusion so quickly it was impossible to reconcile."

Charlene explains how her mom got pregnant before she graduated from high school. The guy was a year older, and they ran off together. She always wanted to travel, and he was a trucker. Turns out babies cramp the trucking lifestyle. So one day he dropped her off at a place called The Harvest Co-op, or what Charlene has always referred to as "The Ranch," located in the middle of Utah, and left her there with her infant baby. Penniless. With no identification.

And Frank took them in with open arms. He welcomed her into "the fold." It was fantastic. They were a self-contained unit. They earned their own way and functioned like a family, and for a woman who came from a small, isolated town where her parents threatened to help her get rid of the baby without seeing a doctor, it's not hard to understand why she ran, and why she stayed where she was for as long as she did.

While her mother might've known her situation wasn't

normal or conventional, it was certainly preferable. Until apparently it wasn't anymore.

"So how did you get out, and what prompted leaving?" I ask, still trying to figure that part out.

"I started my period," Charlene mumbles, and her cheeks flush.

"I don't think I understand."

"My mom worried it wasn't going to be safe for me anymore. We were in extreme isolation, and there were a lot of restrictions. I never left the compound. I'd been told it was dangerous and forbidden. We didn't have identification. We were dependent on Frank for everything, and I was getting older."

It finally clicks as to what she means. "I should've killed that fucker when I had the chance."

Charlene ducks her head. "Don't say that."

"Charlene, that shit is fucked up. Far worse than anything I went through as a kid. That guy needs to be put behind bars or six feet under."

She rolls whatever she had between her fingers faster and faster until it pings on the table. She scrambles to grab it, but I catch it mid-bounce. It's a pearl. I glance up to where her fingers dance nervously around her throat.

"It broke when Da—Frank tried to grab me." She presses the heels of her hands against her eyes, and her shoulders curl forward.

I run a gentle palm over the back of her head. "It's okay. We'll get it restrung again."

"I think I lost half the pearls in the garden this time, or between the stones. We'll never find them all."

"So I'll add new ones until it fits." I never told her that the first time I had the ancient, broken necklace restrung for her, I replaced all but a few of the original pearls since none of them were real. These were. And I definitely won't be sharing that with her, either.

"You've already done that once. You shouldn't have to do it again."

"It's not about *having* to do anything, Charlene. It's about *wanting* to. Whatever you need, whatever you want, I'll do it for you. Don't you get it? I l—"

"Don't!" She scrambles away from me.

Her terror over the RV has nothing on her panic now. She shakes her head, as if she's erasing thoughts, words, and memories. "Please, Darren. Whatever you think you should say right now, please don't. I can't. I can't do this. There's too much. I don't even know." She stands up, smoothing her hands down her thighs. "I need to go home. I have to go home."

I stand too, wanting to reach out and hold on, to keep her where she's supposed to be, which is with me. "I can take you home. Why don't you stay with me? It's safe, and I'll take care of you."

"My mom is here," she says quietly.

"She can stay with us. I have spare bedrooms. If you need your space, you can stay in one of the other rooms, too." I sound desperate. Maybe because I am. I have no idea how to manage this situation, but I feel like I'm losing her, as if I've opened the glass jar and this time when she goes free, she won't come back.

That's not acceptable.

But I can't lock her away or I'm just as bad as the man she ran from.

Everything suddenly fits—the puzzle orders into a picture I couldn't ever piece together properly.

I finally understand how much she hates being tied down to anything, literally and figuratively, apart from her job. She seeks stability in things, not people.

Except for Violet. She's the only constant person I can see. Not even her mother holds that kind of sway with her. I want to know how to be that. I want to know what I need to do in order to be that for her. Because as she shuts down on me and pulls into herself, and the fire I love so much flickers and dies, I'm certain of one thing: if I'm traded, there's a good chance I'll lose her forever. Violet will be the anchor that keeps her from coming with me.

And after everything I've learned tonight, I'm not sure I can blame her for wanting to stay, even if it means I have to leave half my soul in Chicago with her.

BETTER LOVE

CHARLENE

The night I came home from the party, there was a box on the front stoop. I assumed it was from Darren, so I didn't open it right away. But the next morning a pamphlet from The Ranch had been shoved through the mail slot, possibly as some kind of messed-up, highly ineffective enticement. All it did was make me never want to leave my house again.

I learned a very important lesson on my twenty-sixth birthday. Burying the past and pretending none of it happened in no way erases it. In the wake of Frank's reappearance, the carefully crafted façade and the world I'd built for myself crumbled. In its place, I'm left with a past I can't escape, even though I ran from it, a present that terrifies me, and a future that's disturbingly unstable.

The number of memories I'd blocked out, or maybe hadn't been able to process with any kind of reasonable perspective as a fourteen year old, are now alarmingly clear. I see myself through a new lens, without the rose-colored glasses of youth to soften and smooth it all out.

I'm angry at my mother, my father—the real one, and Frank, who preyed on the weak and disadvantaged. They're the people who made The Ranch seem like the better option. In the wake of Frank's reappearance, I feel more alone than ever, even though I have perpetual calls and messages from my friends.

I feel extremely *other*, alien, like I no longer fit where I used to, and I'm embarrassed and humiliated by a past I had no control over. I don't know how to blend in anymore, or even just exist.

On Monday I stand at the front door, dressed for work even though my head is in a fog. I want to ground myself in this slice of normalcy. My hand is on the doorknob, but I can't seem to turn it. I sift through all the memories of The Ranch and fixate on the fence that surrounded the compound, meant to keep us all safe, but all it did was trap us in a life so narrow it was like living in a pinhole.

My head aches as things start to make sense in a way they haven't before. My fear of being trapped, of needing stability, the importance I place on my friendship with Violet, not wanting to leave Chicago and my built-in family, my inability to let Darren get too close. My head is a mess of memories, and my heart is bleeding with emotions I can't filter.

"Sweetheart?" My mom puts her hand on my shoulder.

"I'm afraid to leave. I'm afraid Frank is going to be out there, and he'll take me back to The Ranch, and I'll never get out again."

"That's not going to happen, honey. I won't let that happen, and neither will any of the people who love you." She leads me away from the door and takes me to the kitchen, where she pours hot water over one of her homemade candies.

I stir the water, watching the candy dissolve at the bottom of the mug. "I want to be normal. I want everything to go back to the way it was before all the memories came back."

"I'm so sorry, Char-char. If I could do it all over again I would make different choices. I would find a different way."

"I know."

I understand, sort of, why she chose the path she did. She put herself in control of her own life, she took the reins so no one else could, and she never stayed in one place so Frank couldn't catch up with her.

I call Mr. Stroker and request to work from home this week. I only have a few client meetings, so it shouldn't be too difficult to reschedule them. I also never ask to work from home, so he is more than accommodating—and concerned, of course.

I flounder for an excuse. Telling him I've suddenly developed acute agoraphobia as a result of being stalked by my not-real cult leader father sounds farfetched and could lead to more questions. So I tell him I had an allergic reaction to a new lotion, and it caused a full-body rash.

In the wake of the Daddy Frank episode, Darren has upped my security from the alarm system to a live bodyguard. So far he remains parked outside at night, and during the day he sits on my front step and makes sure the only people who come to my door are ones I want to see.

My mom leaves on Wednesday, very apropos, after my insistence that I'll be fine on my own, especially now that I have a bodyguard and Violet's been stopping by on a daily basis. I love my mom, but she gets antsy staying in one place for more than a few days at a time, and she's driving me crazy. Besides, I'm not keen on rehashing all the memories from The Ranch or hearing again how sorry she is that Frank found us on account of her audition. It's not like she could've known that Frank had finally jumped into the twenty-first century by getting a laptop and a Facebook account.

I don't even feel like I know myself anymore, and trying to

explain that is difficult. My mom thinks the answer is to get out of Chicago and travel with her. The idea of running certainly has it's appeal, but then what would I have? I don't want to leave behind all the people I care about, the family I created for myself in Violet and the girls, and even Darren.

I don't know what to do about him, either. I've made such a mess of things.

He calls several times a day, but I can't answer. I'm afraid to. I know what he was going to tell me. But I can't decide if it was coming from a place of honesty, or if he was simply trying to give me a balm that would somehow soothe me, erase the pain and fear and uncertainty of everything that made me who I am. And I'm unsure who that even is anymore.

I want too much to let him love me.

But admitting it won't prevent him from being traded. Loving him won't stop him from moving halfway across the country. And if he goes, he takes half my heart with him.

He will regardless. So I don't know why the words scare me so much.

Maybe because all the love I've known has been tied up in so much weirdness and instability. Maybe I think as soon as it's real, it will fall apart. And if he stays, I have to acknowledge all the ways I've kept us in this constant state of stasis.

I spend all of Thursday watching terrible reality TV, trying to feel better about my shitstorm of a life. I don't know how to unbreak myself enough to be able to love the way I want to. I mentally unpack my childhood at The Ranch, followed by the freak show that was my teenage years, until I stumbled upon Violet in my first year of college. And in doing so, I see all the pieces of myself and how they fit together in a jagged-edged puzzle of crazy.

I'm sheltered but not. I created normal where there wasn't. I made a family so I wasn't alone. And then I found Darren, the man who molded himself into what I needed, who changed as I required, who kept his emotions locked down to protect me from myself, who never once put the lid on my jar. In a lot of ways we were safe for each other, until it all came crashing down, as happens when emotions are given room to breathe and grow.

I can't allow things to continue like this, with him constantly altering his needs to suit mine. But now that I see things clearly, I realize that how I operate is exactly what he's used to. I put restrictions on us, and he abided by them.

If I keep doing this, I'm just as bad as the people who raised him. And that's not what I want to be. Because I love him, and as scared as I am of what's coming, I don't want to lose him.

By Friday I'm restless. I've binge watched every terrible reality TV show available. After six straight hours of *Garage Wars*, I clean my house from top to bottom and fall asleep at four o'clock in the morning, only to have nightmares about being trapped at The Ranch again. Except there's no way out anymore because instead of a razor-wire-topped fence, the perimeter is lined twenty feet deep with recycled junk, and every time I try to climb to the top, the stacks fall and bury me.

I decide to switch to game shows after that for a few hours. Every time I nod off I have another nightmare, though, so I consume a pile of my candies, hoping to find some calm. I miss Darren. All I want is to curl up in his arms and let him protect me. But I worry as soon as I do, he'll turn into another Frank, and then I'll be trapped for the rest of my life.

It's not rational. It might not even be sane, but the fear takes hold and roots itself in my brain.

Around noon my stomach rumbles, and I make my bleary way to the fridge. The box of wine my mom left for me has probably turned into vinegar by now, and I've eaten all the food Violet left me yesterday. She's supposed to stop by after work with fresh donuts, which is all I want to consume right now, but that's still hours away.

There's a convenience store down the street. They'll have

Twinkies and Ho-Hos. I can make it there and back in less than twenty minutes, especially if I drive. Nothing bad will happen.

I get a load of my reflection in the mirror. I look like I've been on a serious bender. My eyes are bloodshot, and my pajamas are a wrinkled mess. I end up taking a very long shower and changing into a pair of leggings and a shirt Darren bought for me. I brush and braid my hair, because drying it would take too much effort. Then I grab my purse, phone, and keys and open the door.

I've forgotten about the security detail—don't ask me how, he's there all day every day—and I suck in a sharp breath and grab for my pearls. But of course they're not there because they broke, again, all because of crazy fucking Frank.

"Miss Charlene, I apologize if I've startled you. Do you need something? A ride to Mr. Westinghouse's perhaps?" he asks, polite and formal.

I consider it for half a second as I glance around at the wide open space and all the potential for danger. All the worst possible scenarios bounce around in my head, such as Frank popping out from behind some bushes with a chloroform rag and dragging me back to the RV with the help of all the co-op women.

"No. No, I'm fine." I back up and slam the door closed, fixing the lock with shaking hands. I'm sweaty, and my mouth is dry. I pop one of my candies, even though I'm not sure they're effective at keeping me calm anymore.

The soft knock at the door makes me scream.

"Miss Charlene? I apologize again for startling you. Is there anything I can do for you?"

"How do I know you're not part of Frank's RV gang?" I shout through the door.

"I've been hired by Mr. Westinghouse to ensure your safety, Miss Charlene."

I know he's telling the truth. He's been standing outside my door all week. Also, Darren texted me his picture and his personal details.

"Prove it!" I yell. My voice is super pitchy. Clearly I'm losing it. Again.

Less than a minute later, there's another knock on the door. "Miss Charlene, I'm going to slide my phone through the mail slot. Mr. Westinghouse is on the line and he'd like to confirm that I am indeed here for your safety."

I catch his phone before it hits the floor and stare at the screen. Shit, Darren Facetimed. I take a few deep breaths, wishing I was more put together and that my hands would stop shaking.

"Charlene?"

I keep the phone pointed at the ceiling and drop to the floor. "One second." I put my head between my knees because I feel dizzy. I haven't spoken to Darren since my birthday, although he calls and leaves messages on a daily basis to make sure I'm okay.

"Firefly?"

The nickname makes me want to cry because I finally understand what it means. I'm his firefly. The one he wants to catch and keep, but can't.

"Just another moment."

"You're worrying me."

I lift my head and tilt the phone down until his face comes into view. I'm unprepared for the rush of emotion that comes with seeing him. I want to reach through the screen and touch him. I want the safety of his arms and the warmth of his lips against my skin.

"Hi." My voice is raspy and tremulous, like the rest of me.

He scans my face, assessing, his icy eyes dark and lips turned down. "Are you okay? Did something happen?"

I have so many things I want to say to him. Questions, admissions, fears I want to unload so he can assuage them. But all of those get stuck in my throat, and I go with stupidity instead. "I . . . no. I need groceries."

Relief is followed by a wash of sadness. "What do you need? I can pick it up and bring it over." He pauses and clears his throat. "Or have it sent if you'd prefer. You can order online if that's easier and use the credit card I gave you to pay for it."

I don't know why I didn't think about ordering groceries. Maybe because my mom was here until a couple of days ago, and between her and Violet, they've been taking care of feeding me. Not that I felt like eating much. Donuts are my go to. I want Doritos with onion dip, but they remind me too much of Darren.

"I have my own credit card."

I look down, away from his sad eyes and the lost look on his face.

"I know this is difficult for you, Charlene, and I understand your need for space, but when you're ready to talk, know I'm here, waiting for you. In the meantime, whatever you need, please don't hesitate to ask either myself or Luther."

"Luther?"

"It's his phone you're holding."

"Oh. Right." I feel bad that I didn't even remember his name.

After a few more moments of quiet he finally asks, "Are you okay?"

"I . . . no."

His voice hardens. "Has Frank tried to make contact?"

"No." But I don't trust he won't try again. He's too crazy not to. I'm sure he's laying low, biding his time, waiting until I let my guard down.

"Okay, that's good. If he does, will you call me? Or at least tell Luther?"

"Yes, Darren." I raise my eyes to the ceiling, hoping to keep the tears floating instead of falling.

"Charlene." When I meet his two-dimensional gaze, he gives me a small, strained smile. "I waited my entire adult life for you to come along and make sense of my world. I'm prepared to wait as long as I need to for you to accept that."

"I'm not ready." *I need you.*

"I understand."

"I have to go." *I'm in love with you.*

"I'll be here when you're ready to stay." He ends the call before I can.

After a few minutes, I open the door and pass the phone back to Luther, thanking him.

"Can I take you anywhere?"

"I'm fine, thank you." I go back inside. I'm not hungry anymore. I touch my throat, wishing I had more than a few unstrung pearls, the reminder of Darren that I've carried with me over the last several days. I don't know how to do this without him, or with him.

VIOLET STOPS by after work with supplies. I should probably buy stock at Krispy Kreme donuts considering how many I go through these days.

"How you hanging in there?" She passes over the box of donuts, which I hug as if they're my best friend, rather than the person who brought them.

I lift a shoulder and set the box on the counter. Flipping it open, I admire the beautiful array of donut magic. I'm starving since I polished off the last box in the middle of the night. I should probably consider ordering groceries like Darren suggested, but I'm worried Frank will intercept and find a way to get to me, even with Luther standing guard outside my door.

"Have you talked to Darren yet?"

"This afternoon, yes."

She looks surprised. "How'd it go?"

"It was . . . okay."

She taps her nails on the counter. They're pink and blue with

Alex's number on the index finger. "Okay how? What did you talk about?"

"Groceries."

"Really? You talked about groceries?" Violet sighs. "I know this has to be hard for you, Char, but you can't cut him out, or everyone else for that matter."

I swallow a massive chunk of donut. "I'm not cutting everyone out. I just need time. You don't understand what it's like."

"No. You're right. I don't, not at all, and I never will if you don't talk to me about this. I'm your best friend, Char, and considering what I witnessed the other day, I think maybe I can understand why you would never want to talk about what life was like when you were growing up. But I'm not sure hiding from it is going to make it any better, either." She takes me by the shoulders, forcing me to look at her. "We all love you no matter how fucked up your childhood was, just like you love me despite the fact that I'm clearly unable to censor myself *ever*, and I constantly embarrass myself and everyone around me. Let me do what a best friend is supposed to. Let me help you through this. Please don't shut me out."

"I'm not trying to. There's so much I don't want to remember, so many things that make sense now but never did when I was a kid."

"You don't have to try to make sense of it alone, though, do you?"

"I'm scared."

"Of what?"

"I don't know who I am anymore."

Violet's eyes are glassy. "You're my best friend, and you've been like a sister for almost an entire decade. You're loyal and fun and always up for an adventure. You think you like to try new things, but really you like routine and predictability. And you're terrified of accepting help, so you carry the weight of the world on your shoulders, which is pretty annoying for the people who love you and want to help. But I'll forgive you for that since you deal with me on a regular basis and I can be a pain in the ass too." She hugs me hard. "You're still you. Nothing has changed except maybe now we can all understand you a bit better than we did before."

18

OPEN THE JAR

DARREN

I'm a miserable asshole without Charlene. I know this because Alex has told me more than once this week to stop being a dick. It's not intentional. I'm not trying to be a cocksucker of epic proportions, but it's off season, and my plan was to have Charlene at my place almost full time by this point. I'd been on track before her birthday, and now she's not here at all.

Alex has tried to get me to talk on numerous occasions over the past week, but he can't help me, and he can't understand, not really. So I've mostly been stewing in my own frustration at not being able to protect Charlene the way she needs me to.

Her chair is empty. The book she was reading the last time she was here is still sitting on the table. When I'm really desperate for some piece of her—which is pretty much every

226

waking moment of every day—I'll sit in her chair with her blanket and flip through to the earmarked parts.

Ironically, none of her favorite parts are smut, despite the content of the books she reads. It's all the sweet moments—the first kisses, the grand gestures, the breakups and the reunions— that she reads over and over.

I'm currently at the gym, trying to run out the frustration that comes with not having what I want or need. Lance jumps onto the treadmill next to mine, and I give him a nod, then up the speed to nine miles an hour. He cocks an eyebrow and starts off at a leisurely six and a half miles an hour jog.

"You doing okay?" he asks.

I make a sound, no commitment either way, because I'm actually pretty fucking shitty right now, and I don't feel like talking about how fucked up my life is, or my girlfriend's life, if she's even still that.

We run in silence for a few minutes. Lance slows his speed while I sprint. My lungs are about to explode, but I'm unwilling to slow down because that will mean talking.

"You were raised by your grandparents, aye?"

I glance over at him for a split second and nod, then stare at the TV hanging above me.

"I don't know if you're aware, but my aunt became my legal guardian when she found out my mum was beatin' the shit outta me fer missin' goals. Or whatever pissed her off, really."

I stumble a step and grab the rails, lifting my feet from the belt, I straddle the edges, this time giving him my attention and dropping the speed on my treadmill so I don't end up flying into the wall. "I'm so—"

He lifts one hand to stop me and drops his speed even more with the other until he's walking. "Don't apologize. It is what it is. Some people are just fucked up and they shouldn't be parents."

"Tell me about it."

I'm not sure why he's sharing this with me, of all people. I like Lance well enough, but I think he tolerates me more than anything else.

"I didn't understand how you and Charlene worked, but, uh, Poppy kind of set me straight on a few details."

"How so?"

He rolls his shoulders. "I had it in my head that you liked to . . ." He exhales a long breath. "Hurt her."

This time I punch the stop button. "What?"

He does the same, but instead of looking at me, his eyes are on the flashing numbers of his screen. "Like . . . hit her."

"You think I would hit Charlene?"

He runs a rough hand through his hair. "No, like spank her and shit."

That hot, tight feeling in the back of my neck eases up a bit. "Oh. That's not how things are with Charlene. Despite how it may seem, she's very . . . innocent, which I'm only starting to understand better these days."

I've probably just spoken more consecutive words to Lance than I have in the past three years he's been on the team. And my newfound understanding isn't helping me out much, considering yesterday's brief Facetime conversation with Charlene is the only one we've had in the past week.

"So, uh, based on the way you seem like you're either trying to murder that treadmill or yourself, I'm guessing things aren't all that good with Charlene right now."

I grit my teeth, annoyed that I'm so transparent, and that he's calling me out on it.

He nods, as if he understands my silence. "I don't know how things went down for you as a kid—like, when you went to live with your grandparents or what—but I was fifteen when the beatings finally stopped. From what I know, Charlene was a teenager when she went from one fucked up situation to another. I'm not saying it's the same thing."

He runs both hands down his face. "Fuck. Poppy should be the one having this conversation with you. She's a fuckton better at this. Look, what I'm trying to say is that I spent a lot of years trying to forget all the bad shit by keeping it locked up here." He taps his temple. "I'm pretty sure some of it is blocked out, at least that's what my therapist says, like my brain is trying to protect itself from the worst of it."

He exhales a long breath. "Look. I know I'm rambling, but maybe it's the same for Charlene? Or maybe it isn't." He rests a hand on my shoulder, his eyebrows pinched, a heavy swallow making his throat bob. "All I'm saying is that sometimes we shut ourselves off from the things we need when we're afraid to lose them the most. We're all kind of broken, and we all need a little saving sometimes, aye? Poppy seems to think you two are meant to save each other." He rolls his eyes. "I sound like a fuckin' asshole, but Poppy's usually right about this kind of thing." He nods, more to himself than me. "All right. Good talk, Westing-house. I'm gonna get outta yer face now before you give me a beatdown."

He drops his hand and walks away, leaving me to ponder what he's said, and how much I want him to be right. Part of the reason I haven't been pushing myself on Charlene is my uncertainty about whether I'm all that good for her. But maybe Poppy's right and all of our broken parts do fit together.

It's with that thought in mind that I drive to Charlene's after my workout, with a quick stop on the way. When I arrive, Luther is posted outside the front door. He has a twin brother named Damien, and they've been trading off shifts this week at her house.

It's the middle of the afternoon, and Charlene should technically be at work, but I know from Alex that she's taken the week off. I'm also aware she hasn't left her house since her birthday party.

Luther nods his acknowledgement as I knock.

"Charlene?"

Her muffled voice comes through the door after a long minute. "Darren?"

I press my palm against the warm steel, aware she's almost close enough to touch. "Can I see you?"

It takes a minute before the door opens the three inches the chain latch allows. Her eye appears in the crack and darts down and back up, shooting around my face.

I hold up the bag. "I brought some things for you."

She stares at me for a few seconds before she bows her head and closes the door. The lock clicks, and she steps back as she opens it so I can come inside. She looks exhausted. Her eyes are red rimmed, hair piled on top of her head in a messy bun. She's wearing a pair of the leggings I bought her and a shirt. I try not to think about whether or not she's wearing cotton cheekies under those leggings.

Charlene's fingers go to her throat, but drop right away when she doesn't find her pearls.

"I wasn't expecting you."

"I know." I'd apologize for coming unannounced, but it would be insincere.

I set the bag on the counter and start emptying it so I have something to do with my hands that doesn't include hugging Charlene, which is what I want more than anything. That and to kiss her.

Charlene frowns as I set the bag of Cool Ranch Doritos on the counter. "What is this?"

"I picked up a few things I thought you might like."

"Oh." She seems genuinely shocked, which is odd.

"I also picked up some takeout in case you wanted something aside from snacks." I pull out the Styrofoam and Saran-wrapped box containing her favorite penne alfredo from the restaurant we frequent close to my place.

"You came here to feed me?"

"And talk, but Luther mentioned that you hadn't had a real meal in several days, so I felt it might be a good idea to bring you your favorites, soften you up a little after my arriving unannounced." I'm nervous, so I start peeling the cellophane from the takeout. "Are you hungry?"

"Not right now." She wrings her hands.

I imagine this level of anxiety is overwhelming for her, so I decide to cut to the chase and spit it all out. I prop my fists on the counter and take a deep breath. "Look, I know you think you're a mess, Charlene—"

"I don't *think* I'm a mess, I am one."

"But you're my mess, and I'm yours, and nothing has changed that. Not for me. Has it changed for you?"

"No, but—"

"If it hasn't changed, there shouldn't be a but. Why can't we be a mess together? Why do you feel like you have to go through this on your own? Let me be here for you."

"But what if you leave?" she asks softly.

I frown. "Why would I be here if I was planning to leave?"

Her fingers go to her lips. "What about the expansion draft?"

"You mean if Vegas takes me?"

"Yes. What happens then?"

No one ever gets what they want if they don't ask for it. "First of all, I don't think it's going to happen. There are two other players who are younger, faster, and better than I am, and they've brought on someone new to Vegas to keep Lucas, the owner, from making a bunch of stupid-ass decisions, which includes pulling someone as old as me over to a brand new team. But, should the unthinkable happen and I do have to go to Vegas, I want you come with me. But only if that's what you want. And if you don't, we try to make the long distance work, or maybe I take early retirement so I can stay right here."

"But you'd have to break your contract."

"The money doesn't mean anything, Charlene. Nothing means anything without you. I want you however you come— broken, messed up, in leather, lace, satin, cotton pajamas . . . However you are, it's just you I want." I step around the island, closing the distance between us. "I keep telling you that, waiting for you to hear me."

Charlene's eyes are wide. She pulls her bottom lip between her teeth, looking every bit the elusive firefly she often is. I understand it better now. I get her in a way I never could have before.

I cup her face in my hands. "I know you want to run from this. I know this whole thing scares you, but understand this, Charlene, I love you. That's the only truth you need. Everything else in that head of yours is white noise. All the worries are pointless. I want this with you, and I don't care if it's messy and fucked up and no one understands it but us." I smooth my thumbs over her cheeks. "Be with me in this, Charlene. No more of this you live at your house and I live at mine. If we're going to be together, let's just be together."

"Wait, what?" She frowns. "You want me to move in with you?"

That her first reaction appears to be confusion isn't reassuring, I drop my hands and step back, giving her space. "You were staying at my place more than here over the last couple of months. Moving in is the next logical step, isn't it?"

Her fingers go to her mouth. Her panic isn't what I want to see, but I've dropped a pretty huge bomb on her without any kind of warning, after a week of not seeing or speaking to her beyond daily texts to see if she's okay. Maybe pushing my entire agenda on her wasn't the best plan.

"You're asking a lot all at once," she murmurs.

"I'm not asking you to do much more than you already were." Except give up her house and share my space with me on a permanent basis. Not unreasonable after two years. Although maybe just managing our relationship and making sure we're stable first would've been a good start. It's possible I've jumped the gun here, but then again, sometimes Charlene needs to be pushed.

"What if we fight?"

"I expect that might happen on occasion, since I can be an asshole. There are four bedrooms in my house. I anticipate there may be nights I have to relocate, depending on how badly I piss you off."

"I'm not joking, Darren."

"Neither am I." I try to smile, but I'm sure it falls a little flat.

She closes her eyes and turns her head away. I don't know if I'm winning her or losing her. I'm about to tell her she doesn't have to decide in this moment, that she can have more time if she needs it, mostly so she won't say no.

"This isn't easy for me," she says softly.

"It's not easy for me either, but what specifically is so difficult about this for you?"

Charlene drags her fingers back and forth along the neckline of her shirt. "For all the years you spent with no doors or privacy, I spent the same amount of time locked away from the world. Love and dependency were imprisonment." She lifts her gaze. "I'm afraid to be trapped again."

"I'll never put the lid on your jar."

As soon as I say the words, I understand that's exactly her fear—that she'll lose her freedom again. I can only imagine how she felt after she and her mom left the compound, and they only had each other. It would've been a new kind of prison—one created from the fear of being dragged back to the hell they'd escaped. Although from what I understand, Charlene didn't perceive it as hell until she was out of it.

"I don't know what I have to do to prove to you that I'll love you and take care of you in whatever capacity you need me, but I won't walk away unless you tell me to." I press my lips to her forehead. "You know where to find me when you're ready."

My feet feel like they're weighted with lead soles as I head for the door. I've said what I came here to say. There's nothing else I can do to convince her.

She grabs my sleeve. "Where are you going?"

"Home."

"That's it? You're not staying?" She seems confused again.

"I'm not going to push you more than I have, Charlene. I know what happens when I do, and I'm not willing to take that risk." I pull her to me. All her broken pieces and bent edges fit with mine. "Call me when you figure out what you want." I inhale the scent of her shampoo and press my lips to her skin for the briefest moment before I untangle myself.

I don't want to leave, but I can't stay—not unless she's ready to let me in all the way. Luther is on the front step when I open the door, staring out at the neighbor's yard. There's an older woman in a pair of booty shorts weeding the garden. I'm pretty sure it's for Luther's benefit. He's a good looking motherfucker.

"Wait!" Charlene grabs my arm and yanks me back inside. She pauses to wave at Luther before she closes the door in his face.

I stare down at her. Even with her messy hair and wrinkled outfit, she's flawlessly flawed. It doesn't matter if she tells me the only reason she wants me to stay is because the apocalypse is coming; there's a reasonably good chance I'll say yes.

She grips my shirt as if it will keep me from moving. "I don't want you to go."

"Then give me a reason to stay."

She stares at her feet—her toenail polish is chipped—and slowly looks back up. "Can we ease into this?"

"You can't lube up for moving in."

She rolls her eyes at my terrible joke. "I wasn't expecting this. I was ready to deal with the feelings part of us, but then you blindsided me with the whole moving-in thing."

"I figured I might as well lay it all out there for you, so you know where I'm at."

She chews her bottom lip and nods. "I can't give up my night with Violet and the girls. They come over to my place, and we hang out and stuff, and if I live with you, we'll have to do that at your place."

"Those are the same nights I'm out with the guys, and we never come to my place."

"Maybe that should change."

"Do I need to remind you what happened the last time they ended up at my place?"

She manages to blush and give me the evil eye at the same time. "I don't want to sell my house right away."

"Property is a smart investment. You can rent it out indefinitely." I run my fingers through her hair, the need to touch her too overwhelming not to give in. "Whatever you need to make you feel safe, Charlene, you can have it. If you need a house in your own name, then keep it. But don't expect me not to buy you things. You're everything I need, and I'm going to give you everything I think *you* need."

Charlene seems to fight back a sob as she wraps her arms around my neck. "I love you, in case you weren't sure."

"I hoped." I press my lips to hers for a moment and then pull away. I slip my hand into my pocket and retrieve the necklace I've been carrying with me the past few days. I went in search of all the fallen pearls after her mother took her home and brought them to a jeweler the very next day. I picked up the necklace three days ago and have been carrying it around with me ever since.

Charlene's eyes soften, and a lone tear slides down her cheek as I clasp it behind her neck.

"I love you more than you can comprehend. I'll give you anything you want, Charlene. Just stay with me, let me love you like I'm supposed to, let me be exactly what you need."

"You already are."

I kiss her, and my whole world seems to come together and fall apart at the same time. She's everything. She's all the missing pieces I need to feel whole.

CANDY ADDICT

CHARLENE

Darren and I don't make it farther than the kitchen counter before we're naked and all over each other. Make-up-slash-love-declaration sex is the best. Not that I want to have more arguments or breakups, but love declaration only happens once. All the anxiety and stress of the past week is erased by each kiss and touch. I believe Darren when he says he'll never put the lid on my jar. He's always been exactly what I need, and now that he knows about all the good and bad parts of me, it feels like he's truly mine.

An hour later we're stretched out on the couch in the living room. Darren has on boxers, and I'm wearing the shirt he arrived in. The rest of our clothes are scattered around the kitchen. I reach into the bowl next to me and unwrap a candy. I'm already relaxed, thanks to all the orgasms, but I'm a little hungry post sex, and too lazy to go to the kitchen for a snack. And too comfortable wrapped up in Darren.

I pop the candy in my mouth and settle back against his chest. I toss the wrapper, aiming for the coffee table, but I miss, and it flutters to the floor.

Darren reaches down and picks it up, inspecting the opaque square. "What kind of candy is this?"

"It's herbal." I pull myself up a little higher so I can kiss his neck. His skin is salty in contrast to the sweetness in my mouth.

He twists a little so his mouth is close to mine and sniffs while frowning. "Where'd you get them?"

"My mom makes them." I don't usually eat them when I'm with Darren, since I like the kind of anxiety he evokes in me.

Darren curves his palm around the side of my neck and presses his lips to mine. When his tongue sweeps out I part my lips, allowing him inside. He strokes against my tongue a few times before he pulls back, still frowning. He repositions us so we're sitting up. "Stick your tongue out for me."

"What?"

"Your tongue, stick it out."

"They're an acquired taste," I mumble, but I do as he asks, the candy sitting on the end of my tongue.

He pops it in his mouth, rolling it around, which could be kind of gross since it's been in my mouth, but then again, he does put his tongue in there, among other places.

After a few seconds he spits it into the wrapper. "How often do you eat these?"

I shrug. "I don't know. Usually a few a day."

His eyes go wide. "A few a day? How long have you been eating these?"

I don't understand why he's so shocked. "I don't know. My mom has been making them as long as I can remember."

I didn't think it was possible for his eyes to be any wider. "You ate these as a kid?"

"They're calming." Now I'm defensive about it. I love these candies.

"Uh, yeah, they would be since I think they're made from weed."

"No they're not," I scoff.

"I'm pretty sure they are. How do you think they get that green tinge to them?"

"They're herbal."

"And the herb they're made with is *weed*."

"How would you know that? You're not allowed to use recreational drugs," I point out.

"Correct, but I've spent enough time around Alex's dad to know what weed smells like, since he's a chronic pothead." He doesn't say anything else, possibly waiting for me to process this information.

I have to cover my mouth with my palm since I'm incapable of closing it. The greenhouses at The Harvest Co-op, aka The Ranch, flash through my mind—endless rows of gorgeous green plants, the smell of skunks, the barbed-wire fence, how we were located out in the middle of Buttfuck, Nowhere. All of it suddenly makes sense.

"Holy fuck," I say from behind my hand as the truth settles in. "Oh my God. My mother turned me into a pothead."

"Maybe there isn't any THC in them," Darren offers.

I think about how I've been this week—all the candies I've eaten and how much I've been zoned out and napping like it's my job. How many donuts I've consumed.

I consider how I'm relaxed for hours after I eat those candies, and how they always seem to heighten that tingly feeling in my body, particularly the one between my thighs when I'm nervous. I have to wonder if they're somehow related.

I almost always have one with my tea right before I go to bed when I'm at home. I can still sleep like the dead—the flaily dead —even with all my afternoon naps.

I drop my hand from my mouth. "I'm a pothead."

"There are a lot worse things to be."

"I've been carrying those around with me everywhere. I've taken them on planes, Darren! Oh my God, what if I'd been arrested? My mother is my dealer!"

Then it dawns on me that Darren had one in his mouth. "Shit. Now you have weed in your system! What if you test positive at the next drug test?"

"It's off season. There aren't any mandatory tests anytime soon, and I had, like, three sucks of a candy."

A little of the unease dissipates, but it fires right back up. "What if I'd offered them to Sunny and Violet? They're both pregnant!"

"You haven't given them any, have you? Or any of the guys?"

"Well, no, my mom said it was best not to share them, but I could've ignored her, and then I'd be feeding a baby weed, or ruining NHL careers!" I'm starting to feel lightheaded even though I'm sitting down. "I need to get rid of them!"

"Whoa." Darren grabs my arm before I can reach the bowl of candies. "I don't think it's a good idea to throw those out."

"Well, I can't keep them now that I know what they are!"

Darren pulls me back into his lap. "Calm down, firefly."

"I don't think I can." *Shit*. I'm at risk of hyperventilating. And all I want to do is simultaneously eat all of those candies and flush them down the toilet.

He kisses me softly. "Take a deep breath and listen to me, okay, Charlene?"

I nod and do as he asks, sucking in as much oxygen as my lungs will allow, then breathing my weed-candy breath in his face.

"You said you've been eating those as long as you can remember?"

"Since I was a teenager, I guess?"

He tucks a few hairs behind my ear, tracing the shell with his fingertips. They're softer than usual because he's not training as hard.

239

"So you've been eating these every single day for the past decade?"

He picks up the discarded candy from the coffee table. Peeling it off the wrapper, he holds it to my lips. "I think you should eat this."

My mouth waters in anticipation. "Oh, God. I'm an addict."

"It's just weed, Charlene. It's not like you've been shooting heroin your entire life, but I wouldn't suggest quitting cold turkey. It might be a good idea to cut down a little, though." He taps my lips, and I open my mouth, allowing him to pop the candy back in.

I feel instantly better, which I realize is not possible.

"Okay, so tell me about these candies. Your mother's been making them since you were a teenager?" Darren rearranges me so I'm straddling his lap, facing him.

I think back to when it all started. "Earlier than that. When we were at The Ranch, we grew all our own food. We had greenhouses, and there were some I wasn't allowed in, but I caught a few glimpses here and there. Harvest time was always busy. My mom would be gone all day and sometimes late at night. Then they'd make candies and box them all up, and trucks would come and take them away. Jesus . . ." I pause for a moment, remembering very clearly the night we escaped. "When we left the compound, my mom had a car waiting for us, and we had three backpacks—two of them filled with candies and some money, and the other had my stuff. That's how we survived until she found a job."

"That was pretty resourceful and a lot fucked up."

"This is crazy." I can't believe I've been eating weed candies for years and didn't know it, and that my mom failed to mention it.

"Do you think they're still making those candies?" Darren asks.

"Yes. Definitely. There was a box of them on my front porch on my birthday. I thought it was a birthday present from you, so

I left them on my counter and finally opened them the other day. I was going to throw them away on garbage day because there's no way I'd ever eat anything from The Ranch, but I haven't had a chance yet. Let me get them."

I find them in the garage and bring them back to the living room. Darren opens the box and peeks inside. My mom's candies have a tiny logo on the wrapper. I'd never thought anything of it until I note the letters stamped on these mint green wrappers. Darren unwraps a candy, inspecting it.

He looks up at me. "If I'm right about any of this, we might've found a way to get rid of Frank."

GOING DOWN

DARREN

When I look back on the night I met Charlene, I don't think I ever would've pegged her for a pothead who was raised in a commune, but then people only let you see what they want you to, until they take their masks off.

Still, this is the kind of thing they base reality TV shows on. In fact, if they haven't already, I'd be surprised.

"I should call Robbie," I tell Charlene.

She looks a hell of a lot shell-shocked. I can't say she doesn't have a right, considering she just found out she's been carrying around illegal narcotics in the form of candies for over a decade. And that her mother is a manufacturer of weed edibles, and may very well be a dealer.

I call Alex to see if his dad is around. They've been visiting Chicago a lot lately with Sunny and Violet both being pregnant.

"Yeah, man, my dad's here. What's up? Everything okay?"

"Yeah, things are okay. I have some questions for him, though. Would it be okay if Charlene and I stopped by?" I check the time. It's the middle of the afternoon.

"You're with Charlene?"

"I am."

"That's good news. And yeah, of course you can come over—both of you, obviously. Miller and Sunny are here with Logan, and Skye and Sidney are supposed to be over soon for a barbeque. We're all hanging out by the pool, so bring a suit."

"Great. Thanks. We'll be by in a bit."

Charlene packs a beach bag with a bathing suit and changes into a lavender sundress, with my help, of course. She seems to be on autopilot, which isn't all that surprising. We take my car to Alex's place with the box of candies from The Ranch and a few of the ones her mom makes, for comparison's sake.

Violet meets us at the front door. She looks from me to Charlene and cocks a brow. "Please tell me this means I don't have to stop at Krispy Kreme tomorrow."

"No more trips to Krispy Kreme," Charlene replies with an embarrassed smile.

"I'm glad that's over, because it was getting awkward. The same kid works every morning, and he was starting to remember my order." She rubs her still mostly flat belly. "So does this mean you're officially back together?"

Charlene looks up at me, so I put my arm around her shoulder and pull her into my side. She feels good there, right, like she fits. "Even better. I dropped the L-bomb on her."

Violet does some weird little dance and shakes her hands around in the air. It almost looks like a toddler who has to pee. "It's about fucking time! We all knew you two loved each other. I'd say I don't understand why it took so long to figure it out, but considering how screwed up you both are, I'm just glad you got there without turning into Bonnie and Clyde and going on a murder spree."

"It could still happen," I deadpan.

Violet points a finger in my face. "Don't do that. Remember, I'm the one who knows how not-sinister you really are, so that face isn't going to work on me. Also, I'm prone to nightmares at this stage in my pregnancy, and I would appreciate it if that didn't include my best friend starring in them as some kind of female version of *Dexter*."

"You're the one who mentioned murder sprees."

"Right. Okay. Topic officially dropped. Come on in. Alex and Miller are trying to teach Logan how to use a hockey stick. The poor kid has barely mastered walking." She shakes her head and motions for us to follow her to the backyard.

Logan seems more interested in hitting Miller in the shins and smashing flowers than the red foam puck they keep pointing out, but he seems entertained, if nothing else.

Sunny's reclined in a lounger with Daisy and Skye on either side of her. Their conversation comes to a halt when they notice us, and I realize Charlene probably hasn't seen them since her birthday. I lean in and press my lips to her temple.

"Don't worry, firefly, they love you exactly as much as they did before, if not more."

She tips her chin up, eyes meeting mine. "How did you happen to me?"

"I believe your best friend hooked up with my best friend, which likely wouldn't have happened had Alex not won a bet and room to himself."

"I remember Violet telling me about that. What was the bet, anyway?"

"Who could come up with the longest word in an online game of Scrabble."

"Seriously? I expected something so much more . . . interesting."

"It was a long bus ride. We were bored. Alex got lightning. It was impressive." I press a kiss to her perfect lips, promising myself we're going to make out later. For hours. Like teenagers.

I step back as Skye and Daisy converge on Charlene. Sunny's still working on sitting upright. She's looking really pregnant these days.

"Darren!" Robbie motions me over to where he and Sidney are sitting in the shade, watching their sons be dads.

"They're starting early, huh?" I nod to Alex and Miller.

"Pretty sure Miller thinks Logan's going to be drafted by the time he's in pre-school," Sidney says with a smile.

Alex takes a break from getting slammed in the shins with the hockey stick to grab me a beer. "Everything okay?" He glances over at Charlene who's corralled in a corner with Sunny, Violet, and the moms.

"With Charlene? Yeah. We figured it all out. Just took me getting my head out of ass to make it happen."

"That's good. Vi was worried about both of you this week."

"So was I, but I think we've got it all sorted. She's agreed to move in with me, which I'm taking as a good sign."

Alex's eyebrows pop up. "Whoa, that's a big step."

I nod and rock back on my heels. "Yeah. It's about time, right?"

He laughs. "It really is."

"Thanks for sticking by me. I know I'm not the easiest person to understand, but I don't think Charlene and I would be where we are if it wasn't for you."

"I didn't really do anything except give you some advice."

"You've done a lot more than that, Alex. Watching you and Vi grow together, being part of this family—" I motion to his backyard, full of the people Charlene and I both care about. "This is how I figured out how to love Charlene. So yeah, thanks." Jesus. I sound like an asshole.

Alex frowns, brows pulling down, and he blinks repeatedly before he claps me on the shoulder. "I'm gonna hug you now, so don't punch me."

I laugh, but it gets caught in my throat with a whole bunch of other emotions when he really does pull me in for a hug. He slaps me on the back a few times, though, just to keep it manly.

EVENTUALLY I MANAGE to get around to talking to Robbie about the weed candies. I want to make sure I'm right about the ones from The Ranch—or The Harvest Co-op as it says on the wrapper—before I go calling it in to the cops. I also want to verify that the candies Charlene's mother makes are the same, and that we can keep her out of this.

Of course Robbie is only too happy to check out the stock. He opens the box of candies, almost giddily, and picks one up. His expression turns serious. "Where did you say you got these?"

"I'm guessing someone from the RV left them on Charlene's doorstep the day of the party."

"Would Charlene know where they got these from?"

"They're the ones who produce it, according to Char."

"Really?" Robbie's eyes light up, and he calls Charlene over.

This prompts the entire group to congregate around the two of them while she explains what happened when she was growing up at THC—the acronym now making a lot more sense. Robbie listens raptly, as does everyone else.

"This is all very interesting," he murmurs once she finishes explaining what used to go down at THC. "And how old were you when you and your mom left?"

"I was fourteen and a half." Charlene chews on her bottom lip. "My mom took a couple of bags of candies with her. I think maybe she sold them, and I started eating them, but I'm not sure if these are like the ones my mom makes."

Robbie perks up. "Makes? As in still?"

"Um, yeah. She sends them to me every month. I didn't realize they were weed candies. She said they were herbal, and I

246

thought it was more like a cough drop, but apparently I'm a pothead, so . . ." She stops rambling and looks around the group, her cheeks flushed.

"Nothing wrong with being a pothead." Robbie smiles. "Unless you're a professional hockey player. Then you have to wait until you're retired to enjoy that kind of relaxation." He taps on the arm of his chair. "You wouldn't happen to have one of the candies your mom makes, would you?"

"Um, sure. I have some in my purse." Charlene roots around in her bag and retrieves a handful of candies. "These are from the last batch, so they might be a bit stale."

Robbie unwraps one made by Whensday and one from THC and sets them side by side on the table, inspecting them closely. "Very curious," he murmurs.

"What's curious?" Charlene leans in to get a closer look.

"See how the coloring is slightly different."

"Mmm-hmm, the ones my mom makes are greener."

"It could be a purity thing." He pops the one made by Whensday in his mouth.

"Robbie! What're you doing?" Daisy asks.

"Research, darling." He grins. "I have a few theories about these candies, and I should know in about forty-five minutes if they're correct or not."

"What's the theory?" Charlene asks.

"A little over twenty-five years ago, right when I took the position at MJ Labs, edibles were growing in popularity. There was a company we'd been struggling to locate that began producing candies much like the one I'm eating. They cornered the market, but we didn't know where they came from and couldn't track the supplier. The recipe was flawless—the perfect balance to induce relaxation but maintain productivity. No matter how much we studied them, we couldn't replicate the recipe. Then a little more than ten years ago, the quality began to suffer. Something about the production had changed, and we couldn't figure it out. I may have the answer now."

"Which is what?" I ask.

"Charlene's mother leaving is the reason the quality suffered. I think she may very well have been the pioneer of the ultimate in edible candies."

Forty-five minutes later, Robbie is pretty much convinced this is the case. And based on his ridiculous smile, and the coveted bowl of chips he keeps stuffing in his face, I'm thinking Charlene has developed quite the tolerance for those.

He says he has to do a few more tests to make sure he's correct, and he'd like to bring the candies back to the lab in Canada so he can compare them, but it appears as though Frank has been funding the co-op through illegal marijuana manufacturing.

LIFE ON THE UPSWING

DARREN

All it took was one anonymous tip—I placed the call because Charlene couldn't bring herself to do it—and Frank's entire operation fell apart. The media were all over THC like rabid dogs. Charlene couldn't handle watching any of it. Part of it had to do with the memories, but she worried a lot about the girls she'd grown up with, and how they would handle suddenly being thrust into a world that had changed so radically while theirs had remained narrow and isolated.

I learned a lot about how Charlene dealt with their escape, and how the internet and her mom's job formed the basis of her sex education, which explains pretty much everything about her bedroom antics.

I couldn't stand to see Charlene upset, so I pulled some

strings and set up an anonymous fund to help the khaki ladies reintegrate into society. We were able to secure housing where they could all remain together, if that was what they wanted. Unsurprisingly, most of them opted to work at a local greenhouse facility.

Charlene's mom decided not to participate in the *Momma Domme* reality show, thank fuck, and instead she took an external consulting role with Robbie's Lab, which pays well enough that she decided she would retire from being a career Dominatrix, except for a couple of her favorite clients, anyway.

But the best news came at the end of June—well, it was the best news for me, but not for King, our goalie, who ended up traded in the expansion draft. This means I have two years left with Chicago, and then we'll see what happens after that. I won't take Charlene away from Chicago or the people she loves, so if they don't renew my contract, I'll retire. Alex knows that, my agent knows that, and most importantly, Charlene knows that.

I climb the steps to my front door and key in the code, having just finished a morning workout with Alex. We'll be getting together again later in the afternoon for a barbeque at his place.

"Charlene? I'm home!" I smile a little. The new-car smell hasn't worn off on saying that in the month since she moved in.

I wait for her reply, but all I get is silence. Her car is in the garage—her new car, the one I bought for her as a move-in gift—so she has to be around here somewhere. Excessive? Maybe, but it's a nice car, and she deserves nice things for putting up with my shit on a daily basis.

I drop my hockey bag by the laundry room door and head for the living room. Sometimes she listens to music while she reads or works in her chair, but she's not there. I find her in the kitchen—she is wearing ear buds—concentrating on something.

I pull one of the buds free and she startles, nearly falling off her stool.

"You know we have a whole house sound system. You could

save your hearing and some heart palpitations if you used that to rock out to..." I lift the bud to my ear to catch the tune. "Madonna?"

She snatches the ear bud from me. "It's retro."

I smile at her pink cheeks and survey the counter. "What's all this?" The surface is covered in various candies and boxes of Fruit Roll-Ups. Maybe she's been into her candy stash and has the munchies or something.

Charlene claps her hands together excitedly. "I thought we could try something new!"

I raise a brow. Since moving in, Charlene has started pulling out the *I thought I might like it but I changed my mind* toy box. Fifty percent of the time she decides she still hasn't changed her mind, but the other half . . . well, let's just say it's been a stimulating transition.

I motion to the array of candies. "You want a sugar high before we have sex?"

She purses her lips, then licks them as her eyes dart around. She squares her shoulders, apparently finding her resolve. This should be interesting.

"No. I thought maybe we could play dress up."

I look at her and then the counter, trying to figure out what the fuck she's talking about. "I don't get it. What are we dressing up?"

"Your cock." Her tongue hits the roof of her mouth when she says cock, purposely making it sound liquid. So of course mine hardens, until her meaning finally registers.

"No."

She pouts. "Come on, it could be fun!"

I cross my arms over my chest. "Absolutely fucking not."

She opens her mouth, likely to argue her case, but I put up a hand to stop her. "I don't give a shit if Alex lets Violet emasculate his dick with costumes. That's their thing. It's not going to be ours."

"But I worked so hard on this." She holds up what appears to be some kind of cape.

I've heard about this—not because I want this kind of information, but because sometimes Charlene shares things she probably shouldn't with me. Apparently living together gives me *extra* information privileges. I'd be fine without them, but Charlene is chatty before bed at times.

As I take in the array of cape-like designs, I'll admit—in my head and never out loud—that she's been very creative. "Still no."

She bites her lip, clearly trying to come up with a way to convince me to let her dress up my dick like a fucking superhero. Her eyes light up, and a coy smile appears. "I'll let you tie me up."

For half a second I get excited by this prospect, and then I cock a brow. "No you won't."

She runs a hand up my chest. "With the yellow satin ribbons."

As enticing as her offer may seem, I know Charlene. "I'll get one wrist tied to the bed and you'll change your mind like last time." She was so cute, and anxious as hell by the time I freed that one wrist. It took me about thirty seconds to make her come. I also got a sweet blow job as a concession.

"I won't change my mind this time, I promise." She parts her legs and pulls me between them.

She really doesn't want to give up on this, apparently.

"Okay," I concede. "I get to use the yellow satin ribbons. *Then* you get to dress up my dick with an edible costume."

Her brows pull together, and I fight a smile. This is clearly not going the way she expected.

"Do we have a deal?"

She huffs. "What about anal instead?"

I scoff. "Baby, you love me in your ass. If I'm going to let you make a fool out of my dick, I better be getting something phenomenal in return."

She chews on the inside of her lip and starts slipping buttons free on my shirt. Her knees press against the outside of my legs. "What about anal against the window in the front room?"

I like everything about that idea, except the landscapers are here. Usually the whole point is the illusion of an audience, but I have an issue with that today. "No."

"No?" She tips her head to the side, regarding me curiously. "Why not? The landscapers are working on the garden right under the window, aren't they? You love that."

She hops off the stool before I can stop her and rushes for the front room, stripping off her shirt as she goes. I chase after her, her bra smacking me in the chest and dropping to the floor.

Charlene's all giggles as she glances over her shoulder and pulls her shorts and panties down, kicking them off.

"You're not playing fair, firefly."

"Says the man who likes to make me wait all damn day for an orgasm." She wiggles her ass and slaps her palms against the glass, causing the landscapers to look up. Which is when the reason I said no becomes obvious.

The company who does my landscaping hired a new kid. He's in his early to mid-twenties and has full sleeves.

She spins around, wearing an amused smile, and thumbs over her shoulder. "So it's okay when it's the Ramsbottoms and their poodle wandering by, or ancient Bob, but this new guy is a problem?"

"You're not checking him out while I'm fucking you."

"You think I'm going to check him out?"

"I've seen the way you eye my tattoo artist. This kid looks almost the same, except less broody."

"I was trying to figure out the design on his arm, not check him out."

"Still no."

She throws her hands up in air. "Oh come on! Stop being so difficult."

I laugh and thread my fingers in her hair. "I'm always difficult." I brush my lips over hers. "I appreciate your creativity, but you already own my balls. You're not dressing up my dick."

"I'm trying to be fun, Darren." She pouts. It's cute. And she's obviously already worked up, considering the way she's rubbing her thighs together.

"Stay right here, and don't move."

I go back to the kitchen and grab one of the bar stools. Charlene is exactly where I left her when I return, rolling her pearls over her lips. I give her a dark look as I set the stool down in front of the window and hold out a hand. "Have a seat, Charlene."

She releases her pearls and slips her palm into mine, allowing me to guide her to the stool where she sits, facing the front yard. The landscapers are working on the bushes to the right. I adjust her position so her ass is hanging over the edge and I have the access I need.

"Hands on the window," I whisper in her ear.

She complies, palms flat on the glass.

I slide a palm under her chin and tip her head back so she has to look at me. I run my other hand down her spine and between her thighs to circle her entrance.

I bend to touch my lips to hers. "Hands stay on the window and eyes stay on mine or I stop."

"Okay." She nods and arches her back, probably trying to get me to finger her. Too bad I'm not in a hurry to make her come. I spend the next ten minutes making painfully slow figure eights around her clit and entrance, but not penetrating. I know exactly the moment to back off so she doesn't go over the edge.

"Darren," she whines and lifts her right hand from the window.

"Hands, firefly. Yours stay where they are if you want mine to stay where mine are."

She moans and slaps her palm against the window. The landscapers have moved on at this point, but she doesn't know that.

I go back to doing figure eights around her clit. "It's a good thing the floor is hardwood. You're making quite the mess right now." She's dripping down my fingers.

"You're so mean," she grumbles.

I laugh. "Weren't you the one who wanted to play?"

"I wasn't expecting orgasm torture," she shoots back.

That's the moment I push two fingers inside her, find the sweet spot and start pumping, hard and fast. She can't keep her hands on the window, and for a second I consider stopping again, but we're spending the afternoon with friends, and I don't want her pissed off at me. So I keep pumping, and she starts coming. She latches onto my arm, nails digging in as her mouth falls open and a low moan bubbles up.

I drop my mouth to hers. "Does it feel good?"

"Oh my God, yes." The S draws out, long and low. And still, I keep pumping, and she keeps coming.

I could have her like this, but I want her wrapped around me, so I spin the stool and fumble with the button on my jeans. Yanking down the zipper, I free my cock, part her legs, line myself up, and push inside.

"We're finishing this upstairs so I can fuck you like I love you."

"Whatever you want, Darren."

"And you're not dressing up my dick. Ever." I grab two handfuls of ass and pick her up.

Her lips find the edge of my jaw as I carry up the stairs. When she gets to my ear she whispers, "You have to sleep sometime."

I chuckle ominously as I stretch out on top of her on our bed and grind my hips into hers. "I think you've forgotten who the lighter sleeper is between the two of us."

Her eyes flare, and she starts to tremble again, likely a combination of the sudden spike of uncertainty and the grinding. I dip down and press my lips to hers. "I love you, little firefly."

"I love you, too."

"Don't forget that when you wake up tied to the bed one day soon."

Another nerve shattering orgasm steals her breath. I wait until she comes down again before I kiss her, and love her, and tease and torment, and love her some more.

EPILOGUE

FIREFLIES
FOREVER

DARREN

ONE SUMMER LATER

"Someone smells like he could use a diaper change!" Sunny scrunches up her nose and passes off baby Lane to Miller. "It's your turn this time."

"You gotta keep an eye on Logan and make sure he's not feeding Wiener all the cocktail wieners or we're going to have bigger problems than this stinker right here." Miller holds the screaming baby at arm's length, his face contorted into a grimace. "I think it's the broccoli soup that does this to him." He heads for the cottage.

"Logan!" Sunny calls out, and I follow her gaze to the table of food set up about twenty feet away.

Her son is indeed feeding cocktail wieners to Wiener. He pulls the treat away every time Wiener gets close so the dog has to jump for them, making his ears flap and Logan burst into a fit of giggles. It's cute, but if the dog gets the human treat, the cottage is going to smell like rotten dog fart for the rest of the weekend.

"I'll take Liam; you deal with Logan," I offer. Turns out the reason Sunny looked so pregnant at the end of last season was because she was incubating two babies instead of one.

Sunny glances from Logan to the squirming kid in her arms to me.

"I can handle it," I assure her.

Prior to all of my teammates having babies, I hadn't had much exposure, but when your best friend has a kid, it sort of forces you to figure out how to become an honorary uncle. I may not be one-hundred-percent natural around kids, but I can definitely watch one for a few minutes without the world coming to an end.

Sunny passes the little guy off to me. "Thanks. I'll be right back!"

"Take your time." He's half asleep, or at least he is until he's out of his mom's arms and into mine. "How's it going, buddy?"

He shouts nonsense in my face and cranes to find his mom.

"She'll be back. She's dealing with your older brother. He's getting up to no good over there." I have no idea how much he understands, but his little fists jab out, reaching for my sunglasses.

I find a lounger and rearrange Liam so he's stretched out in my lap, feet pushing into my stomach.

"Look at you." Charlene smiles as she crosses the lawn, a beer in one hand and some kind of girly drink in the other. She drops into the chair beside mine and pulls out her phone, snapping a bunch of pictures. "You better be careful, Mr. Westinghouse."

"Why's that?" I tickle the bottom of Liam's feet, and he bursts into a fit of giggles.

"It almost looks like you're enjoying this. People will start asking when you're going to knock me up."

"You let me know when you're ready for that, and we can jump on the baby bandwagon."

She laughs, but her expression shifts to contemplative. "Are you serious?"

"I want whatever you want, Charlene. You know that." I give his little tummy a tickle, and he giggles again and then farts. It doesn't sound dry. "Oh, you just did that, didn't you? I guess I better trade off with Miller." I lean over to give Charlene a quick kiss. "I'll be back in a few."

She grabs the front of my shirt, keeping our lips locked together long enough for her to get her tongue in my mouth for a stroke or two before she pulls back. "I love you."

"And I love you, firefly." I kiss the end of her nose, and she releases my shirt. I take Liam to the cottage and run into Violet on the way.

She's cradling a sleepy-looking baby Robbie. She raises a brow when she sees me holding Liam at arm's length. He definitely crapped his pants—the smell is getting worse, not better.

Violet's all smirky. I assume it's because I'm holding him like he's a nuclear bomb, not a kid, but if the diaper starts leaking, I don't want to wear his crap, thank you very much.

"Better not let Charlene see you with Liam."

"Why not?"

"Because it's baby central in here, and it's only a matter of time before her ovary clock starts ticking."

"Oh, well, nothing to worry about there. She's already seen me, and I already told her I'm happy to knock her up whenever she's ready."

Liam lets another fart rip, and Violet and I grimace at each other.

"Come on," she says. "Let's get that taken care of before he explodes all over the place."

I follow her down the hall to Robbie's bedroom, which is right next door to hers and Alex's. She pats the changing table, and I lay Liam down. He's started squawking, probably annoyed because he's marinating in his own crap. Violet puts Robbie in his crib, and I step back.

"Oh no, this is all you." She motions from me to Liam.

"What? I can't—"

"Seriously, Darren? It's poop. If you knock my bestie up, you're going to need to learn how to do this. Might as well start now. Don't worry. I'll walk you through it." She pats me on the shoulder.

I give her the eye.

"You don't scare me, Westinghouse. Deal with the poop."

I sigh. I guess she has a point. If Charlene decides she wants to have kids, I'm going to have to change some shitty diapers along the way. I unsnap the onesie that reads *iPood*, ironically enough.

"Okay, let's get the wipes ready. Liam is notorious for his ass explosions, aren't you, buddy?" Violet coos at him, and he smiles and claps his hands together.

I prepare the wipes and look to Violet. "What next?"

"Time to get your hands dirty. Okay, you're going to pull the tabs on the diaper, and the trick is to slide the top of the diaper down and then grab Liam's ankles and lift them before he can jam his foot in the dirty business. Got it?"

"I think so?" I follow her instructions and gag a little as I get a glimpse of the damage. Violet walks me through cleaning him up, which is just . . . fucking nasty. Liam seems to think it's hilarious, though.

Violet's all smiles as I go for wipe number fifty. "Did you bring the ring this weekend?"

"Yeah."

"You gonna pussy out again?"

I've had the ring for a few months. "I'm waiting for the right time. I don't want to push Charlene into something she's not ready for."

"Seriously? If she didn't run screaming at the offer to be knocked up by you, I'm pretty sure it means she's ready. Besides, I hear Randy's been looking at rings, and he and Lily are the co-founders of the Anti-Marriage Brigade. If you propose first, it means you get dibs on wedding dates."

"You think Randy's going to buy Lily a ring?"

"Make sure his wiener is pointing down," Violet instructs as I slide the fresh diaper under Liam's butt. She nudges me out of the way and finishes up. "I think what people want can change with time and perspective. You and Char are a perfect example of that. We can all make ourselves scarce tonight if you want. It's supposed to be nice out. There are always fireflies by the water when the sun goes down."

I mull that over. "You really think she'll say yes?"

Violet fastens the snaps and picks up Liam, patting his little fresh butt. "When I met Charlene, she didn't date a guy for more than three weeks. She never settled down and wasn't interested in long-term boyfriends, which, considering what she's been through, isn't much of a surprise. But everything changed with you, Darren. If you ask, she'll say yes."

"Okay." I nod, resolved.

She smiles and pats my cheek. "Now go wash your hands so they're not covered in crap residue, and maybe your face, too."

By NINE O'CLOCK, Alex and Violet still haven't reappeared from putting Robbie to bed. I have my doubts that Sunny and Miller will be back since the twins were fussy at dinner. Lily and Randy are likely doing what Lily and Randy do best, and with Poppy in the early stages of pregnancy where all she seems to want to do is take naps, she might be done for the night, as well.

I'm not sure Violet had to work all that hard to give me and Charlene some privacy.

Charlene snuggles into my side on the glider, and we watch the sun disappear behind the trees from the deck outside our bedroom. "Remember when we used to stay up until three in the morning and drink our faces off?"

"I certainly do. My favorite part was always getting you up to the room at the end of the night. You're such an adventure in the bedroom when you're drunk." I run my nose up her temple and kiss her cheek.

"I always went into it with the best of intentions."

I can feel her smiling. "Let's try all the things!" I mimic her voice.

"I do not sound like that when I'm drunk!"

"You do, and I love it. You're so fucking adorable when you're trying to be a little firefly." I chuckle. "We could do shots if you feel like letting your freak out."

Charlene snorts. "I think I'll pass. Those babies are like roosters at the crack of dawn. I can't imagine nursing a hangover and dealing with all of that craziness." She motions to the sounds coming from inside the cottage.

We're silent for a few minutes, enjoying the peace and the quiet—apart from the occasional burst of crying coming from one of the bedrooms, anyway.

"Alex said the cottage next door is for sale."

Charlene shifts so she can look at me. "You want to buy it."

It's not a question.

"This place isn't going to be able to handle all of us for much longer."

"Not with the way Sunny and Miller keep populating the future NHL draft," Charlene agrees.

Sunny's currently pregnant with baby number four, and very determined to have a girl. Based on Alex's competitive nature,

I'm pretty sure he and Violet will be trying for baby number two soon. Even Randy seems to be warming to the idea of having a family. Although I think it's a lot easier to picture it when you're surrounded by your teammates, who are essentially your family. Which is something I've started to do lately.

"It might be nice to have a second cottage for summer get-togethers, especially since my contract expires at the end of next season."

"Chicago could renew."

"Maybe, but if they do, I think it'll be for a year at a time." I stare out at the lake, considering all the options for our future. Charlene and I have talked about this often over the past year—what I'll do when my contract with Chicago ends. "I don't know if I want to play without Alex."

Charlene kisses the edge of my jaw. "You are such a sentimental softie."

"I'm pragmatic."

"You can call it that if it helps you feel better about it. There's no shame in loyalty."

"I'm pretty sure he's going to retire at the end of next season."

"He has too much to lose now."

"He does. He'll go into sportscasting, and I can try coaching, and we can stay here where all the important people are." They're too much a part of both of our lives—the stability we both need, the good example of what a family should look like that neither one of us had growing up.

"I don't like to think about any of the guys getting traded," Charlene says softly.

"I know." I press my lips to her temple. The idea of anyone not being here is difficult to fathom, but it's a reality we'll all have to face. "They'll all be back eventually. Chicago is home."

"I hope you're right."

"I think I am."

The sound of babies finally settling gives way to crickets. I'm nervous now, edgy, this thing I want to ask her making my throat tight and my palms damp. I think we're at the place we need to be.

"Oh!" Charlene sits up and points out into the darkness. "Fireflies."

I take the opportunity for what it is and stand, holding out a hand to her. "Let's go catch one."

We take the stairs down and cross to the beach where it's darkest. Charlene is still, her eyes scanning the inky night for a tiny green glow. When she spots it, she jumps and claps her hands around it.

"Did you get it?"

"I don't know."

I come up behind her, ducking down to rest my chin on her shoulder, and we wait, patient and quiet to see if her palms light up.

"I think I missed it," she whispers when it seems to be taking too long.

"Just wait." I slip one arm around her waist and kiss her neck. And sure enough, a minute later her palms glow green in the inky night. She opens them immediately, and the firefly rises into the air, giving me the opportunity I need.

I clap my hands around empty air. "I think I got something," I whisper.

I hold my clasped hands out in front of her, lifting the top one to reveal the small velvet box.

"What is that?" Charlene strains to make out what's in my palm in the darkness.

I flip the lid open, the moonlight catching on the ring, making it sparkle as I come around to stand in front of her.

She lifts her wide, uncertain gaze to meet mine. "Darren?"

In my head I've done this a million times, practiced all the words I want to say to her. I drop to my knee in the sand, hoping I've got this right, that I know her as well as I think I do.

"I'll never put the lid on your jar, Charlene. I love you too much to do that. I know I already have you in all the ways that count, but I want this with you. I want your fire and your softness, your innocence and your adventure. I want to love you and protect you and take care of you, exactly as you do for me. I want to watch you glow every day for the rest of my life. Say you'll marry me. Be the only forever I need. Please."

Charlene's fingers lift to her lips and then drop to her pearls. Her eyes are soft and glassy as she takes my face between her hands and bends to kiss me. "Of course I'll marry you. You're my only forever."

CHAPTER ONE: DARREN POV

WHY DID I WRITE THIS?

I loved writing Darren and Charlene, and I wanted to spend a little more time in his head, so I wrote the first chapter from his point of view, and thought readers would love seeing that first date from his perspective.

BONUS CHAPTER 1

JUST A COFFEE DATE... AND AN NDA

DARREN

I'm early. Twenty-four minutes early to be exact. I drive by Charlene's house, my GPS telling me I've arrived and then indicating I should make a U-turn. I keep going, all the way down the street until I can make a left and circle the block. It's a nice enough neighbourhood. The houses aren't in disrepair, there are no creepy looking fuckers standing on their front porches smoking cigarettes in bathrobes.

I park down the street and check my reflection in the visor mirror. I look exactly as I did before I left my house, nervous, but still put together. I root around in the messenger bag sitting on the floor in the back seat, checking once more for the paperwork. I debate whether I should bring it to the door with me or leave it in the car.

I should wait until she invites me in, I decide. Then I can go back to my car to get it. I blow out a breath, more nervous than I've ever been for a date before. Charlene isn't just a random woman. My best friend is already dating her best friend. It's an added layer of complication.

But I'm willing to deal with that because Charlene is unlike any other woman I've had the pleasure of spending time with. And memories of what it felt like to kiss her—make out with her —for the better part of an hour, have consumed me since the night I met her. So I'll take complicated if it means I get to kiss her again.

At ten to ten my patience wears thin and I shift my car into gear and roll the hundred feet down the street to her house. I pull into her driveway and cut the engine. "You got this West-inghouse. She said yes to seeing you again so you're already ahead of the game," I assure myself.

Fuck, I'm nervous. And giving myself a pep talk like an asshole.

At eight minutes to ten I get out of my car and approach her door. I wipe my damp palm on my pant leg and ring the bell. There's a mat under my feet that says WELCOME! in cursive.

The door opens and my mouth goes instantly dry. I'm unpre-pared for the vision that is Charlene. Jesus Christ she's stunning. She's wearing a pair of jeans that hug her lean, luscious curves like a second skin. Her long sleeved shirt is a buttery yellow and has a gauzy quality to it. A breeze wafts through her foyer and ruffles her gorgeous auburn hair, which is loose around her shoulders. The last time I saw her I had my hands in all that soft, luxurious hair.

I'd love to have it wrapped around my fist. I'd love to hold it tight while I guide those plush, glossy lips along the length of my cock. *Dammit.* I need to get the head below the belt under control. This is a coffee date that will hopefully lead to lunch and future dates, not a let's get naked and fuck date. Although, I wouldn't be opposed to the latter at all if she happens to be interested.

Her huge hazel eyes meet mine and I try for a friendly, approachable smile. I don't have a lot of experience with friendly or approachable, so the way her eyes flare doesn't help me much with gauging how intense I'm coming across.

"Hi." Her voice is a caress I feel everywhere.

"Hello, Charlene." I hope that doesn't sound nearly as lecherous to her as it does in my own ears.

"Hi." She bites her bottom lip which momentarily fritzes out my brain.

"I'm a little early." Way to state the obvious. "I hope that's okay."

"Yes! Yeah, of course. Just let me get my purse." She turns, but her purse, which is already hanging from her shoulder, bumps against her hip. "Oh, never mind. Looks like I'm all set."

I wonder if she's as nervous as I am. And now I have no reason to invite myself in so I can get the paperwork out of the way and get to the good stuff, which is our date.

I help Charlene into her jacket and free her hair from the collar, trying hard not to be super creepy when I sniff her hair. She smells good. Better than good. I wish I'd thought to bring coffee to her place, then we could drink it here while she signed on the dotted line and we could make out again.

Maybe with less clothes this time. It's been a long time since I've been naked with anyone, let alone someone who jacks me up the way she does just by touching her hair.

I manage to remember what the hell manners are and hold her door open before I take my place behind the wheel. I ask her about her morning and her weekend plans as I drive toward the waterfront, which is closer to my neighbourhood.

I would take her right to my house, but I need to figure out a way to broach the whole paperwork business, and I'm thrown by the fact that she didn't invite me in. Maybe she doesn't really want to be here. Maybe she's only out with me as a courtesy to her friend.

Shit. I never considered that. We'd spent that night at the bar talking. Well, she'd done most of the talking. I couldn't tell you half of what she'd said, not because I don't find her enthralling, which I do, but because I needed to come up with a way to see her again and knowing that I needed to get her to sign an NDA to do that was a little preoccupying.

I pull into a Starbucks drive-thru for lack of other options. I can tell Charlene is confused, but she rolls with it. I drive to the park near the water, mentally working out how I'm going to make this happen so I can bring her back to my house for lunch.

I've never brought a woman back to my house for lunch on the first date. Most of the time it's dinner at a private restaurant, a nice hotel room and a night of decadence that may or may not be repeated. It rarely turns into more because I'm such a private person. I know it's a problem. I know I'm the problem but my family is a nightmare and public relationships mean dealing with things I don't want to, so it's the only way I can manage.

I park close to the water, but leave the engine running. Charlene is definitely trying to figure out what's going on. And for some reason all the things I've done in the past with the women I date seem . . . ridiculous. But I don't know how to do this any other way. So we drink our coffees and people watch and talk about things that don't matter, but do.

Charlene loves sweets but generally tries to avoid them because her cravings get out of control, and the sugar makes her edgy. She loves terrible reality TV. She smells like home and is gorgeous in jeans. She would look amazing naked in my bed.

She tells me stories about Violet that I've heard from Alex's point of view. It's interesting how differently he perceives things considering the way Charlene spins it, Violet is eternally embarrassed by the things she does and Alex is nothing short of obsessed with her.

Maybe a little like I'm obsessed with Charlene. And how

amazing she smells. And how much I want to spend more time with her like this, talking about nothing, drinking coffee, just being.

Eventually the desire to touch her overrides my ability to speak. I hate the fact that there's a console impeding my ability to get closer to her, even though I acknowledge that it's presence will prevent me from doing something stupid.

I skim her cheek, marvelling at how soft and smooth and warm her skin is, and sweep her hair over her shoulder, all that satin softness brushing across the back of my hand.

Charlene's eyes, so wide and expressive, lift to meet mine as she leans into the touch. I mirror the movement, that magnetic pull between us taking over. I tip her chin up until her lips are an inch from mine. "I would like to kiss you."

"I have coffee breath."

It's everything I can do not to laugh, or fall in love with her. "As do I."

She blinks up at me, so sweet and perfect and nothing I deserve but everything I want. "Okay then."

For a moment I fall back in time, to the moment my lips first touched hers. I want that again. I want it to be just like that. Sweet and soft and electric. I sincerely hope it wasn't the beer making it feel like something it's not.

The second her lips touch mine it feels like I'm being electrocuted with lust. I sweep her mouth with my tongue, tasting coffee and vanilla and that same sweetness from our first kiss. And I can't stop. I just want to sink into this and stay here forever. I want to kiss her until the world ends and my past disappears and it's only us, and now, and here.

When I'm at risk of suggesting we move to the backseat I break the kiss. "Would you like to have lunch with me?"

Charlene's gaze is heavy with the same lust that's turning me into a walking, talking hormone. "Definitely."

"Great." I smile, excited by the prospect of bringing her back to my house where we'll have lunch, and then, if she's interested, we can continue this make out session in a more comfortable location.

I reach into the backseat and retrieve my messenger bag with the paperwork. I'm nervous all over again as I produce the folder with Charlene's name printed neatly on the front of it.

"What's that?" All the lust and need in Charlene's gaze turns to wary uncertainty.

"A non-disclosure agreement," I try to sound nonchalant about it so she doesn't think it's a bigger deal than it is.

Charlene's frown grows deeper, as does the line between her eyebrows. "I'm sorry, why would a non-disclosure agreement be necessary?"

Fuck. *Fuck fuck fuck.* I hope I didn't read this wrong. She has to have heard the rumours. Everyone has. "Because I'd like to have lunch with you."

I don't miss the way her fingers creep along the armrest and settle near the handle. "You need a non-disclosure agreement for lunch?"

I run my sweaty palms down my thighs, hoping I'm not fucking myself right now. "I'd like to take you to my house."

"For lunch?"

"Yes."

"Is *lunch* code for something?"

"Code?" I have no idea what she's talking about.

"Yeah, like, is *lunch* a code word for some kinky sex games or something?"

So far Charlene has struck me as . . . sweetly innocent. The way she kisses tells me a lot about her as a partner. She's gentle, soft, she lets me lead until she gets excited and then she gets a little aggressive. I wonder about that side of her, and what else I'll discover if she signs the paperwork.

"No. Although I'm certainly not opposed to kinky sex games if that's what you'd prefer in lieu of lunch." I'll take whatever she's willing to give.

Charlene doesn't respond. Instead she picks up the folder

and flips it open. The agreement is several pages long. Charlene glances at me and raises her eyebrows.

"Take your time. I can wait." I smile again, but it feels a lot like a grimace since I know the contents of the agreement. With most women it wouldn't be unexpected, but maybe I should have prepared Charlene a little better.

I try not to fidget while she scans the contents. It's incredibly thorough, with a whole bunch of clauses. There's even one pertaining to a credit card and a budget for clothing and lingerie because I make a lot of money and lingerie can be expensive. Especially my particular tastes.

After several long minutes Charlene closes the file folder and passes it to me. "I'd like you to take me home."

I smile, relieved that it's going to be so much easier than I anticipated, and produce a pen.

Charlene's expression goes stony as she holds up a hand. "No, you're not understanding. I'd like you to take me to my house, not yours. I'm not signing an NDA agreement for a lunch date—especially this type of NDA."

My buoyant mood deflates and I blink rapidly, my fingers tapping against the manila file folder as I try to figure out a way to persuade her that I think we work well together, and that I want more of her. "But I thought we were enjoying each other's company."

"We were. But there's no fucking way I'm signing this, so if you want to have lunch with me, you'll have to do it without an NDA."

In all the years that I've produced this document no woman has ever said no. Over time have they decided they couldn't deal with my need for secrecy and my inability to give them more of myself than what they expected? Of course, but not one woman has ever contested signing this agreement. "It's meant to protect us both," I tell her.

"It's not a condom, Darren. It's an NDA. The next thing I know I'll have some kind of tracking chip and I'll be tied to your bed."

I try to picture that, Charlene tethered, but I can't. She's too much of a firefly, flitting around, shining her light for the few who are lucky enough to capture her for as brief a time as she'll allow. "Would you like to be tied to my bed?"

"Not if I have to sign an NDA."

I love how irritated she looks right now. "And if you don't have to sign an NDA?"

She shrugs, intending to come across as nonchalant but the flush in her cheeks and the way she crosses her legs tells me more than her wordless response.

I decide to be honest as I'm able. "I'm a very private person, Charlene."

"So am I. Doesn't mean I make all the people in my life sign an NDA because of it. If you want to have lunch with me, you can do it without asking me to sign away my rights."

Her chin is tipped up, defiance warring with lust. She wants me like I want her, but she wants her freedom just as much. It's something I can relate to in ways she can't understand and likely never will, because there's no way she'll stick around long enough to know the real me. But for today I'm willing to concede and pretend that this will be more than a few weeks that will become sad, fond memories.

"Okay, no NDA," I agree. "But I have rules for dating, Charlene."

"So do I, and we can discuss them over lunch."

How was I to know that one lunch date was all it would take for me to fall hopelessly in love with her? Or that it would take me more than two years to fully understand that Charlene had managed to become as necessary as the air I breathe.

A NOTE TO MY READERS

In 2008 I started writing what would become my first published novel (duet, actually). It wasn't Pucked, it was Clipped Wings & Inked Armor. If you've read it, you'll know it's the polar opposite of Pucked; heavy instead of funny. I needed a break from all the depressing, snot sobbing angst, so I started writing what eventually became Pucked. The year I wrote it, Chicago won the Stanley Cup, and then the year I published, they won again. Not saying I had anything to do with that, just kind of a cool coincidence.

If you've made it to this note, then you've been on quite the journey with me and the Pucked gang. I have loved every minute of writing this series and I'm so proud of this bag of WTF that came out of my brain.

The other day Debra Anastasia, who has been on this very wild ride with me the entire time I've been writing, told me that Pucked Love was me writing with my seatbelt off. And that's pretty damn accurate.

The Pucked Series is where I let all the crazy out. It's outlandish, wild, ridiculous and just so much fun. Of course there are ups and down. Of course there are challenges to overcome, but I think the best part of writing this series has been how much these characters feel like a family. It's Violet's insanity and her lack of filter, it's Alex's Zero Fucks Given attitude that she sometimes says and does embarrassing things. It's in the way this unlikely group of characters supports and loves each other through all the good times and the bad that makes them difficult to say goodbye to.

Pucked Love is . . . nuts. I'll be honest, when I started outlining this pile of crazy I was like OH SHIT. What the hell have I done? I don't write BDSM. I might make little jokes about it, but that is not my wheelhouse. I write super consent-y sex where everyone is in control at all times—I mean, no one is actually in control during an orgasm, but there was no way on earth I was going to write BDSM with any kind of seriousness, so I had to get creative. I think Darren and Charlene are my favourite couple (although I say that with every book). I'll always love Alex and Violet because they're where this all started. Obviously I love all the couples for very different reasons, Miller and Sunny for being so freaking sweet, Randy and Lily for ruining all those bathrooms, Lance for being so broken and Poppy for saving him from himself with love and kindness and her quiet strength. But Charlene and Darren are a successful couple because of the people they have in their lives, not just because they're right for each other and to me, that makes them extra special.

I hope you loved this finale as much as I did. I hope the epilogue gave you a look into everyone's happy future. This Pucked family will take up a big place in my heart and I'm so glad I've had an opportunity to share so many laughs and tears with all of you over these past three years.

Don't worry, it doesn't end here. There are always new stories, new characters and new families to build and fall in love with. Thank you, though, for being a part of this, no matter when you jumped on the crazy train with me.

Endless Pucking Love,

Helena

Read on for a preview of A LIE FOR A LIE, a brand new Pucked Series Spinoff

ABOUT THE AUTHOR

NYT and USA Today bestselling author, Helena Hunting lives on the outskirts of Toronto with her amazing family and her two awesome cats, who think the best place to sleep is her keyboard. Helena writes everything from emotional contemporary romance to romantic comedies that will have you laughing until you cry. If you're looking for a tearjerker, you can find her angsty side under H. Hunting.

Scan this code to stay connected with Helena

OTHER TITLES BY HELENA HUNTING

Pucked Series

Pucked (Pucked #1)

Pucked Up (Pucked #2)

Pucked Over (Pucked #3)

Forever Pucked (Pucked #4)

Pucked Under (Pucked #5)

Pucked Off (Pucked #6)

Pucked Love (Pucked #7)

AREA 51: Deleted Scenes & Outtakes

Get Inked

Pucks & Penalties

All In Series

A Lie for a Lie

A Favor for a Favor

A Secret for a Secret

A Kiss for a Kiss

Lies, Hearts & Truths Series

Little Lies

Bitter Sweet Heart

Shattered Truths

Shacking Up Series

Shacking Up

Getting Down (Novella)

Hooking Up

I Flipping Love You

Making Up

Handle with Care

Spark Sisters Series

When Sparks Fly

Starry-Eyed Love

Make A Wish

Lakeside Series

Love Next Door

Love on the Lake

The Clipped Wings Series

Cupcakes and Ink

Clipped Wings

Between the Cracks

Inked Armor

Cracks in the Armor

Fractures in Ink

Standalone Novels

The Librarian Principle

Felony Ever After

Before You Ghost (with Debra Anastasia)

Forever Romance Standalones

The Good Luck Charm

Meet Cute

Kiss my Cupcake